This is a work of fiction. Names, characters, businesses, places, events and incidents are either the product of the author's imagination or used in a fictitious manner. Any resemblance to actual persons, living or dead, or actual events is purely coincidental.

Wry Treason

Pat Marlow

Wry Treason

Vanguard Press

VANGUARD PAPERBACK

© Copyright 2023
Pat Marlow

The right of Pat Marlow to be identified as author of
this work has been asserted by them in accordance with the
Copyright, Designs and Patents Act 1988.

A CIP catalogue record for this title is
available from the British Library.

ISBN 978 1 80016 760 5

Vanguard Press is an imprint of
Pegasus Elliot Mackenzie Publishers Ltd.
www.pegasuspublishers.com

First Published in 2023

**Vanguard Press
Sheraton House Castle Park
Cambridge England**

Printed & Bound in Great Britain

I would like to dedicate the book to Volodymyr Zelenskyy and the people of Ukraine in recognition of the great courage and tenacity of all Ukrainians, facing the unlawful actions of a tyrant. I hope the epilogue the book reflects the ultimate outcome.

Acknowledgements

The welcome advice from Simon Clissold and the Scallywags, regarding the mysteries of Cyberspace.

Prologue

Ivan Kapalski leaned back in his leather chair, closed his eyes, and sighed.

"What is it," he asked himself, "about powerful men that makes them lust for more — always more? Is it not enough to be surrounded by sycophants who fall over themselves to earn a nod of appreciation? Is it not enough to have antagonised most civilised countries in the world, and to have interfered in their election processes? What good has that done? Our methods are transparent. We are exposed. We end up exchanging threats with an ignorant idiot and providing arms to a regime that is internationally despised. Are we flourishing as a result of all this? No. Am I any different? Yes, I am, and I know others who are."

The 'safe' phone in his pocket suddenly signalled a call and he listened.

"Ivan? It's me, Pieter. Can you talk?"

"Yes, go on."

"It's Alicia. I'm afraid she died this morning. I thought you ought to know. The funeral will be in a few days. I've told as many of the family as I can."

"It was, I think, expected."

"Indeed, and it was peaceful."

"I'll try to be there. Give me times and details when you can. Thank you."

He switched off and thought about the family he had left behind long ago, uncles and aunts, now dead, brothers and sisters? Sad to say, apart from Pieter, he didn't even know where they were. They avoided him. Cousins? Well, there was one in particular: a girl with blonde pigtails who had gone to Oxford and never come back. She must be about thirty-eight now. He knew all about her: where she lived, what she did, whom she had married. Time to get in touch. He stood up and stared out of the window at the city he loved. So much had changed, not for the better. The feeling of vulnerability was strange and unfamiliar. Suddenly, he knew exactly what he was going to do. The time had come, but he must be so careful.

Chapter 1

Jake Scott worked for MI5. Essentially, he was an investigator, a high calibre technologist, appointed by GCHQ. With the advent of cyber intelligence, most of his work was done at a desk. Jake knew as much about hacking as anyone in the country and sometimes only he was trusted to seek and interpret certain information from specified sources that came into Thames House day after day. It worked both ways. Root access was Jake's special skill but detecting penetration by others into the firm's top-secret files was just as important as being able to investigate theirs. He loved his job. When the baby had arrived, he had booked a week's leave. He was back at his desk after three days.

His wife Kate knew perfectly well that to complain would be unfair. She understood that the nature of his work would test their relationship and would be difficult at times, but she loved him. Well, they loved each other, and mutual trust was an un-written undertaking, never to be forgotten. She herself had been on maternity leave from her job as a Detective Inspector with the Metropolitan Police Force and that was certainly not a nine-to-five job, but they had managed their erratic timetables well, through mutual understanding and acceptance

When Jake suggested that she should go and visit her mother for a week or two, Kate was reluctant. Her mother lived in Paris and even with the most meticulous planning, the journey with little Ben would be difficult. On the other hand, her mother had not yet seen her grandson, and it would be rather nice to introduce them.

"I'll take you to Heathrow — the flight will be less than an hour. I'll make sure someone meets you at the other end and drives you to Emily's door," promised Jake.

"But he doesn't have a passport"

"Actually, he does. I've sorted it. There are some perks with this job."

"You seem to have it all planned. Are you going to install some floozy into the house while I'm away?"

"Yes, she's a blonde with huge tits, and there's no milk spurting into my eye every time I try to kiss her. She can cook, too — a bonus."

"Great — that gives me the right to find a holiday companion with money and muscle, who has an occasional haircut, with a noticeable six pack."

"What do you mean? That's cruel. I can't help being tall and skinny. My strength is in my brains. Is Ben asleep?"

"Yes — come on. Help me make the bed."

"I thought you'd never ask." They tiptoed upstairs. The next day Kate was on the way to Paris.

"It seems funny being here without them," observed Griff from Jake's sofa, "but there's the still the faint smell of baby — you know, not nappies, but that nice small of baby talcum powder. How long will they be away?"

"She only went this morning. She stayed with a friend near the airport overnight and would have been driven there early. We didn't fix a return date. I kept avoiding the issue. I just hope to God we can sort this quickly before she comes back. I feel that I'm expected to prove my innocence. And that's not right, is it?"

Griff sighed and threw a newspaper onto the table. Working for MI6 took Griff out of the country on many occasions. They frequently worked together and had been friends for years

"Sadly, in our field, I'm afraid it is. Has Hubert found anything specific? I mean something tangible or is it just an instinctive thing? If he has, he needs to talk to us in MI6. You know that, however much our masters trust us, there must be no room for doubt. They've been bitten before — Burgess, Mclean, Kim Philby, Blunt — even Sir Roger Hollis, Head of your Security Division was still under suspicion till the day he died. All a Soviet agent has to do is sow the seeds of doubt to cause mayhem. A few feasible allegations will do."

"They are remorseless, Griff. We know they are targeting state systems, tuning in to our exchanges with the United States and European allies. We are on the lookout for that sort of thing all the time but quite honestly, although we have one of the safest systems in the world, they can disrupt our lives in so many other ways as you know — bugger up banking systems, close down train services, interfere with elections, flights, hospitals. We're constantly on the lookout. I spend hours looking at my own computer here at home searching for viruses and cyber-attacks. It's doing my head in. That's been going on for months, but suddenly it's more than that. Hubert is onto something at the heart of the Intelligence Services, and he thinks I am being used as a vehicle by someone who has the same suspicions as he has."

"I don't understand. If this someone is onto it, why would he not come forward and alert us?"

"Because he or she doesn't know who to trust"

"But the stuff planted on your laptop at work… You're the expert. Surely you can trace it — analyse it."

"Of course, as soon as I get my computer back. It might be an invitation. I don't know. I can't discuss this with Kate. That's why I persuaded her to take a break. I know she's worried about me. It's not fair on her at all. Hubert tends to play his cards close to his chest. Maybe he does suspect me. He hasn't mentioned it to anyone else I work with."

"He desperately wants to trust you, Jake. You are the best he has, but he'll look like an incompetent idiot if you suddenly bugger off to your luxury Dacha outside Moscow."

"I don't even speak Russian and I hate vodka."

"What about caviar?"

"Love it."

"I rest my case. Look, Jake — the very fact that he has appointed me to keep an eye on you proves that he knows you are above suspicion. He knows we're close. He just wants to protect you, but at the same time, he has at least to appear to go through the set procedure. He knows I speak Russian fluently."

"Maybe it's a double bluff. It's you he really suspects. In fact, you are rather dodgy — and yes, you do speak Russian."

"Yeah, but I'm a lousy actor." Come on. Let's go out and have a drink and plan our strategy. We need a list of suspects. Who has access to your computer?"

"Laptop, it's on my laptop. Anybody, even the cleaners. It's usually on my desk, but it could come from anywhere, as you know. They don't even need to be in this country. There are safeguards, but you never know. Nothing is safe these days."

"Yes. Okay. We need to isolate everything that you didn't record or research, and set aside the rest to see what is unfamiliar and then work out how and why they want to implicate you."

Jake laughed. "Stick to languages, mate. As you know, all sensitive stuff, the highly confidential stuff involved in serious work, is on the mainline which is just about impregnable. This incursion into my private computer which I use for day-to-day trivia was, far as I can tell, an acknowledgement from someone, certainly no expert, that a message purportedly from me had been received. The message concerned Westminster security and with it was a request to clarify some aspect of it, including an innocent-sounding message about intelligence links to Washington. It originated in Moscow. In the scheme of things, it was an innocuous straightforward message, and it beats me how he noticed it at all. Quite honestly, at the time, I barely glanced at it. Nothing significant. I thought it was some joke from one of the New York pals that I sometimes exchange insults with. Hubert must have been nosing around my office, but why bother to check my laptop?"

"That's ridiculous. The intelligence world knows everything there is to know about Westminster Security. That proves this is rubbish. Whoever has set you up is out of your league. Hubert will be well aware of that. Maybe someone is just testing the testers to see if they pick things up."

"You think it was a set-up? Oh, I don't know. To hell with it, let's go and get drunk. I'll have a serious chat with Hubert in the morning and then resign and get a job with Charlie Knowles. I'd make a first-class cop."

*

At nine o'clock next morning, Jake parked his car in the usual underground space allocated to him. Griff was in the lobby waiting and together they made their way to Jake's office. They had barely sat down when there was a knock on the door. It opened immediately and a male entered, closing it behind him. He nodded a greeting to Griff, handed Jake a small white sealed envelope and spoke.

"I have instructions to remove you from the premises without delay, Mr Scott." He nodded at Griff. "If you would both follow me, please."

"What! Why? Who the hell are you? Identify yourself," Responded Jake, jumping to his feet. He tore open the envelope and read the contents of a brief note.

The stranger continued, handing Jake a larger envelope. "This contains a copy of your contract and your resignation letter. Please return the second without delay."

Jake hurled the brown envelope across the room and knocked back his chair.

"Who the fuck do you think you are? How dare you? I have my own fucking car, thank you, now get the hell out of my office."

"I'm sorry, sir, but I believe your car belongs to the company. Please come with me. I am just obeying orders."

"Orders from whom?" asked Griff. "This is outrageous."

"Never mind, Griff," said Jake quietly. "Let's just go. You needn't drive me home, whoever you are. I would rather a bastard like you didn't know where I live. You can drop us off at the nearest tube."

"And you can send all his belongings to me at MI6," instructed Griff. "On second thoughts, I will send someone I can trust to collect it."

In the car, they sat silently staring out of the windows, until Griff said, "Hang on a minute — where are we going?

17

We said the nearest tube station. That would be...
Temple."

Jake kicked his ankle and shook his head slightly.
From his pocket he carefully fished out the folded piece of
paper.

Griff took it and read, "This will be a shock. I had to
do it this way. Trust me. Be overtly furious. Slam doors,
but just do as he tells you. I'll explain soon."

It was signed with the initials of the Head of Section.

Griff stared straight ahead. "I guess we're on the way
to Bloomsbury," he muttered. "That's where he lives."

"Really? How the hell do you know where he lives? I
don't."

"Doesn't matter, I was wrong. He's looking for
somewhere to park now and I haven't a clue where we are.
Gather up your belongings."

The car stopped at a small but exclusive-looking 'Art
and Antiques' shop, with a puzzling absence of any kind
of painting or antiquity in the window. The driver turned.
"If you could get out here, gentlemen. Someone will pick
you up in a minute or two." They climbed out and he drove
away without another word.

Seconds later, the shop door was opened and a grey-
haired man with a large nose appeared at the door. "Mr
Scott? We have a parking area at the back, and someone is
waiting for you there if you wouldn't mind walking
round." Minutes later they were seated in a car with Hubert
Edwards (known in intimate circles as Uncle Hubert),
Head of Section, at the wheel.

"I won't apologise for all the subterfuge," he said. "I can assure you, Jake, that you are not under suspicion as far as I'm concerned, but as far as the rest of the world goes, it could be very useful to us if you would turn traitor for as long as it takes to convince the author of the message on your laptop that you are at least approachable. The stuff I found concealed there originates from Moscow. No doubt about that. But the thing is, it's amateurish. It lacks the kind of sophistication we've come to expect from our friends in the bad lands. It's a mystery we must resolve. You don't speak Russian, and your work can't possibly benefit them. They have equally skilled experts of their own, but for some reason, they've designed this to persuade you to make contact or at least be available for them to do so. They can't imagine for a moment that it would put you personally under suspicion, but there is definitely an invitation there. Is there anything you're not telling me?"

"Of course not, and if you hadn't seized my laptop, I could have investigated it myself. Whoever it is must be well aware that we're not going to be fooled by any of it. It's such an obvious ruse. I can't think what good I could possibly be to them either. So, what am I supposed to do? Can't we just challenge them? Ask them what the hell is going on?"

"Challenge who? We don't know enough to risk a response. Not just yet. Your laptop is here you can take it away. We're going to play along — draw them out. So, consider yourself suspended — under suspicion." He

19

paused. "The thing is, Jake, I do believe there is a bad apple somewhere in our organisation. I sense that whoever is doing this knows, too. That rules out some random smart-ass schoolboy computer buff. We just have to play along. I strongly suspect that whoever is doing this is on our side. We do have sympathisers in Moscow who are not at all happy with the direction the President is taking or the friends he is making. If we start making something of this and demanding answers, it might get someone into trouble.

"Just in case there is much more to this than meets the eye, just play along. Stay at home. See if you're contacted. You remain on the payroll, of course. The Press might get wind of it, although you won't be named, and getting another job without a CV will be nigh on impossible, although it might help this bloody pantomime if you applied for one or two. I'm pretty sure it won't be long before you're approached. How you're approached remains to be seen. If it turns out against all my expectations to be an unfriendly approach, you will be immediately and publicly re-installed. It could go on for weeks, but it might be all over in a few hours. Who knows? As things stand, at the moment, nobody else in the service has an inkling that anything is happening. I put a brief hint in a circular this morning, mainly so that they will know we've taken the bait. Quite honestly, Jake, I'm fully expecting you to be back at your desk in no time at all, but I have to cover all possibilities. If there is no contact from whoever they are, within say, a week, then we just forget the whole thing."

"That creep who drove us here," Interrupted Griff. "Who the hell was he?" Hubert chose not to respond.

Jake continued. "So you are assuming there are in fact two unknowns — one a bad apple, as you call him or her in our organisation, and someone else who is aware of the above, who thinks we should know, but can't contact us directly, which means that he or she might be in Moscow. I really don't like this, boss. You know Kate is on her way to Paris right now, but she won't stay there for long. What am I going to tell her when she comes back? There's the baby. I don't want to put my family at risk. Could you not just have ignored it? Shown them you are confident that I would never do anything to harm my country. Do I have to agree to this? Because I'm inclined not to."

"You don't have to, of course," said Hubert with a sigh. "Look I need to get home. Take a taxi wherever you want to go. I do understand, Jake, it is entirely up you, but we've set the scene now. I've seconded Griff, with the permission of MI6, and you and Kate will be shadowed throughout. She will be perfectly safe, I promise you."

"Did you know about this, Griff?" asked Jake angrily."

"No, he didn't," said Hubert. "It seemed better to put you both in the picture together."

"There are times when I really don't like the way you operate," observed Griff, "but if Jake is in, so am I, and I too may have to lie to my partner, but I think he expects that. He knows where I work."

At that moment, Jake's mobile vibrated noisily in his pocket, and he took it out and looked at the screen,

"It's a French number. Must be Kate. Excuse me a moment."

He put it to his ear and turned away from them. "Hi, darling."

"Is that you, Jake? No, it's not darling, it's her mother. Where is she? She hasn't arrived. The plane landed hours ago and there's no sign of her — or Ben."

Chapter 2

Little Ben had been a perfect traveller, but once at Charles de Gaulle Airport, before waiting at the Carousel for her suitcase, Kate had been obliged to find a ladies' toilet with baby-changing facilities. Consequently, by the time she emerged, there were only two isolated cases circulating slowly. Neither was hers. She stood helplessly, wondering what on earth to do. She turned as a female voice behind said, "Don't panic. I saw you go to the toilets and realised you might take some time, so I picked up your case for you. Sometimes if they need the carousel, they remove any left-over cases as a security measure."

Kate was so relieved that she didn't think of asking how the young woman had known which case was hers. She simply assumed that this was the escort arranged by Jake. She had stayed with an old friend the night before because that friend lived close to London City Airport and the flight was early. Her friend's husband had driven her to the airport in good time, and she had been one of the first to check in.

Ben had been as good as gold on the flight and was now cosily snuggled against her in a sling.

"Look, just wait here and I'll get a luggage trolley," urged her helper, "and then we can share a taxi."

Kate was glad of the help. She assumed that the pleasant young woman had the address of her mother and settled into her seat expecting a journey of about half an hour. The girl had identified herself as Natasha and seemed a little edgy.

"Look! I'm going your way, but would you mind if we made a stop at my apartment? I left my phone at home. I was in such a hurry this morning. It's a very quick detour."

Natasha spoke to the taxi driver, and he replied at length, sounding quite angry."

"I'm so sorry" she said. "He can't park in my road, and he has another customer waiting to be picked up. He can drop us off at the corner, as long as we get a move on, and I can phone for another taxi from home."

The taxi stopped outside a block of flats, and they climbed out.

"Well, he must be in a hurry," remarked Kate. "He didn't even ask for the fare."

"Ahh yes, well, I have an account. It's like an Uber Taxi. Come on, let's get inside and then go on our way."

Natasha's flat was basic. No pictures, no cushions, very little furniture. She motioned for Kate to sit down. Kate did so, holding Ben close with the distinct feeling that things were not quite right. She felt in her deep coat pocket for her mobile phone. It wasn't there.

"Natasha — my phone. It isn't here. It can't possibly have fallen out of my pocket. Who are you and why am I here? What's going on? I am a Police Officer......"

"I know, Kate, I know, currently on maternity leave. I know all about you — and Jake"

"Does Jake know I'm here?"

"Not yet, but he will soon."

"Did he ask you to do this? Why?"

"Please just listen to me. I will give you your phone in a moment and you can speak to him. You are quite safe here. No harm to you is intended. My partner is a pilot. You will meet him later. We are not Russian and neither of us feels any obligation, any need to be loyal to the Russian Security Service, but we strive to appear to be loyal and obedient servants of the State." She laughed.

"We play our parts well, but our loyalty is to the SBU, which is a Ukrainian service. My mother is Russian, but we live in Sebastopol in the Crimean Peninsula, which, as you know, Russia annexed in 2014. I speak both languages fluently. Most Ukrainians are bilingual. The languages are very similar. It is because my mother was with her parents in Grozny, in Russia, when I was born, that I have a Russian passport."

"Yes," interrupted Kate. "Well, this is all fascinating. But why am I here and what does it have to do with Jake?"

"Please listen. I'm trying to explain. My father was British. He was a lecturer at the Aviation University in Kiev. We spoke English at home but never outside. I am not happy with the way Russia treats my country; there is a great deal of unrest in Ukraine. There are rumours in Kiev that the country is still in Russian sights. We have been a democracy since 1990, and ever since Russia annexed Crimea, we have felt under threat. Russia does not like the thought of a pro-European democracy next door. It just might make his citizens envious."

"Is your father still lecturing at the university?" Kate was becoming curious.

Natasha didn't reply but got up to remove the empty coffee cups. "Would you like another?" she asked and then sat down again. "My father just disappeared. He used to disappear for weeks at a time, anyway. We never asked where he went because he would never tell us. He's probably dead, we think. He was invited to go to Moscow to give a talk to students there. He didn't arrive — well, that's what they say. We spent months trying to find out what happened. The Russians seemed anxious to find him too. There were posters of him everywhere and requests for information on the television. Strangely, they never attached his name to the photos, but it seemed clear that the Russian authorities wanted him almost as much as we did." She paused. "He was never found. In the end I gave up — or appeared to give up. I think I was offered my job partly to shut me up or so that they could keep an eye on me. I never put a foot wrong. I am very careful. It's years now since I saw my dad. I think they are satisfied that I am not a threat, but I will never give up hope." She smiled and tickled Ben's chin.

"He is such a lovely baby. I would so love to have one if ever I feel that it would always be safe and secure."

"My partner Rudi is a pilot in the Russian Air force."" She continued, "We met at the university in Kiev. I, like your Jake, studied computer sciences. My job in Moscow is to check the category and source of incoming information and make sure it is filed with the appropriate department or departments — and to identify anything which hints of a threat, or which might be an attempt to breach security. They trust me now, you see.

"I am under strict instructions not to make any written notes of the contents of any incoming reports or communications. I am not permitted to take a mobile phone into the office or any other device, which may result in details being recorded. There are various codes to which I have access that provide whatever information I need to decipher them. I happen to have a photographic memory, which is quite useful." She sighed.

"Believe me, most of the stuff I deal with is mind-numbingly boring and there is nothing top secret of course, but over the last few weeks, it has been difficult to ignore certain information concerning your own Security Services. I believe they have been infiltrated and you need to know this, for all our sakes. I can't tell you more just now. I think you need to speak to Jake and get him over here, then Rudi will come and explain it all."

"But Jake is busy, he can't just drop everything."

"No — he is not. He's not busy right now. He has been suspended."

"What? How do you know that?" She felt in her deep coat pocket again. "My phone - do you have it? Give it to me please. At once."

Jake answered on the first ring, and she spoke his name immediately.

"Jake, it's me. I'm fine — so is Ben, but something strange is going on. Are you really suspended? Can you call my mother and tell her I've been held up? Do it now and then call me back."

In England, Jake sighed with relief and looked at Griff. *She sounds okay. I have to call her back. She must be in Paris. Grab some stuff and meet me at the airport as soon as you can. There's bound to be an afternoon or evening flight. There's something going on. I don't think she's in any danger. It was her 'don't mess with me' voice. I'm calling her mother now.*

"There's a flight at three-fifty from London City," said Griff, getting to his feet immediately. "I often catch it. We have two hours. Gate 16. See you there."

*

Griff grabbed his bag from the chair next to him, paid for the several cups of coffee they had consumed and called a taxi. Jake was already on his way out, still speaking on his phone. Two taxis turned up simultaneously and they went their separate ways.

*

"I am totally pissed off about this," muttered Jake two hours later as they waited for their flight to be called.

"Well, we'll sort it," retorted Griff, flinging a newspaper at his friend "Read that. In the scheme of things, our problems are trifling. Read the paper and think how lucky you are. Kids are starving or being indiscriminately slaughtered all over the world and their parents can do nothing. I have nightmares about it.

"Kate and Ben are fine, and Hubert will put things right, I'm sure." He paused. "Come on, there's time for a quick drink at the bar before we're called. I can't stand those little bottles they have onboard, and you need to keep your spirits up, literally."

Chapter 3

Hundreds of miles away in Idlib, a small child was in pain and cold, very cold. He could see his mother's hand stretching out towards him from under the rubble. He could just touch it with his fingers. Her hand was cold, too. The fingers didn't move. His whole body was hurting but he tried not to cry. He wanted to watch his mother's hand — see it clearly, just in case the fingers moved, even a tiny fraction. It was difficult not to cry. He remembered her holding his face in her hands, stroking his cheeks with her thumbs, silky and warm. They were so used to seeing death now. Every day there were more bodies. His papa had planned to take them away from Idlib, this terrible place, to take them to Turkey to safety, but the bombs had caught him just before he could arrange it. That was just two weeks ago. His mother cried herself to sleep night after night, but then stopped and searched for the strength that she knew she needed if they were to survive this nightmare. That's what her husband would have expected of her.

"Why are they killing us all, Mama?" he had asked.— "What have we done?"

"We have done nothing, Kerim," she had replied. "President Bashir al Assad is angry with some men here - enemies of the state. He doesn't know which of us they are, so I suppose he kills everyone, just to make sure." She had taken his face in her hands. "We are not safe here, Kerim, but there is nowhere for us go now that your father has gone. We may be killed, little one, but do not be afraid. You and I will always be together, and Heaven is a beautiful place. We will always be together."

There was a wave of pain, and he closed his eyes and drifted into an uneasy sleep

When he opened them, everything was different. It was warm, and he was lying on something soft. The pain was gone. He opened his eyes, and an angel was looking down at him.

"Hi," she said. "You're awake. How do you feel?" She spoke in his language and her voice was gentle, and her hair was golden.

"Where's Mama?" he asked "She must be here. She said we would always be together, she promised."

She smiled. "It's all a bit chaotic right now," she said, "but tell me your name, and her name and I'll see what I can do. The doctor will be round soon. Can you sit up and drink some water?"

"Doctor? Am I not in heaven? Is this a hospital? "They must have found Mama. She was with me. She was hurt. Please help me I must find her."

He struggled to get out of bed, but the pain came again, and he cried out. The angel put her arms around him and stroked his head.

"You must try to be calm. I promise I will try to help you. There are so many hurt people here — children too, and not enough beds or doctors to make them all better. We can only keep you for a short time. Let me help you to sit up, and you can tell me as much as you can, your name, your mother's name and where you lived. When I finish here today, I will go and see what I can find. I'll try to find the ambulance men who rescued you." She paused. "But listen, little one, there is so much damage here. Sometimes it is difficult to find anything." She looked at his sad little face. He was so beautiful, so innocent. How could that monster do this to his own people?"

"My name is Kerim. Do you know the big mosque in the middle of Idlib town?"

She shook her head. "No, but I can ask."

"They never bomb the mosque. When you find it, if you stand in front of it, our house is in a street on that side." He pointed his left hand. Go down there. Lots of the houses are broken and it is very dirty and dusty now. Ours will be broken, too." He looked at her appealingly. "It is eleven houses down on that side." He gestured his right hand. "I was upstairs with Mama. I was going to bed. We were talking, and suddenly there was a terrible noise, and it began to fall. I could see her arm." His eyes filled with tears, and he turned his face into the pillow. His body shook with sobs. The angel lifted his slender little body and held him in her arms."

"I'll help you, Kerim. Don't cry. I'll help you. I will."

She took an escort with her. Doctor Marc Gould was exhausted, but concerned for her safety, he insisted on accompanying her. Besides, he knew the way to the big mosque.

"You're away on leave for a few days, yes?" he asked as they picked their way through the debris in the narrow streets.

"Yes — can't wait, a blissful week in civilisation. Hot scented baths, poached egg on toast and the *Telegraph* crossword for breakfast. How could I have taken all that for granted when nightmares like this are going on all over the world?"

"And your pilot friend?"

"Yes, he should be doing the pick-up and delivery to an RAF airfield in Yorkshire somewhere. I think we do a refuel on the way. I don't know where. When do you finish your stint?"

"I'm doing two more months, and then if I'm still alive, I'm going home for a while. My wife and kids need to see I'm in one piece, and I need to re-assemble my physical and mental stamina. Look! This is the street."

It was like a row of broken teeth. "It doesn't look too hopeful. Poor kid. You are fluent in the Syrian Arabic. Is that why you decided to work here?" Marc enquired.

"Yes, it seemed the obvious thing to do. I have the nursing qualifications and experience and although my dad

33

was against it, I knew I had to do it. We had relatives here — my cousins, but they got away in good time. I still feel that part of me belongs here."

"Lucky for Idlib, I'd say, but when you get home for your well-earned break, don't feel obliged to come back too soon. You've been amazing. You've done more than your share."

She was about to reply when they were approached by a local woman carrying half a loaf of bread and some onions.

"Are you looking for someone?" she asked. "I was wondering about my neighbours." She nodded towards number eleven. "I saw them take Kerim out — the White Helmets. I think he was alive. They found his mother. Yildiz, later, the same day — I don't think she was... alive but... Do you have news?"

"Do you know where they took her? Kerim is in my hospital. I came to try to find his mother. He will be fine, but he's distraught, of course."

"It was an ambulance with a green cross. There are three hospitals in the area. I don't know where they went..."

Grace was already on her way back to Dr Gould. She turned and waved at the woman. "Thank you so much — and good luck. What's your name? I'll tell Kerim."

"Semra. I'm Semra. God bless you, too."

Back at the hospital, Grace went straight back to the children's ward. There was no sign of Kerim.

"Where's the boy that was here?" she asked an aide.

"We had to release him. His broken ribs are bound up. He has cuts and bruises, but he'll be fine. We needed the space. Five more sad little casualties for this ward any minute - sorry — must go."

"Where was he going — do you know?"

"Sorry — haven't a clue. He's only just gone. You may catch him."

Grace was heading for the exit at speed. She knew she had half an hour before she was due to be collected to go to the airfield. She simply had to find him, otherwise she knew her time at home would be filled with guilt and regrets.

It was luck rather than strategy that solved the problem. Kerim had been given a makeshift crutch to help him walk. It was a slow process. The pavement was crowded with people. By the time Grace caught up with him, on his way home, of course, he was exhausted and crying. She took the crutch and dropped it on the ground where it was seized by a hospital orderly. "Help me get him back to the entrance," she begged him. The orderly picked up the child and strode back as if Kerim weighed nothing. Grace carried the crutch. Equipment was scarce.

There was a taxi by the double doors. The driver waved. "Nurse Grace?" he yelled. She nodded and he opened the rear door.

"Put him in first," she instructed the orderly. She thanked him, handed him the crutch, and climbed in beside Kerim.

"School Airfield, please"

The driver, who was used to the comings and goings of foreign volunteers, took off with his hand on the horn. He didn't speed because hapless pedestrians, alert for sporadic attacks from above, tended to race in all directions for cover when they heard aeroplane engines. Russian planes usually. They sounded so much more purposeful than the small single engine plane that taxied to a halt on the grass runway in the grounds of what had been a school in the days when Syria had been an orderly, civilised country.

Grace climbed out of the taxi and gave the driver a hug. He smiled, lifted Kerim out and set him on the ground, then turned the car to head back. The pilot climbed out of the cockpit and jumped down. Grace ran over and they kissed, holding each other tight for a few moments.

"Christ, Grace. Every time I land here, I wonder if you're still alive. Is that a child sitting on the ground? Is he coming with us?" Grace nodded

"Right." There were no questions. The pilot strode over, and picked up Kerim, then carried him carefully to the plane and placed him inside the cockpit door. From there, Grace, now on board, picked him up and strapped him into a seat. By this time the engine noise was speeding up and they were moving.

"An eleven-minute turnaround time — not bad. I'm heading for Ankara and then Sicily for a re-fuel. We'll be in a safe zone shortly. There's a bag of fruit and some choc under the seat. Maybe our passenger could do with some of that. He weighed nothing."

Grace sat beside Kerim, who was looking confused and frightened.

"Listen, Kerim. I'm taking you to safety. I didn't plan to do this, but I have to go home for a little while and I didn't want to leave you. This little plane is going to England"

"But my mama. I want to find her. She promised we would always be together and now I have left her. Please take me back. I have to find her."

Grace told him about her visit to his street, about what Semra had told her — that his mama might be alive, maybe in hospital. She told him that she would be going back — that she would do everything to find her but asked him what he thought his mama would have wanted her to do. "I think she would have wanted me to do exactly this, Kerim — to make you safe."

"Will you let me come back with you, so we can look for Mama together?"

Grace was silent for a while.

"If the bombing stops, and it is safe, then yes. I promise. And it will stop, Kerim, one day. I don't want to lie to you. I want you to trust me and I do promise faithfully, that one day, we *will* go back and find your mama or — what happened to her. In the meantime, you are going to stay with my mama, who is kind and funny and loving, and she will look after both of us. Now try to sleep. Take this pill, which will stop the pain in your ribs. We have a long journey ahead of us, in more ways than one."

They touched down outside Palermo at a private airfield. Ian took them into the rather smart terminal and suggested that a doctor check Kerim's injuries. Grace was only too happy to agree, as she needed to make a couple of long-distance calls. The first was to the Red Cross headquarters. They kept scrupulous records and agreed that if Yildiz had been identifiable, they should be able to find her details — given time. They promised to call back.

When Kerim had been checked and pronounced damaged but intact, they decided to have a meal and get some sleep.

Kerim stared at the dish of meatballs in gravy with rice and green beans. He looked at Grace. "Is this all for me? Do we share? What is it?"

"Well, I think the meat is goat and it is all yours. I have the same, look, and so does Ian. It's all they had left, but I it looks tasty — try it."

Kerim took a hesitant forkful of meat and then another. In no time at all, the plate was clean and he turned to Grace with a smile on his face. It was the first time she'd seen him smile. "It was delicious. The best food I have ever eaten. Thank you." The smile faded. "I wish Mama was here. She often made me eat more than she did, and I know she was hungry."

"We're going to try to sleep now. Come on. Let's find a little bed for you. I'll wake you in the morning with some orange juice. I'm in the next room. If you wake in the night, just come and snuggle in with me."

Grace and Ian sat at the bar and had a glass of wine. The call from the Red Cross came just as they were about to go to bed. It was not good news.

"How am I going to tell him, Ian?" Tears were running down her own cheeks, for a woman she had never met.

"We tell him nothing yet, darling. We need to give him time. You're going to have to stay with him for a while. You need the break anyway. He lost his father just a couple of weeks ago. How old is he — about seven? All he has known is conflict. This is too much for him to take in. At best he will be fostered in England with a family of children who leave food on their plates and are rude to their parents. It will be an enormous cultural shock. He is one of thousands, Grace. This is happening all over the world. All we can do in our own little world is give this child love and keep him safe. Come on. We need to sleep, and we have an early slot tomorrow."

Tomorrow, Grace thought, *I'll have to come to terms with the fact that my life will never be the same again*. She thought of the White Helmets, an organisation recently formed to assist the people of Syria. They worked tirelessly to protect and rescue the victims of Assad's relentless bombings, maligned, and attacked as they were by both the Syrian and Russian leaders, both intent on driving out the ISIS invaders, regardless of the cost in human life of the Syrian people. *I must come back,* she thought.

Chapter 4

Over in France Jake and Griff, clutching their hand luggage, stood together at Charles de Gaulle Airport back-to-back, looking for anyone who might be approaching them purposefully. It was very busy, and Jake was getting edgy. They were, as instructed, standing by the notice which indicated waiting taxis. Both jumped when a stranger suddenly passed and then turned quickly.

"Mr Scott? I thought you would be alone. It is what I requested."

"Yes, well, hard luck. I have little regard for requests made by someone who has kidnapped my wife."

"That could be considered a short-sighted attitude in those circumstances, Mr Scott, but your wife has not been kidnapped. She is with my girlfriend, awaiting your arrival. If she had decided to leave, she would not have been detained. Perhaps you could introduce me to your companion."

Griff chose to respond himself. "My name is Richard Griffiths."

"May I call you Dick?"

"No, you bloody may not. I am here as a friend of Jake's and to assist him with the language. His French leaves a little to be desired and we didn't know what to expect." This was untrue. Jake spoke French fluently, but they both intended to keep their powder dry. Griff's Russian was perfect and they both rightly suspected that this was a possible development resulting from Hubert's suspicions and Jake's sudden dismissal.

"So, what happens now?" asked Jake. "I would like to be re-united with my wife and child as soon as possible. You will receive nothing more than my name until I see them." He closed his mouth firmly and stared at the stranger.

"I'm sorry! My name is Rudi, by the way. Come on — let's go. Mrs Scott and Ben are waiting for you." He held out his mobile phone, which revealed a picture of Kate, with Ben on her lap and a glass in her hand, sitting on a sofa, apparently chatting to someone off screen. She looked relaxed.

Rudi rattled off directions to a taxi driver. Both Jake and Griff mentally noted the address, and within half an hour, Jake had his arms around his two most important people in his world. Griff waited for his turn to give them a gentle hug, listening carefully to the quick exchange between Rudi and his girlfriend. All was well so far.

"I don't know what's going on, Jake," said Kate "Natasha seems to know more about you than I do. Have you been fired? What the hell have you done? Why is Griff here? For heaven's sake, I really need answers."

He held her close. "Calm down. I haven't been fired — It's just a device to find out what these two are up to.

Believe me, when I am re-employed, I will expect at least double my old salary. Hopefully it will be sorted very soon. What you need to do now is go to your Ma's. She's worried. She thought you'd be there for lunch and it's nearly bedtime."

He looked at Griff. "Take her, will you please, Griff, and on the way, you can tell her what has happened and what brings us here. She needs to be in the picture." He leaned forward and tickled Ben's face. Ben kicked his little legs vigorously and gave his daddy a smile. *There's something about a baby's smile*, thought Jake' and his heart swelled with love.

Griff was back in an hour, having left Kate to think of a convincing excuse for her delayed arrival. Luckily, all Nana had wanted to do was talk about the baby. Meanwhile Jake had been offered sandwiches and coffee, all of which were welcome. He had satisfied the two Russians or Ukrainians or whatever they were, that Griff was trustworthy and indicated that if he was not included in discussions, there would be none.

"Well! Now that you have set down the rules," said Rudi, "perhaps it might be the appropriate time to tell you that we are here to help you, and that if our masters ever found out what we are proposing to tell you, we would disappear — permanently. We have very little, if anything, to gain from this, but we feel that we need to do what we can."

"Then let's hear it," said Jake — unconvinced.

Rudi explained in detail, with one or two interruptions from Natasha, about what she did and what had first set alarm bells ringing.

"They have files on just about all of you," she said, "at least those who are significant members of the agencies. You are watched, and lines of communication are hacked. We have addresses and telephone numbers. You know that, of course, you do the same for the Russians, and both sides have means of interrupting, diverting, disguising — it's like a game."

"Too right," interrupted Rudi with a wry smile. "It makes me furious — guys with nothing better to do than to play computer games, while I have to go out night after night trying not to kill people — regardless of my instructions."

"But that's a speciality of your lot, isn't it?" said Jake. "Please don't pretend you are not assisting Assad, in his search for ISIS. Is blanket bombing really the answer? Does it not upset you to think of the children who are being slaughtered in Syria?"

He stopped as Rudi sprang to his feet

"Do you think I want to? I have to do it. I hate it. I try to avoid streets and homes. I hate what I do. So many times, I have saved my cargo until I was in the countryside where it would do little harm — but they can tell. My comrades are the same. We do not enjoy this, or even understand why it is happening. The President is power-crazy. He wants to rebuild the Soviet Union. All our wealth goes on building the power of the army, creating

43

new missiles. The country is falling to pieces, food is short, jobs are scarce — I think he wants to be able to rely on Syria for support, I don't know, but I am in the Air Force and do what I'm told to do. The only safe places in Idlib and other cities in Northern Syria are the mosques. We have strict instructions to avoid the mosques."

"So, there is safety for those who get to a mosque in time. What about children?"

"They normally don't go into mosques until they are at least seven, but of course they would be given shelter in an emergency. There is a separate area for women and children. The trouble is, they don't have time. There is little warning. We fly in over the border at all times of day. Look — do we have to talk about this? I came to warn you. Maybe if what we tell you is useful, Natasha and I can seek asylum here or in England, but that is not our prime purpose. I assure you. It's just a pleasant thought." He put his head in his hands.

"Okay," said Jake. "Tell us all about it — Natasha. First, were you responsible for planting that rubbish into my computer? It didn't fool anybody, by the way. We're just playing along."

"Yes, it was me," interrupted Natasha, "and I expected you to be at least curious enough to investigate"

"And your motive?"

"Entirely altruistic. I'm beginning to wonder why myself."

"I'm sorry," said Jake. "It's been a stressful time lately, and I can see you are not in the happiest situation either. You're taking risks and showing great courage. It's not within my remit to offer you any kind of sanctuary, but I know people who might help."

He looked Griff, who shrugged

"Right," said Rudi and fired off a sentence to Natasha in Ukrainian. She nodded.

Jake glanced at Griff, who gave a slight nod.

"The first inkling I had that you might have a traitor in the camp," said Natasha, "was when I picked up a file marked with this heading." She handed Jake a piece of paper on which was written "CIT STA RES/3.3." "Does that ring any bells with you?"

Griff leaned across, studied it for a minute and then sat back.

There was a silence as Jake concentrated on the reference, looking puzzled.

Rudi looked across at Natasha and made a comment in Russian

"Give him time," remarked Griff, also in Russian. "Did that message emanate from Millbank?"

"Da," nodded Natasha, and then looked up, startled. "You speak Russian." A statement, not a question.

Griff grinned. "I needed to trust you," he continued in English. "This is more my domain. I'm with MI6. I guess the CIT STA refers to the Hotel 'City Stay' in Salisbury. The RES is reservation, and the 3.3 is March 3rd. The mystery is, who in MI5 is making reservations for two assassins who flew over to London, drove one hundred and fifty miles, did the job, and then hightailed it home to

Moscow? It seems pretty careless to send a message like that from Millbank. I got it straight away but that was because you had warned me, I suppose. Can you tell me anything about the file?"

"Nothing that makes sense. It had a long numerical number, but I didn't make a note of it. Someone approached my desk and I quickly switched over."

"We need to get back, Jake. We can put down your sudden disappearance to a stomach bug, but we need to let Hubert know that he was right.

"We need some safe way to communicate with you two." He looked at the Russians.— "You've taken chances and we appreciate it. If there's any way we can help you, we will. Give me a bit of time. There are people I need to talk to."

"Just a minute, Mr Griffiths," said Rudi. "I think you should wait a while. How well do you know your people? Who can you trust? Who is Hubert? We chose Jake because Natasha believes in him. He and Natasha are both experts in the same field. She persuaded me to agree to make contact with him, but whatever you do back home, please leave us out of it. You can't choose to disclose our identities. That is for us to decide — when and how, if at all."

"I think we know who to trust, Rudi," interrupted Jake. "My boss has been perfectly straight with me. He will be waiting for me to report any developments. It was he who realised that Natasha's message to me was an invitation, but I will agree to keep your identities secret, until you are ready. How can we keep in touch?"

"If it is a complicated matter but not urgent, we'll write to you. Good old paper in envelopes with stamps. Strange, really, in these days of advanced technology that the old ways are the safest. I have your address. If it is something more urgent, I will email a signal to Kate, then we can use a safe phone line. Natasha will give you her mother's email address and phone number in case you need us. We know that is safe. Nothing should come from your laptop, Jake. Just carry on with the charade for a day or two. You have been suspended. It was all a silly misunderstanding. Stay at home, try to relax, and then go back to work as usual."

"He's right, of course, Jake," said Griff. "We can't trust anyone — like that guy who took us from your office? Did you know him?"

"No — never seen him before, and he seemed very confident — almost as if he was in charge. God, this is awful. Suddenly I don't know who my friends are. We need to get back anyway. Can you get us a taxi please? We might just make the last flight back." He stood up and held out his hand. "Why should I trust you? I don't know why, but I do. I also appreciate the fact that you have trusted us, and I give you my word that we will not let you down. Hopefully we'll meet again when all this is sorted."

Griff went straight back home to see his partner and change clothes but was at Jake's door early next morning.

"Okay, so what's the plan? Have you been in touch with Hubert?"

"No. I called to arrange a rendezvous but there was no answer. I'm going over and over in my mind what happened yesterday. About our new buddies, now presumably back in Moscow. Do we believe them, Griff? Or are we both being massively naïve and stupid? Yesterday they seemed kosher, now I'm having doubts."

"Of course, you are. We are trained to disbelieve everything which doesn't have a visible stamp of approval — a certificate of origin or a validation by Her Majesty the Queen. That is what we are for. On the other hand, we're pretty good at telling very convincing lies ourselves and there is no reason to think that they can't do the same thing. What we must do is analyse and eliminate — so what could they possibly have to gain, by getting you over to Paris? They must have known you would be there like a shot if you thought Kate was in danger."

"I was the one who persuaded her to go. They picked that up from my laptop and took advantage of the chance to talk to us on neutral territory. But what's in it for them, Griff? Sowing the seeds of doubt about the firm? I'm just a deskman. This is not within my remit. For all they know, I might be the mole. I did believe Rudi, though. His reaction to my accusation of blanket bombing was spontaneous and genuine. He does hate what he is expected to do."

"Yes, he's kosher. I had a chat to him before we left Okay. So, we get in touch with Uncle Hubert but keep quiet about this for the time being, yes? There have been no developments. You just popped over to Paris to make sure Kate was okay. She had stopped to do some shopping." He paused "Hubert will naturally want an update. Leave that to me. I'm just a little surprised that he hasn't been in touch. I'm going to the office. I'll try from there. You may as well go home and type out the recording you have on your phone. I'll see what we have on the Ukrainian outfit — and her father."

Chapter 5

Grace's mother Sharon was waiting at the door when Ian dropped Grace and Kerim on the pavement outside. He had to get back to the airfield. There was another mission that afternoon, thankfully not to Syria. He waved a greeting at Sharon and smiled encouragingly at the little boy, who, clutching Grace's hand, was looking apprehensively at this home of Grace with its neat front garden and shiny black front door. It was so much bigger than the little haven he had shared happily with his parents, and he silently prayed that his mother was somewhere safe. He must find her.

Grace had explained the situation to her mother. "Don't be too effusive," she had said. "He is in a state of shock and desperate to find his mother. Sadly, he never will, but at the moment, nobody can take her place. Just be friendly and calm. Don't, for heaven's sake, try to hug him."

"Give me credit for some sensitivity," Sharon had replied quietly, realising at once that this little boy had become Grace's new project and was likely to become part of the family for some time. There were of course official channels to approach, but they could wait.

She held out her hand, smiled and said formally, "Welcome, Kerim, I am happy to meet you. Will you come in and join us for breakfast?"

Grace translated.

"Thank you," replied Kerim and took Grace's hand as they walked towards the front door. In spite of his ordeal, he was curious. This was another world. In his seven years, he had never been further than a few miles from Idlib. Inside the front door there were wooden tiles in a strange zig-zag pattern on the floor, and some stairs going up. The stairs had a carpet with no pattern on it. Maybe these were poor people. The carpets in Syria all had beautiful patterns.

They didn't take the stairs; they walked ahead into a room with wide windows that looked into a pretty garden. It was a kitchen, with tables, chairs and cupboards, and a fridge — bigger than the one at home, and other white machines, one with a round window in it. All very clean, and there was a nice smell of food. He was very happy to sit down to eat eggs on toast and a large glass of orange juice.

"More toast and butter?" enquired Sharon, noticing how quickly the food had been devoured.

"Yes, please," he replied and smiled at her.

She breathed a sigh of relief and smiled back. *The way to a man's heart*, she thought, *however young he is*, and began to plan lunch. He spoke very little English, but she could see from his manner that he was beginning to relax

They left Kerim in the living room, wide-eyed, watching a suitable film for children involving spaceships

51

and weird puppets, which seemed familiar to him. He was comfortably ensconced on the sofa and when Grace checked half an hour later, he was sound asleep.

"So!" began Sharon, "What's the plan? Does he have papers?"

Grace explained how and why she had brought Kerim to England "It wasn't exactly a spur-of-the-moment thing. It was as if it had been planned. Everything fell into place. There was no time to sit and think about it. To leave him was unthinkable, anyway. You would have done exactly the same thing in my place."

"Probably." Sharon sighed. "It's heart-breaking to contemplate what's going on there, and not only there. All over the world, children are being abused, starved, killed, abandoned. I've stopped going to church. Why should we demand our daily bread? We're just a greedy fat ungrateful race perpetually complaining about trivia."

"We're not all fat," observed Grace, who had heard her mother's views on topics like this more times than she could remember. "And all we can do is help whenever we can. Now! What about that guy you know who runs the boys' home? We know he has contacts who can help with papers."

"Spike — yes. I'll get in touch. When are you due back?"

"When I'm ready. I'm not employed, I'm a volunteer. I will go back, but not until he is settled. I'm going to have to tell him his mother didn't survive at some point, but not yet. Could you phone Spike today? We could pop over.

He'll need a bit of time to prime his young residents but they're all good kids."

"Spike has a way of bringing out the best in people," her mother observed. "He once said that to have a bad start in life can be a benefit if you deal with it in the right way. You're much more likely to appreciate the good things in life, and to develop that empathy that helps you to understand other people's problems. Those boys are a credit to him."

"Yes, they are, and heaven knows. His start in life was particularly tragic."

Spike's parents had both been killed in a horrendous car accident. With no relatives, both Spike and his younger brother had been placed in a boy's home, run by the Catholic Church. It was the home from hell, managed by a priest who was sexually exploiting the smaller boys. The body of Spike's little brother Joey had been found dead outside the building, beneath a window. Spike, ten years later when he had the strength and resources, and with the aid of members of the Metropolitan police, had been relentless in his search for that priest. Now, his catharsis was to run a model home for orphan boys, giving them every opportunity to live a good life and respect others. It was funded by a very successful boatyard, from which Spike occasionally used one of the boats to pick up young illegal immigrants in France and reunite them with families over here. When Sharon called briefly to explain the situation with Kerim, he was only too happy to help.

"Come on over," he said. "Today would be great. I'll expect the three of you around lunchtime — and plan a sleepover."

"Er, well, yes. I think we can do that."

"Good, because you may just be able to help me. As it happens, I have a youngster here who has come from Iraq. The story is that he and his parents escaped to Turkey, but when the authorities found out that they were Kurds, both parents were interned; the kid was smuggled out by some bastards who took all his money, so he says, and left him with a group who made their way across Europe to France, which is where Vic picked him up. He speaks excellent English and French and would have no problem communicating with your Kerim."

"I'll tell him what to expect." She paused "Look Spike, is there any chance that you could look after him for a while?" "Grace has promised to stay as long as necessary to see him settled, but I know she feels she ought to go back and help in Idlib. I've begged her to stay at home, but she claims she must do what she can to help those people while the rest of the world turns its' back on them."

"Just come over. We'll talk about it. Must go. We have a lawyer coming in to lecture a group of aspiring solicitors and I thought I'd join them. It's so much easier to break the law if you know precisely what the law is."

They both laughed and Sharon switched off her phone. "Get ready" she yelled at Grace. "We're going on a Bear Hunt."

On the way, they stopped in town at a couple of charity shops and bought clothes for Kerim — jeans, T-shirts, sweaters, shoes, socks and a warm jacket as well as the *Bear Hunt* book that Sharon had noticed in the shop window the day before.

"It's a bit young for him, Mum," frowned Grace.

"It's about life," replied Sharon. "It's about getting where you want to go. However difficult it might be, however many obstacles there are, you go for it, and if in the end, it was all a waste of effort, you learn from it, shrug your shoulders and tackle the next problem. It's written in simple repetitive English so it's educational — trust me.""

The manager of the shop was quite happy for Kerim to change into his 'new' clothes in the changing room and he was beaming with pleasure when he emerged attired and looking good. He held out his hand to Sharon and spoke. Grace translated. "You are so kind. My mama would love you. Thank you."

"Can I give him a hug?" she asked Grace.

"Not yet. You'll know when. He might even hug you first. Come on, let's go. It's a three-hour drive."

Spike emerged from the house as soon as he heard their car. Beside him was a dark-haired teenaged boy, not smiling and looking slightly apprehensive.

When they had all climbed out, Spike approached to greet them shook, hands with Kerim and beckoned the dark boy forward.

"Come and say hello to someone you may be able to help. His English is not quite as good as yours. This is Kerim from Syria. Kerim, meet Ahmed from Iraq."

The boy stepped forward hesitantly and the two exchanged words in Arabic. Grace listened carefully. She spoke Arabic well and noted that Kerim had glanced at her but had not made any reference to the fact that she could understand some of what was being said. She wondered why. The conversation was brief and awkward, mainly about where each other had lived, and how each one had ended up in England lived. There was something strained about it — like a performance put on for the adults, but they were strangers, and their recollections were almost certainly traumatic.

"Shall we go inside?" she said at last to Spike. "It's a bit chilly out here."

"Of course. I'm sorry," responded Spike and ushered them into the comfortable living room at the back of the house. Pippa came in with a tray of cakes, biscuits and drinks.

"You know there are so many rival factions in that part of the world,"— Grace explained quietly to Pippa. "Kurds, Jihadists, Hezbollah, Al Qaeda, Sunnis, Shias... It's a nightmare. Russians, Turks, Iranians intervening in their own interests and in Syria, a President who is willing to sacrifice as many of his own people as necessary to stay in power. Let's wait a while and see if these two are prepared to trust each other. If not, there must be a reason why."

"They're just kids, Grace, thinking like old men," remarked Spike. "It's tragic. It's bloody religion again, isn't it, driving people apart. Ahmed is insisting that he must go to the mosque to pray. I know it would not be right to prevent him, but I'm not inclined to help. There is a mosque about fifteen miles away. I just don't have the time to escort him. I've managed to avoid the subject of visits up to now, but I saw him at a computer yesterday doing research. He knows how to use them, and he's very well educated. There's a grim determination about him. He's on a mission of some kind. I'm sure of it and I think he's decided to strike out on his own. I feel too responsible for him to let that happen."

"So, what precisely do you know about him?

"Only what he told Pierre when he rescued him in France. There's nobody who can verify his story, but he was a mess. Dirty, hungry and determined to get to England. He claims his parents were Kurdish and they planned to go to Istanbul. They were separated somehow. There are certain inconsistencies in his account. I know President Erdogan in Turkey has it in for the Kurds, so why would they flee in that direction? He couldn't explain it, except to say that his father had a cousin in Istanbul. He clams up if there's a hint of interrogation — and I'm not the person to do that anyway. He needs to be cared for and trusted..." He hesitated. "But you know what? Try as I might, I don't trust him, or care for him all that much. There's something about him. A supressed rage, I feel. You know the rules here. We encourage self-respect,

respect for others, responsibility for our own actions, honesty, the courage to own up of we do something wrong. Most things are forgivable, but not betrayal or the intention to do harm. I usually get to know the boys quickly. They trust me, but not this one. I can't risk a cuckoo in the nest Grace." He paused, sighed and leaned forward towards her.

"I've been chatting to Sharon, and I understand that there's a mosque fairly close to where you live in London. Could you possibly have Ahmed for a couple of weeks? I know it's a big ask, but if you could find out just a little more about him? It seems a lot like spying, I know, but there have been a number of bad apples arriving in this country and my school is off-limits to anyone who has anything but good intentions." He looked at her enquiringly.

This was something Grace had not envisaged for a moment, and she took a few moments to consider the implications. It might mean a longer stay at home, time to get to know Kerim better and break the news of his mother's death when he was more able to cope with it, but was she prepared to take on a mystery teenager who had appeared out of nowhere? How would Sharon take it?

"Have you sounded my mum out about this?" she asked

"Actually, she almost suggested it herself. I think it may be a device to keep you at home just a little longer, but she was quite enthusiastic about the idea."

Grace laughed. "Okay, if you can look after Kerim, just long enough to get papers for him — and I know you can do that — I'll take Ahmed home with us, but I will alert the right agencies. He's just a teenager and probably harmless, but if he disappears, they will be aware of him. I'll take him to the mosque and hopefully some kind Muslim will give him a home. I'll stay here for a day or two, while we sort it out, but then I must get back."

"Thanks, Grace. I'll get onto Griff straight away. It's his line of work. It will be interesting to see what he makes of Ahmed. I know him well enough to assume there will be no papers for the boy if he has any doubts at all. Kerim seems straightforward, and you are going to sponsor him. That's great. Don't worry. He's in good hands."

From the window, Grace could see some boys playing football on a marked-up pitch not far away at the back of the house. One of the boys was Kerim. She saw him running frantically towards the ball, get there just before another boy, and kick. It hit the back of the net. There was a cheer and he turned around, arms up in the air. She could see that he was laughing."

Dinner, as usual, was in the very large dining room. All the students were there, chatting happily, and Grace was pleased to see Kerim looking fairly relaxed and talking to Ahmed while he consumed with familiar enthusiasm a meal of roast chicken with vegetables and rice, followed by treacle pudding and custard.

At the top table, it was fillet steak with creamed potato and a side salad accompanied by a very good red wine.

Manna from Heaven, thought Grace and had to persuade herself that she really must return to bread, cheese and lentils with water that never really tasted clean — but not just yet.

Chapter 6

Griff came in, looking thoughtful, and threw his briefcase onto a chair.

"So, what's the news?" enquired Jake, "and why are you looking so serious? I've been waiting for a call all day."

"It's only lunchtime, for heaven's sake. Yes, I knew you were waiting but…" He paused. "I've been busy."

Jake stifled the flippant remark on the tip of his tongue. He could tell that Griff was seriously disturbed about something. Griff sighed.

"It's Hubert. He seems to have disappeared. He's been out of contact since closing time yesterday. I went round to his place. All the shutters are closed. There's nobody there."

Jake stared. "And his office? Surely they have some idea where he is?"

"No — well they're being very cagey, but there's a strict protocol, you know that. There is a direct emergency line between his desk and one at MI6, to which he must respond to the signal without delay. If there is no immediate response, the call is then directed within seconds to the next in line and so on till someone of note answers."

"Yeah! I often wonder what would happen if we all went to the loo at the same time."

"It's not funny, Jake. You know that significant unexplained absences are not permitted for obvious reasons. He's completely out of contact and has been for too long — he and his wife."

"So, what are they doing about it?"

"I don't know. All the usual channels have failed to locate him. What else can they do? There's just a lot of head-scratching. Officially, it's being played down. The last thing we want is to circulate rumours about an emergency situation. If the Press get wind of that, all hell will break loose. The whole place will be in lockdown. Anyway, when it was clear that he was missing, someone from Vauxhall Cross did make the call to Hubert's red phone, but there was no response — nothing. The link to the next phone was broken. There is absolutely no clue as to his whereabouts or activity. That is unacceptable. There are strict rules for obvious reasons. To ignore them is punishable by death — well, not that drastic, but…"

"So, he appears to have broken all the rules, which is so out of character," muttered Jake. "How seriously are your lot taking it?"

"Very! There's not too much obvious fuss. No emergency signal light flashing. They're playing it down. Saying it could be a technical fault. They're inside his mainframe at the moment crawling around like ants but not coming up with much. I've put in a report about out Paris trip — I had to, Jake, and it's in safe hands. They're inclined to take the same view as we did. Not all Russians like the way things are going right now, especially when there is so much animosity from the President of the USA. All we know about Hubert is that he was safely home when we came back from to Paris. All fine. If anything had been amiss, there would have been a signal. The camera shows nothing significant that night or the next morning, but he left very early. Where he went is a mystery: we just don't know. Sarah went off on her own somewhere the day before in a car with someone, a friend, I suppose, but she does that quite a lot. Now she is incommunicado also. No appearance, no message. If she turns up, I'll be contacted immediately. They're working on it. In that area of London, it's almost impossible to track vehicles. We've been in touch with relatives. No one was aware of any intention to travel. Effectively, Jake, my boy, the only hope of finding out what the hell is going on is by keeping an eye on you. You were his last contact and hopefully his next — if he is still alive and free that is."

"Who took him home? What about that antique shop guy? He seemed to be at an old friend."

"He drove himself home. He usually does; but yes — the antique shop guy. They seemed to be old friends, so let's go and see if he knows anything. You've been thoroughly investigated by the way. They have details of that weird message on your laptop. You're in the clear but they want you to keep out of the office for the time being.

And if anyone contacts you — report it to me immediately!"

"So, you've told them all about Rudi and Natasha?"

"Yes, I had to. And although I'm still in 'trust nobody' mode, I'm quite sure those two had nothing to do with Hubert's disappearance. I'd love to know whether they have wind of it though. Should we email Nat's mother, do you think?"

"I've bought a new safe phone," said Jake, unzipping his pocket, "and I'm going to send the number to her now. Hopefully one of them will call us."

"I'm supposed to be going up to the Stables tomorrow. Spike has a couple of kids that need papers sorting out. There's bugger-all I can do here at the moment so I may as well go today Do you want to come with me? It's a two-hour drive and we can discuss developments as we go."

"Mmmm, I'll think about it. All I'm doing at home is pacing up and down wishing Kate was back. I can tell she's had enough of her mother already. I think she'll be on the way soon. I might need to be here to pick her up. But if it's a day trip…"

They left to re-visit Hubert's friend in Griff's car, each silently considering, as they made their way through the traffic, every possible reason for Hubert's sudden and inexplicable disappearance.

"This is the road where that shop is," Griff said. "Look, it's up there on the left, and it seems to be closed."

"It had the closed sign up last time we were here if I remember rightly. There's a light on inside. Let's go round the back."

The small car park at the back of the shop was enclosed by a high brick wall with a pair of equally high metal gates for access which were firmly locked. Griff parked in the lane, climbed onto the roof of the car and peered over the wall. He was about to drop over when the back door of the shop opened, and the metal doors simultaneously slid silently open. The man with the big nose appeared at the door and looked at him enquiringly.

"It's Mr Griffiths, I believe. Are you alone or is Mr Scott with you?" Jake walked in through the open gates and waited while Griff, as requested, drove the car through — 'to avoid the interest of nosy neighbours.' The gates were immediately closed behind him.

"I don't think we were properly introduced last time," said the man, holding out his hand. "I am Joseph Epstein. I've been half expecting you. Hubert warned me that you were likely to investigate when he disappeared. But he trusted you implicitly. You'd better come inside."

"So, you do know something?" said Jake. "Thank God for that. Where the hell is he? Is he safe?"

There was a noticeable absence of any antiques inside. It was a spacious, well-equipped office with a desk, filing cabinets, photographic paraphernalia, and a dark room in one corner.

"I can't tell you much," said Epstein. "Hubert did say that there would be an immediate search for him. He just needed a few hours' start. He trusts you implicitly and he may need your help. He needed a reliable contact. Very few people know what goes on here in my little antique shop. I've told the neighbours I've retired, and they leave me alone.

"Although I've known Hubert for many years, he doesn't come here often. We usually meet for a drink in town, but he knows what I do and has used my services several times."

There was a silence. "We've been very concerned, Mr Epstein. Hubert seems to have disappeared without trace, in a manner, which amongst other things, could suggest to some people that he may be guilty of some sort of — I don't know. I refuse to believe that he is unreliable but the fact that you seem to know a little about what is going on is reassuring and a great relief to me," Said Jake. "What can you tell us? But first, is he safe?"

"Yes. As far as I know he is safe, but he is taking risks. There are things he must investigate. He's called me once just to let me know he made it. If you hadn't turned up today, I was going to get in touch with you, I'm not sure how. Is there any possibility that you were followed here?"

"No, I'm always careful," said Griff, "and my car is checked over daily for any tracking device."

"Good. Then I'll tell you what I can. Have you ever met Sarah, Hubert's wife?"

"No, people in our line of work tend to keep our private lives private. I've seen her just once — at least I think it was his wife, a very attractive woman, but we weren't introduced. He pretended not to see me. We were both shopping at Harrod's."

"Yes, that probably was his Sarah. She is lovely. You wouldn't know that she is Russian, then?"

"Hell no. How did that happen?"

"You knew he spoke Russian?"

"That's no secret. He did languages at Oxford, yes?"

"Yes — he and his wife met when he was doing an exchange term in Moscow. Then she moved over here. She too studied at Oxford. She's been checked out of course — more British than half the Brits really. She won't even go back to Russia to see relatives. She is very disturbed by what goes on these days. The Russians are effectively at war with the West. Not with guns and bombs but with technology. There are incursions everywhere. They seek to gain control and information. Nothing is sacred. Fortunately, you people are onto it. Our secret intelligence systems, I'm told, are second to none, certainly every bit as good as theirs. The United States turf out Russian spies by the dozen every year. But you know all that, of course, Mr Scott. Trouble is, the better we get, the harder they try, and not only that, but they are also not above a thorough cleansing job if they feel it necessary."

"You mean the assassinations?"

"Quite! So Hubert is playing a dangerous game. I don't know whether you have noticed things in this room which might indicate what my skills involve?"

Griff stood up and walked toward an area in one corner shielded by a black curtain and twitched it aside.

"You make fake passports."

"Only half right. They are absolutely genuine passports and I have been approved and licensed by your very own organisation. Sometimes a false identity is vital. Hubert has had at least three so far. At the moment he is, I believe, in Moscow, travelling under the name of Boris Tchenko with an American Passport. Tchenko actually does exist — in the States. He sells books and there is absolutely no reason to suspect him of anything. He's a nobody. All background checks have been anticipated and dealt with."

"So, you can produce American documents too?"

"With the appropriate authority, yes, and French and German ones too. The relevant diplomatic services are aware of each one that I produce, and each has a very special mark."

"Hubert is onto something concrete then, but why all the secrecy? Surely that is going to look suspicious immediately."

"Not really. Your agencies tend not to broadcast their plans. Not at that level anyway. I have no idea what he is up to. I would rather not know."

"But to his immediate colleagues," said Jake angrily. "To the people who should know. To me, for example."

"Exactly," interrupted Griff, "which presumably is why we are here. You were expecting us. Hubert knew we'd come here, so what are we supposed to do?"

"I'm not sure." Epstein sighed. "Quite honestly, this has taken me by surprise too. When Hubert came here, he was in a state. He said something about the Soviet Intelligence Agency - the GRU — setting up networks everywhere, and that the UK is an obvious target. Well, that's not exactly news, is it? There is a department at Moscow University which is controlled by the Russian SVR, that is, as you know, their foreign intelligence service. They have technical buffs who are into everything. He hinted that he was in contact with one of them. It all sounded a bit flimsy He gave no details and quite honestly, I wasn't convinced — but who am I to doubt him? It's just that I've known him for years and he's never been so evasive before. He seemed very stressed, almost frantic. He had told me earlier about the stuff planted in your laptop, Jake. He thought, although it seemed innocuous, it seemed to have been placed there to attract your curiosity. He believes it was a warning of some kind. Could it have something to do with that?"

Jake sighed and looked at Griff enquiringly. Griff gave a shrug. "Well obviously. We'd like to find out what that was all about ourselves, but it wasn't the kind of thing that would put the wind up him. Is there any safe way we can contact him directly?"

"Well, as well as the Tchenko identity, he has a new email address. It's in this envelope together with the name of the hotel where he hopes to stay. I don't need to tell you to be careful what you do. He asked me to give it to you, to read and to destroy it before you leave — all far too dramatic for words and not too convincing. There will be a key word in the message, which you will refer to if and when you contact him. You already have your laptop back. There's probably something on there. I don't want to know any details. He and I exchange information which is relevant only to us. It's not that he doesn't trust me. It's so that I cannot divulge any sensitive information under pressure. Sensible, really, although I often think that it would be nice to be able to reveal something that sounded convincing, rather than wait until they started pulling out my fingernails." He gave a nervous laugh.

Jake nodded. "Fair enough. I do understand. I'd probably tell all as soon as they picked up the bolt cutters, but before we go, Joseph, the guy who brought us here. What do you know about him?"

"Nothing, why? I He was just a driver. Drivers are hired and fired, presumably as and when needed, and after background checks have been made. I hadn't seen him before. Hubert did ask me to meet you at the front, though, and not to indicate that there was parking at the back."

"The guy said he was just obeying orders when he picked us up at the office and gave me my resignation to sign. Those orders were to bring us here, and Hubert was expecting us. Does that bother you? Does that mean that guy knows what's going on? I recall he said someone would meet us here. He seemed to know the way."

Joseph shrugged. "Can't help, sorry. I can only presume that if Hubert trusted him, so should I."

They thanked him and agreed to keep in regular touch.

Chapter 7

"So, what do you think of him?" asked Jake as they drove away.

"He's fine. I checked him out. He does exactly what he said he does. Hubert certainly trusts him — and us. It would have been nice if he'd left us some clues or instructions, though. Is there anything new on the laptop? Presumably that's how he'll make contact.

"Presumably yes. Do you think we should have told him about Natasha and Rudi?"

"Absolutely not! That sort of stuff is way beyond his remit. Look, shut up and let me think." He paused

"You know, the first thing that guy should have asked for when he threw you out of your office was your key card."

"Yes! It was in my wallet, and I was waiting for the demand. It never came. They may have remotely disabled it."

"Odd! Very odd! It's too late now. But I'll pick you up first thing tomorrow and we'll go and see."

*

At eight a.m. next morning, the entrance hall was a flurry of activity as usual but the narrow corridor where the barriers were remotely controlled was unmanned. Only staff had access.

The entry system was designed to be fool-proof. Algorithms and cameras did a much better job than anything a security guard could have done. Muscular receptionists were becoming redundant.

The area wherein the barriers were contained was surrounded by bullet-proof glass. Jake hesitated before holding up his card to the reader screen, which also checked his facial features. The gate swung open silently. Griff also was permitted through without hesitation, using his own card, which was effective in his headquarters too. Hubert had sorted that some time ago. Griff was beyond suspicion.

"Hi Jake," yelled a colleague from down the corridor. "How was it?"

"Er, crap," responded Jake, silently praying that that was not an entirely inappropriate response.

"Yeah, these bloody courses always are." I've got one next week. I think I'll go sick. There's load of stuff on your desk, by the way. I had a quick look but there was nothing I could help with. More bullshit from North Korea."

"Not another threat from Kim Jong Un. I keep telling him that there are enough rockets pointing at his ammunition stock to cause a very loud bang, but he thinks I'm kidding." Jake laughed, shrugged his shoulders, and muttered to Griff, "So my temporary suspension didn't hit the headlines. It must have been very low-key. I went on a course, apparently. What the hell is Hubert playing at? The sooner we find that driver, the better. I'm going upstairs to see what's happening in Hubert's office. Chances are that he will be sitting behind his desk wearing his usual mask of total indifference. If he is, hold me back. I might want to punch his lights out."

But he wasn't. The chair was empty and the non-emergency telephone was the only one on his desk. It was unplugged. Jake sat down on the desk chair, re-connected the phone, dialled an extension, waited, and then said, "Is that personnel?"

There was a pause then, "It's Jake Scott. I'm in the Director's office, could you please send someone up with the complete file on drivers we use, including outside agencies? Presumably all their details will be in there, and photographs and more importantly, their assignments and destinations for the last week. ASAP please. Thanks."

He put the phone down and grinned at Griff.

"Well, at least we know where he is but not why. Kate will be back in a day or two. She just texted me, and by that time, I want to be damned sure we have identified that bloody driver and interrogated him. He is distinctly fishy."

"I agree, but I have a nasty feeling that it's not going to be as easy as you think. When we get back to yours, we should send a message to Natasha's mother and tell them to get in touch. We need to update them urgently. She needs to know that Hubert is on her patch and is one of the good guys." He paused. "I hope."

It was a matter of minutes before a girl came in with a thick file.

It contained a list of names, details and photographs, dating back several years.

"Bloody hell! Half of these must be dead. It's in date sequence, so I'll start with the last page and work back."

"Okay, I'll go and get some coffee."

"And biscuits. I'm starving."

"When Griff arrived with a tray of coffee and donuts, Jake was still immersed in the file, glasses halfway down his nose. He looked up.

"I'm going through the photos, studying each carefully. I'm beginning to think he ain't here. Could you have a quick look just in case I've missed something? He looked about forty, didn't he, so there's no point in going back more than ten years, really. I've gone back twenty."

He sat back munching a donut while Griff concentrated on the files. "Is all this online?"

"Bound to be if you know where to look. But it will be exactly the same. Probably on a stick in a safe somewhere in the cellars with all the other records."

"Well, I suppose there's no point in doing a double check, but you're right. That face is not here. Is it possible that they haven't caught up with the records? Are his details hovering somewhere waiting to be added?"

"No chance! He'd be logged as soon as they instructed him, after rigorous checks. It looks as if Hubert is making arrangements of his own, off record and against every rule in the book. So, is he bad or just so suspicious that he can trust no one? Let's get out of here. We need to get a message to Natasha. Do we need to tell her that you have filed your report? It feels horribly like a betrayal. That's how she'll see it."

"No, she needn't know. I'm absolutely confident that the information is filed in the right place accessible only to trustworthy personnel. I promise. I know how you feel, Jake. These moles can be so clever, and it's easy to think they might be crawling out of the woodwork rather more frequently than we expect, but they are few and far between, honestly."

"Turn round," said Jake. "I want to see if your fingers are crossed behind your back."

*

"Fox Glove," said Jake thoughtfully. "That's the only entry since I last touched this. It must be the contact word"

"Foxglove? It's some sort of weed, isn't it?"

"Yes, digitalis, Dead Man's Bells, they call it. Can be useful or deadly. Lovely to look at, but he's used two words, and it can only be Hubert that put them here — Fox and Glove?"

"Take the words separately then."

"Okay! — Fox — what does that suggest, something sly and wily that only comes out at night?"

"Cunning, yes. Could be him then. What about glove?"

Jake pondered. "Gloves protect you from the cold. So, he is out there somewhere with a cunning plan. Designed to protect us from the Russians."

"At a stretch, yes, and he's given us remote code words, not to be bandied about, but for recognition purposes only, I guess."

Griff grinned. "This is refreshing. I've never done this sort of stuff before. It makes a change from translating bloody documents and sitting in dirty cafés appearing not to be listening to dodgy conversations. What are we going to do?"

"Suppose she and Rudi are big liars and take him into custody immediately. You were there, Griff. What do you think?"

"Yes! I meant to tell you. I've done some research. Her father was at the university in Ukraine. No permanent contract though, and his attendance there was strangely sporadic. What she didn't know was that he was in contact with us. I think she would have mentioned that to us if she had known. He was a good bloke. Disturbing that he just disappeared. We lost contact too. I can't find out much about Rudi. He's just a pilot with a conscience and a thirst for vengeance. Use your new phone and email Nat's Ma. Hopefully she'll come back to us this evening."

"Right, it's done. What's the Latin for fox? We need to compose a message for Hubert just to let him know we're in. We have no alternative but to trust the passport guy. Hubert clearly does."

"Okay, how about this?"

To boris_tchenko@mos.com

Hi Boris,

Just keeping in touch as promised. I hope this finds you in the pink. I'm looking after your garden while you're away. The digitalis is magnificent this year.

All is well at home although it seems strangely empty. I assume you are safe out there, but it would be nice if you came back soon. Any idea when that might be? Keeping the lawn cut is hard work and I have to watch my back. Thankfully I have a friend helping.

Fritz

P.S. How can I get in touch with that driver you used recently? I need a lift to the airport, and I don't think you told me his name.

"Yeah. Just the kind of thing a neighbour would write. Especially if he was pissed off with looking after your garden and didn't know how long he was expected to do it. Nice touch about the driver." He scratched his head. "And 'strangely empty'? So, you think this might have something to do with Sarah? Can we see if she was on the same flight out?"

"Done that. Not that flight or any other that day since."

"Well, let's hope he responds. If there's been no sightings or contacts with Sarah here, there must be a connection. He'll tell us all he thinks we need to know but his messages might be vetted so he'll have to be very careful. Anything from Natalie's mother yet? I don't want to send this until we get the okay from them. When does Kate arrive? Are you picking to pick her up?"

"No. It's all sorted. She's getting a taxi. By the way, I had a call from one of her friends — Grace. She wanted to contact you. She spends a lot of time in Syria. She's a qualified nurse. Her parents came here from Syria when she was small, so she is fluent in the language. I think her mother died when she was very young, but Sharon, her step—mother, is great. Seems Grace rescued a little boy from the bombing and brought him home. Didn't you say you were heading for Spike's today? You'll meet her. She's there with the boy and he needs papers. She just wanted to chat to you about it."

"That's odd. Spike mentioned an Iraqi boy, but he turned up a couple of weeks ago. Vic brought him over from France. He needs papers too, but Spike has reservations apparently. Anyway, I can't possibly deal with that today. I'll give them a call. Things to do, people to see. I will do it when I can. Spike knows that."

Chapter 8

Charlie Knowles was at the end of his tether. While it was the remit of MI6 to deal with potential terrorists, the police were required to observe and report anything suspicious, but there were just too many suspects for them to make an effective contribution. It was nevertheless essential that they did what they could. Charlie had agreed that his own section of the force would report any suspicious activity, rumours, or potential trouble spots during their work or free time, and now that they had a team of very sharp Asian detectives, it made sense to rely on their instincts and observations. They had, of course, good reason to visit the mosques as part of their daily life.

So far, they had been instrumental in preventing five serious threats to public safety, and Knowles was proud of them. Although it was fair to say that most mosques and Muslim worshippers were beyond reproach, one had to be careful and tactful.

Thank God Kate was officially coming back to work, albeit part time. Kate had found a reliable source of help with her baby from the flat upstairs, where two ex-soldiers, Sam and Kipper, were installed. Both were enthusiastic and competent babysitters. Little Ben loved them, and

Kate could check the situation minute by minute on her phone, which transmitted pictures of Kipper making funny faces and Ben laughing that lovely baby laugh.

The drug situation was still a problem, despite useful information coming from a recently acquired Albanian secret agent, and Knowles, realising that nothing was going to change until the law permitted some sort of controlled possession of class B drugs, just did what he could. If people were daft enough to poison themselves, it was their own look-out. As long as he could protect youngsters and alert them to the dangers, that was about it.

What bothered him today was a request from the City of London Police. There was a visit scheduled from a Saudi prince, who insisted that his life had been threatened. He wanted his own armed escort to accompany him wherever he went, day or night. This was completely unacceptable to the authorities here. Details of the 'threat' had not been provided and the last thing they wanted was a bunch of trigger-happy Saudis in the Capital.

"Just tell the bugger 'No' and advise him to stay at home. Make it quite clear that we cannot take responsibility for his safety. It's not a State Visit — that would be different. He'll just have to take his chance.

"In the meantime, the security cameras need to be checked. And operative. I want details of anyone visiting the Saudi embassy, especially if they don't come out." He went on to insist that weapons found on or in the luggage of any arrivals from Saudi Arabia at any airport were confiscated on arrival. "If it's a Prince, offer him a motorcycle escort but insist that all his proposed movements are made known to us in advance and in detail. When is this bloody visit?"

"Next Friday," had been the response, "In six days."

That will give Kate four days. He smiled to himself. *She'll love it.*

In fact, Kate was delighted to be home. She and Jake had, after a very happy reunion, discussed Jake's current situation, and although she was concerned about Hubert's disappearance, she didn't know him personally and in fact often cursed him roundly when Jake was not where he should be, like at home by dinner time. All she cared about was Jake, and it was relief that he had not in fact been publicly labelled as a double agent and traitor. Not that anyone who knew him would have believed it — or would they? Anyway, nobody seemed to be aware of any allegation of any kind. It had been some sort of brief weird diversion.

It was great that Sam and Kipper were happy to take on the responsibility of looking after Ben. They were amazingly good at entertaining him, changing nappies, and preparing perfectly healthy baby meals. Ex-soldier Sam spent a lot of time at the police station, sitting in on interviews when detainees had language problems and was even thinking of taking some exams so that he could expand his services. Kipper with his leg-blade spent more time at home during the week and was very happy to earn some cash. Both had served time in Afghanistan and had not come out unscathed.

Kate couldn't wait to get back in the saddle. She had had a long chat with Charlie Knowles the night before and another with Grace, a long-time friend, who told her about the two new youngsters in her life, one of whom was just a child but clearly very important, and the other, Ahmed, who was a bit of an enigma. Both were at the Stables, a modern, private, self-funded home for boys. Kate had agreed to go round and visit one evening when they were home. It seemed that Grace had agreed to look after enigmatic Ahmed for a short time until Griff had a chance to talk to him.

"I trust your judgement, Kate," Grace had said, "and if this boy is trouble, I don't want to leave him here when I go back to Syria. I would worry about both Mum and Kerim."

"Are you due back soon?"

"No, it's up to me, but I'm being pulled both ways. I want to stay and look after Kerim for a while, but such terrible things are happening out there. They need all the help they can get."

"Well, don't stress. We'll talk about it. If there's any doubt about Ahmed, Griff will be on it like a shot."

"Yes, he's coming to talk to him at Mum's house. Kerim will stay at the Stables for a couple of days, so as not to get in the way. It's nice to know Griff is almost within shouting distance if I need him, but I'll be glad when we know who is going where. See you later."

Kate was tempted to confide in Knowles. She felt uncomfortable about not mentioning Rudi and Natasha and the strange goings on at MI5, but he was up to his eyes in problems already. She concentrated on the visit of the Saudi Prince — not a very important one, she'd never heard of him, a fact that she would tactfully disguise with an enthusiastic welcome. She decided to make an appointment to see him as soon as he arrived at his hotel on Friday but in the meantime, she would pay an advanced visit to see what the security arrangements were like. Sensibly, they had chosen a discreet hotel, out of town, but the staff were in a state of panic as, until Kate arrived, they had no idea at all that a prince was arriving with an entourage of four. No reservations had been made and there were not enough available rooms to accommodate such a large party. Somehow, they had to make space. No hotel would turn away a Saudi Prince, after all.

"Look, keep calm," said Kate. "A coffee and cakes would be great if you have time, and if I can use your office," she said to the manager's secretary. "I'll get in touch with the City Police and find out what's going on."

How on earth could this cock- up have happened? she thought. From what she knew of the Saudis, whoever was responsible for this oversight, if it was one, would live to regret it — or not. She called Charlie first.

"I've traipsed all the way to Richmond to this bloody hotel, and there is no reservation for His Highness or his mates. Are you sure it's the right one?"

"Err. Hell, I don't know. Get to a computer and I'll send details. I'm sure there was a copy of the reservation and price. Three rooms as I recall at about a hundred quid a night each. I'll try to get confirmation from Riyadh. Stand by!" He was back in ten minutes, sounding highly irritated

"I found it and did some research. To begin with there is no such prince as Osama Ben Saladi; no known prince has planned a trip over here, and the reservation was a clever fake, typed out on a photocopy of a genuine letterhead which, at the time, I had no reason to question. I reasonably concluded that the information had been delivered in the usual way — online and by phone, with the usual safeguards, but not so. A packet had been delivered by a messenger on a motorbike, a service the branch had used themselves once or twice and had no reason to suspect. Nobody thought to check. I have no idea what this is all about. I'm about to call Griff. He may know about it and might have some clue as to the whys and wherefores. Anyway, tell the manager not to worry. If anyone turns up, just tell them to bugger off and call us immediately. Better still, lock them up and then call you."

"Good heavens," exclaimed Kate. "Look it's getting late. Could you come over for dinner? I'll tell the hotel manager to forget all this happened. I haven't actually seen him yet, but his secretary is on the ball and I'm sure he'll be glad to. Griff needs to know about this, too. See you later."

When she arrived, Jake had just arrived home and collected Ben from upstairs. He was spooning some unappetising yellow stuff into an eager little mouth. There was more on Ben's little cheeks than there was on the spoon, but they were both happy.

Kate took time to hug them both and help with the feeding. By now Ben had his little hands in the dish of baby food and was squeezing the mulch between his fingers.

"I'll clean him up," said Jake, "while you pour us a drink and tell me about your day."

"I've invited Charlie to dinner — it'll have to be a takeaway, but there's stuff he needs to know. Strange things are happening." Jake was stunned when she related the facts relating to the hoax message which purported to have been delivered from somewhere or someone in the secret services.

"So, there were no immediate checks? They just accepted a message from a guy on a motorbike? What about the phoney hotel reservation? Where did that come from?"

"It was one of the delivered documents. A forged reservation on a photocopy of the hotel's stationary."

"And if you hadn't decided to go and check their security, we would have had an all-stations alert at Heathrow and Gatwick and heaven knows where else, on the lookout for a group of heavily armed trigger-happy Arabs. It must be a diversion. I'm glad you invited Charlie over. I've been thinking that we ought to trust him with what happened in Paris. I need to convince Griff first. He's coming over, too."

"Good! I don't like withholding information from Charlie anyway. I don't think he'll want to get involved quite honestly but we ought to come clean. No one is more discreet than Charlie Knowles."

"Yes, I agree. He might be very useful anyway. And if we ever needed his help, he would be there for us, so it's better if he has some idea of what's gone on."

Chapter 9

By seven thirty, they were assembled. Jake related the briefest details of his own alleged misdemeanours, his temporary dismissal, the trip to Paris and the sudden disappearance of Hubert. Griff followed with the involvement of the mysterious driver and Jacob Epstein.

It sounds like a network of deceit," remarked Knowles. "Have you decided which of these characters is credible? Trustworthy?"

"To be quite honest, no," said Griff, "but I'm almost certain that Natalie and Rudi are okay. I've done as much research as I can, especially into the Ukraine situation. You know there are about two million Ukrainians who live and work in Russia, so it's not unusual for him to have been accepted into the Russian Air Force, especially with his qualifications from that particular Ukrainian university, but do you remember the Malaysian plane that was shot down over Ukraine in 2014? Well, a few days before, a Ukrainian Air Force plane had been shot down from the same Russian-controlled area, by a similar Russian missile. It was launched from that area of Ukraine which is held by Russian separatists. Rudi's brother was the pilot. He was killed, of course. Rudi told me privately

87

when we had a little chat. He was extremely bitter, and nobody had ever explained why or how it had happened, so I'm inclined to believe both of them."

"Gosh! How awful," said Kate. "They didn't tell me that. Well, yes, I'm with you as far as they're concerned. I liked them too, but Natasha is taking huge risks. Can we help them, Griff?"

"Probably, Kate," he replied. "Let's see how it goes, eh? I have problems of my own to sort out regarding a Syrian boy, which hopefully aren't urgent. Our priorities, Charlie, are finding a mystery driver, of whom there is no record, and getting in touch with Hubert, who is either treading on very thin ice or, very skilfully, betraying his country and his friends."

"Let's take one thing at a time then," said Charlie. "First of all, I am not personally concerned with the disappearance of Hubert. That's your province, Griff. As far as this Russian couple are concerned — well that's a bit different — very interesting but not my province.

"Kate has told you about the Saudi Prince business. That does concern me, because that fake message, purportedly from the Intelligence Services, could presage nightmare situations in London. If it is a diversionary tactic, just to concentrate the force's attention on something that is not going to happen, trouble could be brewing elsewhere. You have your own investigation techniques, I know, but I would expect anything relevant to be referred to me."

Griff nodded. "Of course."

Charlie turned to Kate. "You were telling me about Grace and her Syrian boy. He sounds safe enough. What about the other kid, Griff? From Iraq? Perhaps we could help you there? I have a good team of Muslim detectives, out of uniform, who are very keen to justify their salary increase."

"That could be so useful, Charlie. I'm not prepared to sort out papers for him until I've made enquiries and obtained convincing details from him. Spike seems to be pretty sure he's on a mission of some sort. Can we talk about it later and discuss some sort of strategy? I'll be in touch in a couple of days. Right now, I need to concentrate on identifying that mystery driver. Jake and I are going to go through the closed-circuit stuff we have at the office, in particular, the underground park. We can't really ask anyone else to do it as we want to keep any gossip about Hubert to a minimum. If the Press get hold of this…"

"Then everyone's cover is going to be blown in no time at all," finished Knowles. "Tell me what I need to know after dinner, and I'll be on to it tomorrow first thing. Right now, I'm starving."

*

"That," said Charlie, wiping his mouth half an hour later, "was delicious. Thank heaven it wasn't pizza. I am so fed up with those. That beef was so tender and the gravy — perfect. You've been at work all day, Kate, how did you do it?"

"I opened a box." Kate smiled. "All I had to do was heat it up and do a few fresh veggies. Take the box home and show it to Jill. How is the TV detective series going, by the way? The first series was great! Do you get jealous every time she has to kiss her boss?"

"Not really. She says he has terrible body odour. I think that is just to put my mind at rest, but we're fine. She's a great actress but a lousy cook, though, so don't let me forget that box. Now, let's see what we've got. I' was thinking as I ate."

"In your domain, Jake, there are two situations which seem to have arisen from the same assumption, that there is a double agent in the frame. How did it start? Was Hubert the only one to suspect that trouble was brewing?"

"Yes," said Jake. "Hubert was onto something. I could tell he had something on his mind. Something far more serious than careless messages on laptops. But in fact, it was due to that suspiciously amateurish plant in mine that persuaded him to follow it through, because it was clearly designed to persuade me to investigate. It was so amateurish that when Hubert did draw my attention to it, I thought it had been placed there by some hyper-intelligent sixth-form adolescent who was trying to prove his genius by breaking in and applying for a job."

"How did Hubert know about it? Did you mention it to him?"

"No. Quite honestly, I missed it, and having studied it now, I would never have taken it seriously anyway. Hubert must have been searching for something. I leave the office laptop on my desk most of the time. I have my own small personal one in my briefcase. Anyway, he did see it and decided the message was there for a reason. He was already suspicious, you see. He had suspected an in-house problem for some time. He knew damned well I was as sound as a bell and that if I did want to betray my country, I was far too clever to exchange messages with some Ruski on a laptop. He decided that we should draw them out. He did what he thought they wanted him to do and suspended me so that it would be easier for them to approach me. He assumed that they would contact me pretty quickly, which they did, through Kate."

"So, you were, for the attention of whoever was accessing your laptop, summarily dismissed because of a suspicious email, but what was the point?"

"Well, we knew they had access and assumed that they would be checking, but for them to send another email would be pointless. If there was to be a meeting, it had to be a face to face. The next step was up to them, and sure enough, they did check. That's how they knew about Kate's trip to Paris. They knew when she was due to arrive. They rented a flat there for a couple of days, Natasha waited at the airport and bingo.

"Kate would normally have called to tell me she landed, but it was her mother who phoned to say she hadn't. I was frantic and Griff and I were on our way in no time at all; meanwhile, Hubert had circulated a brief notice, mentioning my name and the phrase 'suspension of contract for personal reasons,' so that he or she would know we'd taken the bait.

"When Kate did call and told me exactly where she was, it was a huge relief, I can tell you. Obviously, I didn't want her to be mixed up in this, but they had wasted no time in letting her contact me to let me know she was okay. They knew that I was free to travel because of my reported departure from the Department, and Kate, when she called me, inferred that there was something that I should investigate in Paris, which by then we strongly suspected, so although it sounds complicated, it all worked out."

"Fortunately, by the sound of it, but does that mean that our secret services are an open book to anyone with the right computer skills and the inclination to manipulate our agents?" asked Charlie incredulously.

"Dear Charlie, you know better than that," laughed Griff.

"The mainline computers we use at the office are impenetrable — well, 99.9%. We all have laptops for the usual office chat — safe stuff — notice of meetings, headlines from international agencies, funny political cartoons. They are provided by the firm. I use mine to organise my life at home, get in touch with Kate, pay bills and so on. I booked Kate's airfare on it. If it's something private or confidential, I use my own private one which I keep in my briefcase.

"Anyway, Charlie, you're a cop. Stop pretending to be such a dyed-in-the-wool Luddite. You know as much about computers as any other person who uses them for work."

"Well, we have a special department for cyber offence investigations. I wouldn't know where to start. It's well out of my remit."

"So, you haven't studied the Computer Misuse Act at all? I'd have thought that it was an essential part of the job. International crime is rife."

"And that Act deals with it?"

"As far as possible, but it's ineffective beyond these shores, of course."

"So it doesn't apply between countries?"

"Well, there's no international convention on Internet Regulations, and I doubt there ever will be. Hackers are everywhere. About 44% of cyber-attacks come from China but it's happening all over the world. There are, of course, legitimate hackers, like Jake, just doing a job to identify the bad guys."

"Yes, Charlie, I'm a white hacker — an ethical security hacker," grinned Jake, "and so is Natasha, although the Russians might not agree. Her intentions were 'entirely altruistic' as far as we're concerned. I hope she never has to pay for it. I hope we can find a way to bring them over here. I think that's what they want."

"I'm working on it," said Griff. "But she has family in Crimea. We'll need to get 'em all out. As for what Hubert found, Charlie, it was on Jake's very easily available laptop, and it served its purpose."

"No thanks to me," said Jake. "We all have access-codes of course, but it wouldn't take a genius to break mine. I've changed it now to facial recognition. I quizzed Rudi about that when we were in Paris, but he's a bit like you, Charlie. His speciality is flying planes. Computers are for practice landings and sending harmless messages to his mates. Natasha is the expert and she confirmed that as far as she knew, our service mainline devices have very secure walls around them. She rightly assumed though, that the data on personal laptops would be under observation from time to time, to some extent, just in case anyone was careless. She managed to access mine and kept it under surveillance. That's how they picked up details of Kate's flight. You know the rest...

"Then something appears to have spooked Hubert and the next day he was gone. As far as I know, we are the only ones who know where he is. It will be circulated that he's taken a business trip to Washington, and for the time being, his code name, for those of us in the know, is Claudius."

"Hmm," said Charlie, "something rotten in the State of Denmark?"

"Yes," replied Jake, "but he certainly isn't in Copenhagen.

"Anyway! I, for one, need an early night, and Griff and I have an early start tomorrow. The first thing we need to do is find that bloody driver who nobody has heard of and who has mysteriously disappeared."

*

Griff met Jake in the underground car park and together they made their way to Jake's office to examine the closed-circuit tapes. Since the event leading to Jake's short-term dismissal had taken place only a few days before, there was not much that they needed to examine minutely, and they were able to fast-forward quite lot. Nevertheless, they went through it three times. The driver had not come in via the main entrance, therefore he must have come in with Hubert through the underground car park to an area which very few people had access. The entry code was changed daily and notified to the few people who used it. Hubert's car did arrive on the day but there was no distinguishable picture of Hubert or his passenger. The area to the lift was not covered.

"Why the hell not?" asked Griff

"Because you would be surprised to learn who pops in from time to time. They need to know their movements are not recorded. It's often a condition that must be observed if the visit is to take place at all. It's not unusual for some visits to this country to be entirely under wraps, from arrival to departure. You should know that, Griff. You're in the business."

"Yes, I know, but sometimes if feels as if we fall into our own traps. So, what now? I need to go soon. I need to have a chat with this Ahmed kid at Grace's."

"Why don't you go and sort that? I'm going to contact Natasha's mother from my laptop here, and hopefully

95

she'll be in touch. Natasha needs to know where Hubert is. I sent him that message last night, so we should get something back assuming he is still alive."

"But no mention of Nat and Rudi, okay? We just can't risk their safety. If she wants to contact him, that's her decision."

"But are we risking his safety? It's quite a dilemma, isn't it? I just hope I come out of this without having to chastise myself for wrong decisions for the rest of my life."

"I know what you mean. It's a matter of judgement and instinct, isn't it? Look, we both think the same, don't we. Jake? You are not alone here. We just have to hope that Rudi, Nats and Hubert are on the same side too. We must smoke out the bad guy, and we have to do that logically and carefully. The driver holds the key. I think we need to pay another visit to Epstein and tap his phone lines. I'm going to sort that when I've seen Grace. I'll leave you to it here. See you later."

Chapter 10

"All we can do now," Jake said to Griff, who had returned from his visit to Grace's home looking thoughtful, "is eat, drink, and compare notes. I need to collect Ben from upstairs and Kate won't be long. Pour yourself a drink."

He returned in ten minutes with Ben in his arms, singing a version of "Baa Baa, Black Sheep." "How long is it since we sent the email to Hubert?" he asked, removing Ben's little hand from his nose. "It seems like days."

"About forty-six hours. I think Kate's just pulled up outside."

"Is Charlie with her?"

"No, I don't think so. She's carrying a fish and chip bag. I hope there'll be enough for me."

"There will be. She called earlier and I told her you would be here. She asked how you had got on and I said you'd be here to tell her all about it. She said Charlie wasn't really interested." Griff laughed

"You know what? I think he just might change his mind."

The discussion with Ahmed had not begun well. Grace and Sharon had left him to it and gone to the supermarket. When Griff went in to introduce himself, the boy was about to eat. He had looked up sullenly from his plate of bread butter and cheese and stared at him.

"Why do you not want to help me? Are you going to help Kerim to get papers? He is just a stupid little boy. Why is he worth more than I am?"

"Every life has the same value, Ahmed. It is not unusual for immigrants to be investigated. You know that perfectly well. You know also that my country is happy to welcome as many troubled people as it can possibly accommodate and feed.

"You ask about Kerim who will be sponsored by a friend of mine. You met her at the Stables, I think; she will see that he is cared for, educated, and when he is older, that he will be self-sufficient. He is just a child, Ahmed. Grace will be entirely responsible for his welfare. She rescued him in Idlib. She saw his home in ruins. She met his neighbour who was weeping for him. He doesn't know whether his mother is dead or alive. He is a child who has known nothing but conflict. He has seen horrors that children here could not imagine. Surely you have some sympathy for him?"

Ahmed stared at him for several minutes without speaking, his face expressionless. Then he spoke. "So, what about me? I am entitled to nothing. No sympathy, no kindness, no understanding? You know nothing about me. I see only suspicion in your eyes. I was a child. I had a home in Mosul. My father was an architect. He was killed by the very people who were trying to help us — the

Americans. They bombed the city to destroy ISIS, but bombs aren't selective. He was crushed when his office collapsed around him."

Griff reached out to put a hand on Ahmed's shoulder. It was shrugged away.

"I am very sorry to hear that, Ahmed. Believe me, very sorry. Look finish your breakfast and we'll talk. If I can possibly help you, I will, but my job is to make the right decisions, to make sure, as far as I can, that the people we welcome, are not our enemies and to do that, I need to know all the facts. You are right. I know nothing about you. That's why I'm here today. Help me to help you."

"The facts?" Ahmed shouted. "You want to know the facts. What facts? I wish I could tell you. It was turmoil, a nightmare. One day I was a happy child with a lovely home and loving parents and suddenly I was alone, no parents, no home, no friends, no food. It was as if, in the space of a day or two, I was dragged out of heaven and thrown into hell. Those are the only facts I know"

Griff listened intently. The boy was remarkably articulate. "Well, you have been well educated, Ahmed. Your English is as good as mine."

"Let me help you with the facts about me," Ahmed said coldly. "My mother spent most of her childhood in Washington. She was born in Teheran. Her father was a diplomat, an Iranian, or Persian if you would prefer to call him that. I vaguely remember him. He was a great friend of the Shah. Then, of course, in 1979, the Shah was overthrown. My mother by then had met my father. She worked at the American Embassy. They were both used to Western ways and were determined to move to America, but my father had contracts to fulfil so they stayed. He was also a keen archaeologist. We were in Iraq at that time. He was working on some restoration project in Ninevah and we were living in Mosul, quite happily — and then ISIS came."

There was a long pause. Griff waited

"He was one of the first victims." He paused. "I was at home with my mother. We could see the planes go over. We lived on the outskirts of the city. We didn't know about Dad, but we were worried. She told me to stay inside and went to get her coat. I was in the kitchen. Suddenly she rushed in and pulled me towards the stairs. 'Go upstairs now,' she whispered. 'Go to the attic and hide. Keep quiet. Go now.'"

He got up and went to stand by the window, his back to Griff.

"I need to go outside for a minute," he said quietly and opened the kitchen door. Griff let him go, realising he was struggling with a memory that he didn't want to share. He thought he knew what it would be. Mosul, ISIS and a sophisticated woman, used to having her own way, used to being respected, wearing what she liked to wear, certainly not a Hijab, free to go wherever she wanted to go. Griff suspected already what had happened. *I need to spare him that*, he thought. He waited another five minutes and then went to the door.

"Come and have a cup of tea, Ahmed," he called. "I've heard enough for today. I have a pretty good idea of what civilians in Mosul had to suffer. It keeps me awake at night sometimes and I was hundreds of miles away."

Backed by U.S.-led airstrikes, Kurdish forces had taken back the town of Mosul from ISIS in November 2015, seizing a site where ISIS forces had committed some the worst atrocities during their march across Iraq. ISIS jihadists brutally killed hundreds of people and captured and raped and killed thousands of women and girls. Heritage sites, mosques, churches were ruthlessly destroyed; heart-breaking for an architect interested in archaeology, a man used to creating and preserving, not destroying. Any objections, of course, would have been dealt with in that typical ISIS way. It didn't bear thinking about. Ahmed's father had been killed by the Americans, he'd said, presumably during an aerial attack on 'ISIS's strongholds. It was all very confusing. No wonder the kid was practically unapproachable.

If he had some sort of vengeance in mind, it was hardly surprising, but Griff needed to find out what it was. When Ahmed came inside, clearly now in control of his feelings, Griff was sitting down.

"You hungry?" he asked. "Could you eat something?"

"Well, it's a long time since I had one," Ahmed responded after a minute or two, "but I'd really love a bacon sandwich."

"Bloody hell," said Griff." And for some reason which neither of them really understood, they dissolved into hysterical laughter, and that is how Kate and Grace found them when they arrived back from the supermarket with amongst other things, a large pack of crispy bacon.

It was much later that evening when Ahmed described what had happened to his mother. Both his parents had been Christians, not devout churchgoers, but they lived their lives according to Christian principals. The day ISIS came to their house, his mother was unaware that her husband was not coming home. It was much later that friends of the family had told Ahmed that the building his father had been in was in was destroyed.

His mother had seen the men approaching their house, trampling over their carefully cultivated garden. She almost certainly knew what to expect and had ordered Ahmed to hide. From an attic window he had seen them drag her outside. She kicked, lashed out and spat at them, and they killed her. They stabbed and slashed with strokes from knives over and over again. She was pregnant. Ahmed had only realised later what it was that one of the laughing assassins had taken from her body and held up. It was a tiny, shapeless thing. It was what would have been Ahmed's brother or sister.

Griff was silent but so moved, that tears were in his eyes. The boy had given these facts calmly and with restraint. Griff guessed it was the first time he had spoken of it, but the memories of that horror must visit him every day.

"I didn't want to look, but I couldn't move. They left her there. It was as if I was literally petrified. Turned to stone. I stayed in the attic and when it was dark, I went downstairs. A friend of my dad's came to tell me what had happened to him. He gave me money and told me I must go away. Hundreds of ISIS rebels had been killed but not all. Those remaining would know we were Christians. They would be looking for revenge. There was no special place in their hearts for children. He drove me out of town. And left me with a group of people heading for Turkey. One day I would like to go back and thank him. He saved me, although at the time I don't think I wanted to be saved.

"It's many months ago now but like yesterday. I'm never sure whether I should think about them every day, just to honour them, or try to forget that I didn't have the courage to go out and say goodbye to my dead mother. I need some way of avenging her. I want to remember her as she was when we were happy. She was beautiful, perfect. You want to know why I'm here, Mr Griff? Muslim terrorists are everywhere. They are like a filthy poison polluting the earth. Those people I travelled with. Some of them admitted it. ISIS murderers, pretending to be sad frightened refugees. I came here to kill them, as many as I can. You must understand that. Surely you will not stop me. An eye for an eye, yes?"

Griff could not find the right words. To point out that most refugees were just desperate, helpless people. hoping for a better life, would not have been accepted although it was quite true, but he understood how Ahmed felt, and he also knew that there was a small number of immigrants with evil intent. He'd met one of them. Recalling that particular incident, he could even contemplate wishing Ahmed luck, but that was not a good idea. Not for boy who had suffered so much emotional agony. He would help him somehow.

He asked Ahmed if he might tell Grace about it all, which was agreed. When he left, she and Ahmed were playing chess, which was clearly familiar to the boy who was well in control of the game. He needed to speak to Kate and Charlie. During the course of the day, Ahmed had told him of the trek across Europe. Part of his original story was true. Some Kurds, not relatives, who had known his parents, did smuggle him out to Turkey and his knowledge of English had helped him there. He had cash from a safe at his parents' house and more money given to him by friends. He had managed to keep it hidden in a shabby toy bear that he had carried everywhere. He had made his way along the south coast of Turkey and then crossed to a Greek island. From there he had had joined a group of travellers until they got to France where he was picked up by Vic.

It had taken many months, and a young, cherished and protected boy had turned into a young man who nurtured a feeling of intense loathing. He said that he had been surprised at the care and freedom enjoyed by the boys at the Stables and spoke of his respect for Spike and Pippa. They had restored his faith in humanity. He had mentally registered every detail of the travellers who came to do harm. They had tried to enlist him. To them he was another Arab boy who could be useful, who could speak English and was young and attractive enough to wheedle his way into their target clubs and organisations. They had come to encourage and assist terror cells already established here. Ahmed had had to hide his revulsion and loathing. He'd lied about his life. He actually knew very little about the Quran or Islam but decided to absorb as much information as he could, to do nothing to arouse their suspicion,, but above all, to find a way to destroy them.

There was one thing he thought it better not to tell Griff. When they reached France, they were herded into an immigrant camp. They were there for some days. So many strangers, so many faces, but there was one face that he would never forget: A face that stopped him in his tracks when he recognised the man he had last seen it in his garden in Mosul. He couldn't move as the man approached. He felt faint, sick and afraid, but the man just walked past. The man who had killed his mother didn't recognise him, of course. He didn't know that Ahmed had been watching from an attic window.

Chapter 11

When she returned, Grace had been delighted to see that the unfriendly young man she had brought back from the Stables was suddenly only too happy to talk to her. When Griff had enlightened her, she was speechless with horror at the trauma he had suffered. She had had a long chat with Kerim on the phone and he was more than happy to stay a couple more days with Spike. He was learning the language fast and playing football so well that everyone wanted to be his friend. Maybe he should stay longer. She would take advice on that. Right now, on Griff's advice, she planned to speak to Kate. Griff would be speaking to Charlie Knowles about how they should make the most of Ahmed's special knowledge, whether they should stream photographs past him in the hope that he would recognize someone he had seen on the trek across Europe, or whether they should refer him to a psychologist who might help him to erase those dreadful images from his mind

Charlie was having none of that. "We'll do both, if necessary," he had said when Griff called to update him, "but if you are right, and he has this knowledge, the last thing we want is a bloody namby-pamby do-gooder shrink trying to erase it all from his mind." Knowles insisted, "He can seek them out and we can incarcerate them." He paused. "Mind you, in any case, what we must never do is let his story become public. Islamophobia would be rife, and in all honesty, there are many more of our own godless knife-wielding assassins in this country than there are Muslim terrorists. Gang warfare in London is getting worse and worse. The country is divided by politics, race, and religion, as if any of that really mattered. It's all greed, jealousy, and vengeance. I think I'll become a monk."

He was in his office going over various problems, impatiently waiting for Kate. She arrived promptly at ten.

"How are you and Jake getting on with the hunt for that disappearing driver?" he asked Kate, who was sitting opposite. "Any recognisable faces on tape?"

"Not that I know of," Replied Kate. "I think he would have told me. He was more interested in a message from the Russian girl."

Natasha had called barely twenty minutes after Jake had completed the text to her mother. When she did, he was pacing up and down, thanking his lucky stars that Kipper upstairs was only too pleased to have Ben as and when necessary. Whether or not it was fair to Ben was a thought that plagued him, but Ben was a very happy little baby and the health visitor seemed satisfied.

Sitting down on the sofa, he gave Natasha all she needed to know about Hubert, what he looked like, what name he was using and where he was staying. He assured her that he and Griff were not disclosing any information to anyone about her and Rudi. They had conveyed no information to Hubert, and that it was up to her how to approach him, if indeed she still wanted to be involved at all.

"All I can do is assure you that if you never make contact again, Griff and I will forget you exist. Take care." And he switched off.

Three hours later, he and Jake were enjoying a coffee in Thames House when a ping from Jake's laptop signalled that an email had arrived. It was from 'Boris'. Natasha hadn't wasted any time. Jake read it out loud.

'Good to hear from you, and I am delighted to know you are already looking after my garden. I know it's hard work but I'm sure there's a chap who will be pleased to help. Can't remember his name, but he lives at 85 Albert Road and is very good at digging.

It's rather strange being here but I have something vitally important to sort out. It's complicated and I'm not sure how long it will take. Trust me, Jake. I would never betray you or my country. I can't say more. No doubt rumours are flying but with luck I'll be able to explain soon.

I've just met a lovely girl who is trying to help me to find my way around. Very pretty. When she smiled, the sun came out, but unfortunately, she has a boyfriend. I think he's a pilot. I'm a bit old for her anyway!

If things don't develop very soon, I think I'll head for home. Pray for me, Jake.

The driver you mention, I'm not sure that you should contact him. I don't know where he lives. He just kept turning up. Had all the right I.D. Something about him I didn't like. Give him a wide berth.

P.S. Would you mind checking on my cat Jacob for me tomorrow? He needs feeding every day. I just need to know he's healthy.

I'll keep in touch
Cheers

"I think we'd better visit Jacob Epstein right away," said Griff when Jake conveyed the information. "Hubert seems worried. I must go and collect something up from my office first, but I'll pick you up in an hour."

"Right. I'd better let Kate know I might be late. She won't be home for a while. Luckily Ben seems as happy with the guys upstairs as he is with Kate and me, which is great, although I sometimes feel like a parent *in absentio*."

"Well, Hubert is clearly worried about Epstein," said Griff, "and all that stuff about the bloke in 85 Albert Road…"

"Yes," Jake interrupted. "What the hell is all that about? And the significance of the sun coming out? What on earth does that mean?'

"It means he has been enlightened, I think. She's been able to tell him something interesting. ""Something he's not prepared to risk sharing with us just yet and too risky to put in an email, I guess. As for the address, my splendid office building, for the purposes of postal deliveries, is 85 Albert Embankment. Not a lot of people know that."

"Yeah! Skip the Michael Caine impersonation. I knew that, but he knows you're helping me anyway. Why put that? If anyone in the business picks this up, they'll know straight away that there's an investigation going on."

"Hmm, it does seem a little like unnecessary loose speak and he's rather too evasive about the driver. Either he's protecting us from him, which is unlikely, or he's protecting him from us. In either case, we keep looking.

"Natasha has clearly contacted him. We'll just have to wait to see what she thinks. She knows she needs to tread carefully, but the very fact that he has mentioned her in this email means that he now knows we're in cahoots with a couple of Russians. He doesn't seem too concerned, but it's clear that his mind is on other things. He may well have to resign, you know. Buggering off without any explanation is just not on. We should report it."

Jake picked up his phone to message Kate.—

Sorry darling. With Griff. We have to go out. Keep the door locked if you get home before me. We may be late. I have both my phones. Look forward to catching up later. X

He put the phone in his pocket. Griff had disappeared, so he did some paperwork and then went down to the lobby. He suspected that Griff had gone to collect his small handgun so that one of them would be lawfully armed and prayed that it was an unnecessary precaution.

*

There were no lights on at Jacob Epstein's. There was no car parked at the front and none at the back apart from Jacob's old BMW, parked as it had been before, on the left behind the wall, and the electric gates were closed. Griff had parked the car a little way down the road and their approach to the back door was quiet and cautious. The blinds at the ground floor windows were down. And there was no chink of light behind them. Upstairs, however, there was a dim light in what looked like a bathroom window.

"In the shower?" suggested Jake.

Griff pointed to the drain. There no water running into it and no indication that it recently had. There was no sound at all.

"Try the door," whispered Griff. It was unlocked. Jake went to open it, but Griff put his hand on his arm. "Try the number."

They had tried calling Epstein twice on the way but there had been no response. That meant nothing. It was his business number, not the one he had given them for emergencies. This time Jake tried that number. There was the faint sound of a telephone signal from inside which continued until he switched off.

"I'm going in first," whispered Griff. "As soon as I get in, I'm going to drop and roll. Stay outside till I call you in. If there's a shot or anything else that sounds like trouble, get behind the car and be careful who you shoot if anyone comes out. It might be me."

"Don't worry, I didn't bring a gun. I'm a lousy shot and it's never loaded anyway. This isn't my scene. I'll trip them up. And sit on them."

"Griff gave a faint snort, opened the door quickly and disappeared inside. Jake waited a few seconds and followed him in. The kitchen was empty. There was no sound from anywhere. They checked downstairs. There was no sound of movement. Well, either he's out." murmured Griff, "or… Well, let's go and have a look."

The stairs were carpeted, and they made no sound as they climbed up. "We need to try the bathroom first I think" said Griff quietly and opened the door. The light was dim but there was no need for anything brighter. Nothing there.

When they switched on the hall light, they could see what looked like blood pooling outside one of the bedrooms. Jacob was on the floor inside the door. He was face down with one arm stretching out towards the bedside table. A phone was beside the bed, but he hadn't quite made it. He was clearly dead.

Griff was speaking on his phone. "They'll be here in about half an hour. We need to do a recce quickly. See what's missing. We don't know who did this, but let's hope they left something to help us find out."

They went quickly down to the office, which had been ransacked. Anything of any note had been removed. What had been left in drawers was of no significance or value. Any records he had of passport issues would have been destroyed immediately. Part of his contract ensured that no records existed except those in River House. So, whoever did this had wasted his time looking.

"Did they hurt him?" asked Jake

"They slit his throat. I expect that felt more than just a tickle, for Christ's sake. Did they torture him? I don't know. I didn't want to move him. He was face down. His hands looked okay. We'll have to wait till they have him face up. There'll be an ambulance soon, I expect. There may be signs of bruising. I hope not. I rather liked him. If he caught them unawares, and they knew what they were looking for, it was probably quick. Don't dwell on it."

"Shit," I hate this job. I mean, computers are great, but the stuff you do. Not only scary, but... well, I couldn't cope with much of this. I feel sick."

"Oh, for God's sake, grow up, Jake, and shut up. Let Hubert know what's happened. Ask if there's anything here that we should be looking for." He went to the window and raised a blind. "No sign of an ambulance yet. They won't use sirens. I told them it was too late for any assistance, and we don't want to frighten the neighbours."

Jake had retired to a corner and was busy texting. The response from Boris came quite quickly...

'*Don't want to dwell on it but I am devastated. We have been friends for so long. There are wall lights over some wall cupboards. You can't miss them. There are cameras. The recordings are inside false walls at the back of the cupboards. They are always functioning. Take them and go. Do not disclose to anyone yet.*

Jake deleted the text, went immediately to the cupboards, retrieved the recordings and carefully replaced the false backs.

"Take them and wait for me in the car," instructed Griff. "Here are the keys. As soon as you see the van arrive, I'll be out. Turn the car round and be ready to move."

Jake was happy to follow the instructions. Ten minutes later, Griff joined him, and they headed for home. Griff took a half bottle of scotch from the glove box and handed it to Jake. "Have a swig. It works wonders and you need to pull yourself together before Kate sees you. If she knew what we've just found, she'd have you out of the service and delivering pizzas in no time at all."

"We need to tell Charlie. The neighbours know something is up."

"I know but Six needs time to investigate. Two lots of forces trampling all over the place is not good. Trust me. I'll talk to him tomorrow. Now go on in home, have a bath and a drink, then collect Ben and act normally. See you soon. Whoops! Looks like Charlie is arriving with Kate in the car. I don't want to talk to him just now. Out you get. I'm going."

114

Chapter 12

Charlie had driven Kate home. On the way they had been exploring every conceivable reason why someone unknown had signalled a bogus Saudi prince visit. "It seems to have absolutely nothing to do with the Saudi's. They are as anxious as we are to sort this out and quite prepared to send help. Even offered financial aid if we needed it. Imagine that!"

"Would that stretch to another unmarked police car? We need one especially for me, as a plainclothes investigator. I don't see why I should keep using my own. It's just going to become a target for deliberate scratches."

"You'd be lucky. They Saudis have only just decided that women are permitted to drive. I just can't understand what they, whoever they are, could possibly achieve by concentrating our interest on Richmond. Are we expecting any foreign visitors?"

"I have no idea, and anyway, one of Griff's duties is to give us fair warning of visits like that. Even if it was intended to be totally hush-hush, he'd probably check things out quietly himself and tell you, Charlie, if he thought it necessary."

"Yes, he's good You'd be surprised how many potentates have been and gone without anyone knowing. They usually land at a private airfield somewhere and meet up with Ministers in secret. He never gives me details and I don't want to know unless I need to be involved."

"How about Iran?" she mused. "They and the Saudis are deadly enemies. It's the Sunni-Shia thing. If Iran could damage the relationship between the USA and Saudi Arabia, the Ayatollah would be jubilant. Suppose some hotshot American visitor was bundled out of the Saudi embassy in bin bags. They've done it before."

"So how are you to get an Iranian assassin into the Saudi Embassy?

"Hmmm?"

"What about the Iranian Embassy?"

"It was closed in 2011 after the attack on ours in Teheran. I think the Omani Embassy deals with any problems for them."

"Okay, does Iran have any allies? I'm afraid my Middle Eastern knowledge is sparse."

"Syria, and Lebanon supplies them with arms. They both despise Israel."

"Well…"

"Stop," said Charlie. "Now look! Let's get this into perspective, because right now it makes no sense at all." He leaned back in his chair.

"That message to us, about a Saudi visit, seemingly sent through one of the usual channels, which was not double-checked, as it should have been, must be fake, and heads have already rolled. You know the contents. That turned out to be 'fake news' but rather more than just a joke. There must have been a reason behind it. Anyway, I have concluded that there is no connection whatsoever between that, and the stuff sent to Jake. It's just coincidental.

"The first was in code, to from MI5 to Russia, of which we would have had absolutely no knowledge if it hadn't been noticed by Natasha. and which is a matter for Five or Six to deal with. Not our business.

"Our message, sent to Scotland Yard, was bound to be rumbled within hours. Whoever sent it must have known that, so what was he trying to achieve? Panic? Well, that worked for a minute or two. More intensive security throughout the city — if only we had the resources. Was it an attempt to damage the relationship between us, and them? — the Saudi's, I mean, and if so, why? They were in fact more than helpful and grateful that we contacted them about it." He sighed

"Look, get out please. I really must go. It's getting late. See you early in the morning at the office. There are lines of enquiry I need to make. By the way, did you call the hotel in Richmond before you went?"

"No, I just went. I didn't know how much the staff would have been told."

"But if you had phoned them, chances are we would have known even sooner that it was a hoax." He switched off the engine and took a phone from his coat pocket. "Could you get me Westminster division please? Okay, well, first thing in the morning, please. I'll be in my office at six."

He grinned at Kate. "I'm off. Looks like Jake is back. See you in the morning."

"You won't see me at six. I have a baby to feed. Ten o'clock as usual if you're lucky."

In fact, it was after ten o'clock the next morning when Kate arrived. She had been worried about Jake. He was not his usual self. He was pale and seemed stressed. He made some barely convincing excuse about having eaten something, about feeling tired and unwell. She packed him off to bed and called Griff but there was no response. After a shower and a drink, she went to collect Ben, cuddled him while he drank his milk and then rocked him to sleep in her arms.

*

Charlie waved her to a seat when she arrived at his office. Laver popped on with a tray with two coffees.

"Now that's what I call service," grinned Kate, taking one gratefully.

"That," said Laver, "was mine and it's sugared."

"Yuck! Could you get a couple of biscuits when you get mine then, please? I missed breakfast."

There was a call while they were drinking. The conversation did not last long, and Charlie's face reflected a degree of incredulity that Kate had not seen before. He slammed the phone down.

"That phoney Arab stuff was a message delivered to Westminster Police by a guy on a motor bike. He flashed credentials which they didn't really look at, someone signed for it, but they didn't take details of the bike. It was, they insist, a delivery service that they have used before, but the company in question has no knowledge of such a delivery to them."

"So, they're tracking it?"

"Yes, they have a partial number plate and something about one of his boots is distinctive. The number plate is probably fake, but it's helped them to track him part of the way. They managed to keep him in sight on and off until East Sheen but ran out of cameras. It's mostly residential, so no wonder MI5 can't trace the source. I've asked for the letter to be brought over here immediately. Can you get hold of Jake and bring him up to speed? How is he, by the way?"

"Fine, thanks, although he was quiet after Griff dropped him off last night. I tried to probe, but he wouldn't talk about it.

"I'm seeing Griff later to discuss the kids from Syria. Maybe he can shed light on Jake's state of mind. I know he's worried about Hubert. He's very reluctant to question his loyalty. Apart from anything else, if he does prove to be a double agent, the rest of them will all have to undergo thorough, vigorous and far-reaching background checks all over again." She paused

"Sheen, you said. That reminds me, Grace lives somewhere near Sheen. Griff will be there at about two o'clock to show the kid some mug shots. I had better get going. I probably won't be back in the office today, but I'll be here first thing tomorrow and tell you how we got on. I was taking Ayshe, but now that we know he is a Christian and speaks English, it seems a bit pointless."

"Hm! He speaks Arabic and English, so you don't need her to translate, do you, but what about Islam? He might not be fully conversant with all that stuff, and if it involves going to the mosque, he'll need to know the routine. Besides, she's very beautiful. She might be better at persuading him to do what we want him to do."

"I don't think Ayshe has been anywhere near a mosque in her life. She's a non-practising Muslim. Besides, I'm not exactly ugly. I can be very persuasive."

"Yes, but you're old enough to be his mother. Please don't throw that — it might hurt me. Well, it's up to you, but careful how you go, and don't expect too much. He's just a kid."

"Sure — but he's kid that has suffered unimaginable emotional pain. He's had to grow up very quickly. He's proved that he is brave and resourceful but also cautious. I think he could be very useful to us. It will help restore his self-confidence and pride. And make him feel that there is a kind of justice, albeit inadequate, for his parents."

"Yeah, don't get carried away. You only met him for about half an hour. He might have made it all up. He might have more than just a teddy bear stuffed with money in his rucksack: It might be stuffed with dynamite."

Your cynicism could diminish you," she said, "but I know you better," and left smiling. She had told him Ahmed's story and knew, that, having listened silently, he was deeply moved. Who wouldn't be?

Chapter 13

When Kate arrived, she was shown into the garden where Grace and Ahmed were paying badminton. He seemed to have grown in stature now that he had shared his demons. He was quite attractive, rather like a young Omar Sharif.

They stopped playing when they saw Kate and put the racquets on a nearby table.

"Time for refreshment," said Grace. "What would you like? Orange juice? Beer, gin and tonic?"

"White wine," replied Ahmed with a laugh

"Make that two,'' said Kate. "Brilliant idea, Ahmed. You seem to have grown up suddenly. I'm wondering whether or not Grace is a suitable adult."

"It is so good to be with people who behave like my parents. They loved their food and wine. Got most of it through the American Embassy. I was allowed a thimbleful on my birthday but that seems such a long time ago. So much had happened since. I'm seventeen now."

"A fine man," smiled Kate. "Did you ever see the film *Lawrence of Arabia*?"

"Oh yes ages ago… We all watched it together Mum, Dad and me. It was brilliant. Peter O'Toole was fantastic"

"Yes, and Omar Sharif, you look…"

"A little bit like him?" He laughed "I know. My mother actually met Omar when she was in New York, but I promise you, I am my father's son. To begin with, my parents loved each other very much, and I look even more like my dad." He sighed, got up and walked down the lawn to collect the racquets and shuttlecocks. Kate wished desperately that the conversation had taken a different course.

Grace emerged from the house with a tray of glasses and Ahmed came back looking calm.

He smiled at Kate. "Shall we talk business?"

She returned the smile, took a sip of wine and said, "Right! The first thing to do is to recollect and record every detail of the people you travelled with, those whom you believe to be undesirable. Griff is tied up right now, but he has contacts everywhere and chances are he already has information concerning new arrivals into this country. You came over from France, didn't you? With Vic in his boat to the Stables? Did any of them travel with you?"

"No, but not for the want of trying. Vic just wouldn't have it."

"Vic is very careful. And has sound judgement."

"He certainly wouldn't take any nonsense. They tried bribery, bullying, threats, but the more forceful they became, the more he resisted. In the end, he was about to call the gendarmes and they fled. There was a particular group. I heard them talking about Kingston. They had contacts there. They were planning something big. They talked about a hundred jihadists and a day that UK would never forget."

"Listen, Ahmed, I've just had a text from Griff. He's on the way. Let's leave it now until he arrives. Would you like to go out for lunch? We can take Grace and her mum. I bet it's a long time since you had a beef burger. Do you have another name apart from Ahmed? I thought, as a Christian you might have something more er…"

"Let's say Western." He laughed. "My name is Michael actually. I just used Ahmed because it made life easier when I lived in Mosul. I'm kind of used to it now. Call me Mike if you like."

"No," said a voice behind them as Griff approached from the kitchen door. "If you are to help us in any way, I think you need to remain Ahmed for the time being. I have some photographs for you to study later. Did I hear someone say lunch? It's on me."

Griff had been collecting information without pause for months, turning into years.

The Islamic State ISIS, or as its members tended to call it, Daesh, had existed long before Griff had taken up residence in River House, but from July 2005, when a series of coordinated attacks in London, targeting commuters, travelling during the morning rush hour, he had become almost obsessed with the Jihadist movement.

He had honed his language skills and studied reports following every incident. What appalled him was the fact that the majority of the perpetrators were either British Nationals, or in the country legally. Many of them were involved in activities far removed from religion — drugs, alcohol, prostitutes. Nevertheless, he was aware that recently there was an influx of Muslims from the Middle East who saw 'Londonistan' as a target along with capitals of other countries — including France and Belgium. Griff had close contact with intelligence services in most European countries, all of which were paying particular attention to illegal immigrants, recognising nevertheless that the bulk of them were just desperate displaced people who presented no threat, who just needed help and a little compassion.

His previous conversation with Ahmed had been interesting, but there had not been the time to dig too deep. Now that Ahmed seemed relaxed and eager to help, he could work with him to try to identify particular individuals who came here to do harm. If he could identify them and trace their movements, with Ahmed's help, lives would be saved, he was sure of that, but was it fair to employ the services of a young man who had lost so much already? He would never forgive himself if Michael, alias Ahmed, came to any harm. It was comforting to have Grace alongside. He knew she would put her foot down if she thought he had gone too far.

"So how is little Kerim coping at the Stables?" he asked her as they left the restaurant after a good lunch. "He must be missing you."

"He's fine. I'm the one who's suffering. He loves it there, but he is coming back soon. Ahmed doesn't mind sharing the bedroom. It's big enough for two. It might take a day or two for them to get to know each other, and of course Kerim is much younger, but I'm sure they'll cope."

"Don't worry," said Ahmed. "He'll be fine. I promise not to bully him, and it will be good for me to have a little brother. He can teach me to play football and I'll teach him chess."

It was while they were making their way back after enjoying a good lunch that Kate took a call from Charlie Knowles. He sounded serious.

"Kate," he said. "Would you make your excuses and get back here as soon as you can?"

"Why? What's wrong?" said Kate pausing to listen. Charlie sounded unusually stern

"Is Griff there?"

"Yes."

"Maybe he can enlighten you. On second thoughts, don't ask. Just get back here and tell him I'd like a word with him too when he has time — any time as long as it is today. I've already been in touch with Jake. He's on his way." The phone call ended abruptly.

"Problem?" asked Griff, seeing the puzzled expression on her face.

"You tell me. It was Charlie."

"Ah — right." He paused "Ahmed. Kate has to be somewhere else. We are going to drop her back at Grace's to pick up her car, and then you and I are going to look at some photos."

There were lots of photographs — too many. At first Ahmed studied each of them for a few seconds before turning them face downward onto the table. Once or twice, he looked thoughtful, then shook his head and put the picture down. Griff remained still and quiet. Then, there was a long pause. Ahmed had been studying one face.

"He was there," he said nodding. "Yes definitely, but I didn't get the impression that he was on a mission. His life had gone wrong, and he was looking for new one. They tried to enlist him, but he wasn't having any. Not a bad man, I think." He put it down and continued to study the rest. Griff was watching Ahmed carefully and saw that suddenly, his face paled. He let go one of the photos as if it was red hot and stared at it on the ground. Griff bent and picked it up. There was recognition, he could see that, but more than that, the expression on Ahmed's face was one of revulsion.

Griff waited. "He was the one," Ahmed whispered and suddenly walked down to the end of the garden where Griff could see him retching into the long grass. He waited a while and then walked to Ahmed, pulled him to himself and held him close while sobs wracked the boy's body.

"Your mother?" he asked quietly, and Ahmed nodded.

"He was the one who held up the baby. I have to kill him myself. Please help me. You have his picture. You know where he is?"

Griff shrugged "I know he's in England and I have teams looking for him. When they locate him, you and I will help each other, I promise," he said, and he meant it.

At that moment, his mobile phone sounded, and he looked to see Kate's name on the screen. He switched it off. That could wait.

"Ahmed," he said, "we have to be strong. I am going to do something of which your mama would probably not have approved. I am going to give you a shot of whisky, which I have in my car. It has come in useful once already this week."

He gathered up the photographs and put all but one back into his briefcase. The significant one went into his wallet, and he sent a quick text to one of his colleagues with the reference number. He needed to do no more. The picture would be circulated within minutes.

Ahmed was calm now. There was a distinct look of satisfaction on his face resulting, Griff was sure, from the realisation that the man who had destroyed such a treasured part of his life might pay.

"Come on," he said. "We're going for a ride. I have an appointment with a cop, who might be slightly cross with me about something completely different, but you need to meet him. Go say goodbye to Grace. Tell her you will be back this evening and you will go with her to pick up Kerim tomorrow if she wants, yes? Okay. See you at the car." He yelled goodbye to Grace and Sharon as he walked down the side of the house to his car and waited for Ahmed.

On their way to central London, he told Ahmed about Charlie Knowles, the policeman with a conscience, and also told him a little about Kate and Jake. "They are all good people, Ahmed. I would trust them with my life, and you must too. For the time being you must keep your religion a secret. Avoid discussing your family when you are with Grace. She doesn't know that you are not a Muslim, nor does Sharon, and you must keep it a secret from Kerim for the time being. Charlie will know, as will Kate and Jake, because we will need their help in this. It is they, perhaps, who will come in at the end of our mission and make arrests."

"Rasheed — that man. He will not be going to prison. You promised."

"I will keep my promise as long as you want me to. You may feel at some stage that prison would be a much better punishment. It would be a nightmare for the rest of his life. Terrorists do not have an easy time in jail. If we kill him, it would be over in a minute because his death, if that is your decision, must be sudden and immediate, probably in self-defence. You may not even be there. If I'm the lucky guy that gets to shoot the bastard, I will certainly not waste time telling him why. I wouldn't want to give him the chance to get me first."

"I know. That is not important. He will have slaughtered so many others, in terrible ways. I am not like him. I don't want to watch him die. I just want him dead and for some reason I need to do it. Is it vengeance? I don't know, I just feel this compulsion to kill the man who slaughtered my mother. Maybe my father would want this. He didn't have the chance to say goodbye to us. I hope they are together."

"Were your parents very religious?"

"Ahmed smiled. "No, not at all. We talked about it, though, about the Ten Commandments and tried to remember how many we had broken. I think my dad won. He admitted so may daft sins like coveting his neighbour's sports car and telling fibs to Mum and eating too much. Mum said she murdered thousands of mosquitos, told terrible lies to the woman next door whenever she asked Mum what she should wear and if she looked nice. We very rarely rested on the seventh day. We usually played badminton in the garden. Mum said it was all a lot of nonsense really

"She said that there was overwhelming evidence that a very charismatic man called Jesus had influenced the world in supreme effort to make people kind and forgiving and to love and care for each other, but whether or not he was the son of God was another matter. 'We are just sophisticated human animals,' she would say. Nature causes wild animals to kill each other in cruel and savage ways. They suffer, but it is nature. We each have a conscience, wild animals don't. Maybe God is our conscience. We very rarely went to church, but my parents were good, and kind and I loved them very much."

"I know," said Griff. "Gosh, I think I would have won the deadly sins competition. I must have broken just about every commandment in the book. It's part of my job."

"You mean you have killed people? Are you a soldier?"

"No, but I do work for the government, and I haven't killed anyone yet, but if I had to, to protect my country, I have permission to do so. There would be a thorough investigation, afterwards, though, to make sure I wasn't just trigger happy." He smiled at Ahmed.

"Do you have a wife?" Ahmed asked. "Does she know what you do?"

"I don't have a wife; I have a husband."

There was silence. After about five minutes, Ahmed said, "So, you are…" He hesitated.

"I am what we call gay."

"Yes, I know. I just haven't met one before. At least I don't think I have. Maybe men in Mosul didn't want to be executed, so they pretended to be normal. I don't mean you're not normal. I mean…"

"I know what you mean. Believe me, in Mosul, I would have made a point of smiling at ladies all the time," laughed Griff. "It used to be a lot like that here. Not too many years ago, gay men could end up in prison Thank goodness these days people accept that it is fine to be different."

"You hugged me," said Ahmed slowly

"Yes, I did, but it didn't mean I wanted to — er, marry you. It was just to show that I cared about you. I hated to see you so unhappy, but I understood why you were."

"I didn't mind at all," said Ahmed hastily. "It was comforting, honestly, you can hug me any time you like."

"Thanks," said Griff. "But not too often, eh? We don't want people to get the wrong idea." They both laughed and finished the trip in a comfortable silence, Griff all the while rehearsing the excuses he needed to make to Charlie Knowles for not immediately reporting a violent murder the night before. There were reasons for that which Charlie would no doubt reject out of hand.

Chapter 14

When they arrived at New Scotland Yard, Griff and Ahmed were escorted to DCI Knowles' office. Kate and Jake were already there, talking quietly in a corner while Charlie, apparently ignoring them, was at his desk. He stood up immediately when they came in and held out his hand to Ahmed.

"I am delighted to meet you, Ahmed," he said, "and very grateful to you for offering assistance. These three," — he waved an arm as if to embrace the others — "and I have some important things to talk about, but I have arranged for one of my detectives to show you around. I hope we won't be long, and then perhaps we can join up in the canteen. Kate tells me you might appreciate a glass of wine, and that sounds good to me, although I might have something stronger when the time comes. Ah! Here is DC Laver. He'll look after you. Off you go. See you soon."

When the door had closed, Charlie looked at Griff. "Well?" he said.

"Look, Charlie. It's no good getting upset with me. You know the score."

"Exactly!" said Charlie. "I do. And unless you have forgotten the Home Office Guidelines, we are supposed to work together."

"Of course, we are, and we could not possibly do what we do without Special Branch, but there are occasions when we have to act first and report later. In this case, we had to get in there and seize or identify anything that might be relevant. The body we found was not just any old shopkeeper. It was unfortunate that the neighbours could see that something fishy was going on. We knew at least one of them would be dialling 999 and we needed to remove items and evidence quickly. Sometimes your lot are just a bunch of heavies wearing protective shoe covers. What is evidence to us can be completely overlooked by you, and we needed to preserve it. Quite honestly, this particular case is so complicated that until a day or two ago, even I didn't even know what the victim was up to."

"But that was then," yelled Charlie. "You must have been home or back in your office within the hour. Why didn't you call then? Where did you go? The reality is, Griff, that I have a reported murder to solve, and I haven't a clue what happened, or when or why. Any clues which may have helped to identify the killer, trifling things like fingerprints, or DNA have been trampled on, stolen or otherwise ruined. I want the finger and shoeprints of every bloody member of your team for elimination purposes. I don't know whether I'm dealing with a criminal offence or espionage or terrorism. So, talk."

He slumped back in his chair.

Jake stood up. "It's probably my fault, Charlie. I lost it. Griff took me home. We had waited for his lot to arrive before we left to make sure no one else went in. There is a connection with MI6, apparently. The victim, Jacob Epstein, was on their books, and he was involved with Hubert. It was because Hubert hadn't had an expected message from Jacob that we went to check."

"Yes! Well, I went in myself once it became public," said Charlie. "No clues when I got there apart from a significant footprint. All I know so far is his name. Looked like whoever killed him was no amateur. He left few clues. No significant fingerprints, just that interesting shoeprint. It's all sealed off now."

"I promise you will have a full report today, Charlie," said Griff, genuinely repentant. "And I'm here to fill you in on everything we found" which he did.

Laver had taken Ahmed to the most interesting sections of the building and while they were there, examined closed-circuit television surveillance pictures. While the purpose of the cameras was partly intended to deter offenders, the system was also extremely useful when it came to evidence of offending, and officers at the time were trying to follow the progress of a motorcycle as it made its way through an area of London.

"We make a note of the number plate," Laver explained, "and other things that are particular to that rider, like the colour of his jacket or his trainers, or boots in this case, and then we can pick it up with other cameras further down the road. I'll show you. First of all, I'm going to zoom in, to see if I recognize him. No, I don't, but let's see if there's anything that's particularly distinguishing about him."

"There's a mark on his helmet," offered Ahmed, "just where that bit of hair is sticking out at the back."

Laver zoomed in. "Yes, you're right. I didn't see that before."

"It's like a cat's face, with one ear and a whisker," said Ahmed fascinated, "and a blob over the top."

"Er yeah," said Laver, "you could say that, I suppose. Anyway, we lost him as he left central London, but you see how useful this can be. Come on. We've spent enough time here. Let's go get a coffee."

"Or something," replied Ahmed with a smile.

The atmosphere was a lot less tense when Charlie and the others joined Ahmed and Laver in the bar end of the canteen. "This bit is meant for top ranks and important visitors," explained Charlie, "but there are times when it's packed with all the lads if we get a good result."

"Do you think I could be a policeman?" asked Ahmed.

"Well, let me ask you a few questions. Do you ever tell lies?"

"Yes," responded Ahmed.

"Are you good at judging people — whether they are good or bad?"

"No."

"What would you do if I slapped you now?"

"Slap you back."

"Excellent. I'll get someone to fill in the application form now. You can sign it and start tomorrow."

They both laughed.

"I'm afraid it's not quite that easy. There are interviews to attend and exams to pass and lots to learn. Let's see how things go. Whatever happens, I'm on your side and you can come to me for help at any time. I mean it."

"Thank you, Chief Inspector. So much has happened in the last few days, all of it good. I don't feel alone any more." They clinked glasses.

In Ahmed's absence Griff and Jake had explained in detail to Knowles exactly what they had found at Epstein's, and most of what Griff had learned subsequently from the Russian desk at River House. They had both agreed a strategy for future relevant mutual exchanges when it was appropriate. They were of course each involved in matters which normally would be of no interest to the other.

It was only later in the privacy of Charlie's office that the two of them discussed what Ahmed's contribution might be. He had identified three potential terrorists from the photographs Griff had shown him. There was absolutely no intention on either part to put the boy at risk, but he had mentioned Kingston, and of the men he had identified, one had been seen in the vicinity of the mosque there recently. His movements were being carefully monitored. It was not, to Griff's relief, the man that Ahmed had identified as the murderer of his mother. There was an all-out exercise involving several agents to locate him, and Griff was to be notified, without any delay when they did. For the time being, he decided not to share that information with Charlie.

"He is an impressive young man," Charlie had said. "What he saw would have completely unhinged most kids. I can't imagine how he had the courage, not only to get away at all, but to get here with his sanity intact."

"I think his family had good friends. They must have been horrified. They risked their own lives to get him to the border, and some friendly Turks, who knew what was going on over there, helped him too. He was a young person in need, and they protected him. It does restore one's faith in humanity to some extent, but we too must protect him, Charlie. I know he seems to be well balanced and sensible now, but a confrontation with any of those men might just send him over the edge."

"What I want to do," said Charlie thoughtfully, "is get him together with the team we've set up. I must be totally honest with them. I'll tell them he is a Christian because they'd sus him out immediately anyway. I'll explain to them some of what's happened to him and what we need to do. In effect, he'll have a bodyguard."

"Yes," nodded Griff. "I like that. But ask them not to talk to him about — you know, what happened. Are any of them armed?"

"Yes, one is licenced. He is totally trustworthy and sensible. None of them know what happened anyway, but I'll suggest that they don't ask questions about his past.

The first thing we do is introduce them. Maybe he can pose as somebody's brother. The thing is, it's the gatherings outside the mosques where plans are made; presumably inside it's just the usual routine. Do they sing hymns and say prayers like we do? From what I've seen in films, they seem to spend their time with their bums in the air and their heads on the ground. No disrespect!"

"I think they pray a lot. But I don't know much either. Okay! I'm going to bring him back here later tomorrow. Can you run him back to Grace's when you've finished with him or get someone else to do it? You can talk to him about what we want and introduce him to the team. His little 'brother' will need to spend some time with him first. Will that give you enough time to prime the team?"

"Yes. Most of them are here today. Good."

They shook hands and Griff made his way out, feeling at last that progress had been made on one front and wondering what the hell he could do to find Hubert

Chapter 15

Hubert was sitting in a comfortable chair somewhere in the White House — not in Washington, but in the Moscow Government Legislation building, trying to look relaxed. Sarah, his beloved wife, had disappeared. He was sure they had her, and he could only assume that they knew that he knew. Where else could she have gone, leaving no message or any clue? When she had decided to cut all links with her Russian family after they were married, they both knew they must always be careful. "It's not as if you're just any old Russian," he had said laughingly. "The daughter of a turncoat agent could make a fortune selling her life story." Her father was now, it was assumed, somewhere in the United States, having escaped there many years ago when he had been rumbled. Her mother Alicia had not joined him.

"They wanted to talk to me, but my mother wouldn't have it. I was a student. I knew nothing," she had said. "But maybe they suspect that I have traced him, made some connection. It would be the natural thing for me to do, wouldn't it? And what about him? Might he not try to find his daughter? He had contacts at home. If he is alive, would he not want to find me? They don't know that there has been no contact at all — sadly, not a thing. I have accepted the fact that he is dead. I hope that my name change and my complete silence after all this time has put their minds at rest."

Nevertheless, just in case, the two of them had devised just one or two unobtrusive signals, things that looked entirely ordinary to anyone else — an upside-down plant pot or an empty milk bottle outside the front door. These were signals. They always knew where the other should be. If there was any kind of diversion, there would be a message or a contact number. They sometimes laughed about it but never deviated. It was the clue two days before that had alerted Hubert. When he got home, she was not there. There had been no message. There was a brick outside that looked as if it had just toppled from the doorstep into a flowerbed. That was a signal. He didn't bother to check with the neighbours. There was no message. She should have been at home. They must have her. He had raced upstairs. Her passport was not in its usual place.

He had been to Jacob Epstein's within half an hour. He had picked up a passport that he had used before and which Jacob kept for him in a secure place, and informed Jacob where he was going, but not why.

Just days before, at that very same venue, he, Jake and Griff had discussed the message on Jake's laptop, a message which in any other circumstances he would have ignored or asked someone else to deal with. At the time he felt it was well worth investigating because he was certain that they had a mole in the organisation. He had suspected it for some time. Could this be connected? He had made Jake available by suspending him from the firm in the hope that there would be an informative reaction, and now, against all expectations, here he was in Moscow, of his own volition.

He knew alarms would be sounding. He knew also that he might have to resign. He was breaking every rule. Jacob would let Jake know where he was heading. That was the least he could do. He told Jacob not to disclose his whereabouts to anyone apart from Jake, and only after he, Hubert, was well away. He had given Jacob no convincing explanation and Jacob had expected none. He put his head in his hands; now he had Jacob's death on his conscience. They'd killed a man who had been his closest friend for many years. *Was it my fault?* he asked himself.

They must have got wind of his investigation into the possibility of a Russian Agent being in the Service. Sarah was a hostage. They could possibly have picked up the weird message in Jake's laptop, but they tended to ignore personal devices. The girl Natasha had contacted Jake, so hopefully he was working on that situation. During his walk in the park with Natasha, she had told him what she had told Jake and Griff. It certainly reinforced his own suspicions. If they could identify the mole, maybe he could do a deal — their mole for his wife. It was a long shot. Whatever they wanted from him, he would give them. He wanted his beloved wife back.

A man in a grey suit walked in and held out his hand "Mr Edwards — Hubert — or should I call you Boris? Welcome to Moscow. I hope you are enjoying the wonderful architecture in this beautiful city but I'm sure you didn't leave your desk at MI5 for something as mundane as that, so why are you really here?"

"If you know who I am, then you know why I'm here. My wife has disappeared, and I've come to find her — to collect her."

The man was silent for some moments. "Mr Edwards, what makes you think your wife is here? I can assure you that she is not here in this city, at least certainly not as far as I know, and if she was, believe me, I would be the first to be told.

Hubert stared at him; he had sounded convincing. But he would, wouldn't he?

The man got up and went to the internal phone. "Bring some strong coffee," he said quietly, "and perhaps something a little stronger"

He sat down.

"I know you are probably not inclined to trust me Mr Edwards. I am Ivan Kapalski, head of the security section here. You surely know that. Why would your wife have come to Moscow? She would be welcome, of course, but if she is here…" He shrugged. "Let me try to help you. I am going to ask for all flights from London to be checked. You are free to leave if you want to continue your search, but I would prefer you to stay right here until we can sort this out."

There was something about the manner of the man that was reassuring. Coffee arrived and the two sat in silence until the phone rang. Kapalski listened carefully and then put the phone down.

"They have checked all flights, direct and otherwise, into Moscow. They are now checking other airports for Sarah Edwards. What made you think she would come here?"

"She would only come under duress. Could you possibly check to see if anyone unwell arrived?"

"If they come here half dead, their passports would be checked, I can assure you."

"Yes, of course. Oh God! Where is she? Can I believe you? I was so sure she would be here. She writes articles, you know. Some of them not very complimentary."

"Yes, I know. Quite hurtful sometimes, but if we started kidnapping writers of slanderous articles about us, the population would increase to such an extent that we'd have to build more labour camps. And that would do nothing for our reputation."

Hubert sighed. "We have always anticipated this, you see. She was always a rebel. After university and even before we married, we drew up a list of subtle signals, just in case we sensed danger. Whether we were out or at home. A tied-back curtain, an open window upstairs. I can't remember most of them — until I see them. Sarah had known some people here who disappeared you see — friends of hers. But as the years went by, we learned to relax. Everything seemed safe and sound, but we always knew where the other one was. That evening she was absent when I got home. I had had no message — no note, no call. When she didn't turn up at night, I checked the security system. There was a taxi. The driver went to the door. I thought just to knock, to collect her, but he went into the house. She came out with him not long after. She seemed fine. They left and she didn't come back. I was sure you had her. It was the only explanation.

"I had to get here under an assumed name to find her. I took a taxi. There'll be panic at home. Nobody knows where I am, so I'm in serious trouble, but an announced private visit here was just not on the conceivable. No doubt my immediate future is under discussion as we speak."

"Did you not confide in anyone?"

"No. Before I came, I visited one man. A friend. He's dead. He was murdered yesterday. I suppose whoever killed him wanted information. He had none. There was nothing he could tell, so he was killed. My fault, and if what you say is true, there is no point in my being here anyway. You clearly know who I am and what I do. Are you going to kill me, make me disappear, or let me go home and try to find my wife?

"This man — your friend. Is he in the service?"

"No"

'Did you come here to steal state secrets or to infiltrate our secret service?"

"No, but if I happened to discover anything significant..."

145

Kapalski laughed. "We'd be forced to kill you. This Boris Tchenko seems to have visited Russia before. I wonder what he wanted then. And amazingly, the details on his passport were identical to those on yours."

"I came to visit my wife's family a while ago. I didn't find them," Hubert lied stiffly.

"Without your wife?"

"She won't come here. At least up to now she wouldn't. You have imprisoned some of her friends."

"I sympathise. But please don't quote me. Look, Mr Edwards, I'm going to advise you to go home. I think it best. I'm going to arrange a flight back for you as soon as possible.

"Oh, and by the way. The girl you were talking to in the park, who was she?"

Hubert looked puzzled and shook his head, then said, "Ah, that girl! Sorry, I didn't know what the hell you were talking about. I remember now. I'd put my phone down on a bench. I was just about to turn and pick it up and she was there. She spoke English well. We had a chat. Her father was English apparently." He paused, praying silently that his explanation would be accepted. What he had described had more or less reflected their movements. "I had forgotten all about it."

"Did she say her father was dead?"

"Er No. It was just the impression I got. Quite honestly, I was only half listening. She said that she would love to go to Scotland where her father had lived. I assumed he was dead, past tense. It was just chit-chat. I think she said her boyfriend was a pilot and I laughingly suggested that he steal a plane and take her there."

"So, in spite of your wife's disappearance, you were able to laugh?"

"It was a desperate laugh. At the time, I was just glad to talk to somebody. I had no idea what to do or who to turn to. I thought she might know someone, have some ideas. I had to decide whether to make a fuss, go to the Press or take my chances with someone like you. I decided not to involve her at all and come here in the hope that some of you are decent human beings. I could think of nothing that Sarah had ever done that might cause you to bring her here — I just had this overwhelming feeling of certainty that she was."

"And now?"

"Now I am no longer certain, and I am inclined to believe you, and that makes the nightmare worse, because now I have no idea at all where she is."

Kapalski got to his feet. Hubert also stood.

"Go home, Mr Edwards. I' have arranged a taxi to take you to the airport outside Moscow right now. Your seat will be reserved, and details given to you when you check in." He patted Hubert on the shoulder. "You will find your wife. Trust me. I know it." And with an overwhelming sense of relief, because of the way it was said, Hubert believed him.

He was just in time to board the plane. There was a seat reserved for him at the front of the plane. Someone was already sitting by the window. He sat down, exhausted after two days with little sleep, and closed his eyes. Something nudged his left arm and he saw a hand pass him a piece of paper. It had written on it in Russian in large letters, 'seatbelt'.

The hand looked familiar, the wedding ring looked familiar, but in small print under the large letters was written in English — 'you don't know me.' He gave a huge sigh, smiled to himself, fastened his seat belt, relaxed and slept all the way to Heathrow next to his wife.

Once through customs, they shared a taxi

"I don't want to talk now," she had said, "But could you get Jake and Griff round as soon as you can? Griff knows where we live, I believe, but this involves Jake, too, and it would be nice to meet him. Right now, I need a long hot bath and a vodka and tonic."

"So, you know Kapalski?" Hubert asked.

"Later," she replied. "It's complicated and I don't want to tell the same story twice. I've known Kapalski since I was five. He's my cousin." And she disappeared upstairs.

*

It was with huge relief that Jake recognised the incoming call on his desk phone

"For God's sake, Hubert, where the hell are you? I've been frantic. Natasha said she had caught up with you…"

"Yes, I'm sorry, Jake," Hubert interrupted. "Look, can you get over here ASAP? Bring Griff, he knows where I live. Don't ask questions now. Just get here." The line went dead, and Jake dialled Griff. They were on the way to Hubert's without delay.

Chapter 16

"How did he sound" asked Griff.

"Tired."

"But no clues?"

"No. But we know he's alive and at home, which is a huge relief. If he was guilty of some of the things that have crossed our minds, he wouldn't have called, would he?' Please say no."

"Probably not. God, this traffic is a nightmare. How long before we get there?" he yelled at the driver.

"Are you worried?" asked Jake

"No, not really, not now. I just had visions earlier of finding him somewhere in the same state as Jacob."

"Oh God, please don't say things like that. I spoke to him. Could this be a trap?"

"Yeah! We'll probably be machine-gunned as soon as we enter the grounds."

"Five minutes," the driver had yelled back.

"Okay thanks. Will you take cash?"

"Happily! It's about thirty-five quid."

"Great, I'll hand you forty now and we'll jump Straight out. Thanks, mate."

Hubert was standing at the front door when they arrived. Beside him an undeniably beautiful blonde, who smiled and welcomed them.

It was only when they were settled on a comfortable sofa with drinks that the explanations began.

"It's difficult to know where to start," began Sarah. "If I started at the beginning, you'd be here for a week. Right now, I can tell you that I was born in Russia and had a normal happy childhood. Politics tend not to bother children until they hear their parents discussing them. I had lots of uncles and aunts and cousins. They were mostly unassuming hardworking people. They were proud to be Russian, I believe, and they were, as most Russians are, unaware of international politics. As long as it didn't affect them, they didn't care.

"When I grew up, we moved to Moscow. My dad, who was an intellectual, and had been to university, unlike most of the family, had a job with the government. I didn't really see much of him. His job seemed to involve a lot of travelling but he always had presents for me when he came home. Both my parents played it down, and I was in my teens when I was told that my father had had direct contacts with the Kremlin, but so what? I supposed he was just like one of your members of Parliament. I was fluent in English thanks to my dad, who insisted that it was the universal language that would open so many doors for me. He was right, of course, so I decided that I would like to go to university in England. I was offered a place at Oxford. I was over here when the scandal broke. My father

151

was exposed as a double agent. They say he had been selling information to the Americans. He left Russia as soon as he realised that he was a suspect. He just disappeared from my life.

"My mother advised me not to come home. She said that she had no idea what was going on, but that she thought my father was in America. She had been questioned, of course, but was clearly completely unaware of his actions or intentions. She convinced them that she was shocked and horrified by whatever it was that he had done and was allowed to move into the country. I haven't seen her since then. That was her choice — for my sake. We are not in contact. In fact, most of my relatives have nothing to do with me. They seem to think that living here makes me a traitor, too." She paused and sighed

"Anyway, it suited me really. I met Hubert. I love him dearly, and everything was fine, until the other day. Can I have a refill, please, darling?" She held out her glass and Hubert obliged.

"I have kept Hubert waiting before revealing the events of the last day or two. I didn't want to go through it all twice and you two need to know all that went on. I'm afraid I acted impulsively, and I knew he must have been going out of his mind with worry."

She took a sip, then continued.

"Three days ago, I was getting ready to go to the library. I teach Russian there to a very small group. I saw a car drive through the gates, stop, and a man climbed out of the driver's seat.

"I didn't recognise him at first, he had a hat pulled down which shielded most of his face, but as he approached the door, I saw it and recognised him. It was my cousin Ivan. Ivan Kapalski." Hubert shot to his feet.

"Kapalski was here? On my doorstep"

"Yes, in fact he was in this room on that chair for a while. I was surprised and quite pleased to see him. He used to be my favourite cousin. He asked me if we could go and sit in the car. He wanted to talk to me about my mother and for some reason which I didn't understand, he wanted to check my passport. I grabbed it and my coat. I didn't have time to call you Hubert and I didn't expect to be long. but I did kick the brick as I left, just in case. He drove us away. He told me my mother had died and that I should go to the funeral. I was shocked and upset at first. I wished I had gone before she died, but as I told you, we had no contact. I asked him how he knew where I lived." She sighed. "He knew a hell of a lot more than that. He knows what you do, Hubert."

"Yes, I know he does. We had a long chat in his office. So, what was his motive? Why did you just go like that?"

"Because he wanted me to — and it was true, my mother had died, but it wasn't just that. He had clearly planned the trip. He had everything we needed. A passport in my Russian name, Sara Petrov, a first-class ticket, the seats were reserved, but most of all, he said you were in danger and that I could help you."

"You must have known that was bullshit, Sarah."

"Really? Do you know what position he holds? I dare not risk not believing him, and he is my cousin, Hubert. I like him, I trust him, and I know he is not happy with the way things are. I honestly believe he wants out."

Hubert leaned back into the armchair and closed his eyes. He remembered how Kapalski had reassured him.

"Did he give you any idea of what he wanted from you?" asked Jake

"He saw Hubert talking to a girl in the park. He knows where she works. He knows her boyfriend is a discontented pilot in the Russian Air Force. He knows why. He told me he thought it wasn't just a chance meeting." She paused. "He also knows that information is being transmitted to Russia from your office, Hubert."

There was complete silence for a minute

"My God, you're right. He does know everything," exclaimed Jake and looked at Griff. "We need to warn Natasha. They could arrest her at any time."

"Make contact now," Griff replied, standing up. "Tell her to come here, or France or wherever she can, if she can, and Rudi. Just let us know where. We'll help."

"No, don't," interrupted Sarah. "I said he suspects what she does. He has no intention of revealing it. Don't you see? He's on the same side. If anyone can find out who the mole is, he can. What bothers him is the fact that it's not something he has initiated at any stage. He has no idea who set this up or why. Things are happening over which he has no control, which is his nightmare. He wants to help us to expose whoever it is, and then he intends to leave Russia — if he can."

"Couldn't he have told you all this while he was here?" demanded Hubert

"No, he couldn't. The reason he gave the FSB the Federal Security Bureau for coming here was simply to take me to my mother's funeral. Nobody questioned that, of course."

"Kind of her to die at such a convenient moment. And did you actually attend it?"

She looked at him coldly. "Yes, I did. She was my mother. It wasn't far away and after the service, we had a chance to talk. After that he put me in a taxi to the airport. I had to hang around for a plane for a while, but I had some very nice Russian food and thought a lot about what I was going to say to you. I hoped you would understand. Clearly, I was wrong."

She got up and went upstairs.

Hubert put his head in his hands. He was exhausted, and knew he was being unreasonable. He looked up.

"Would you two like to order a taxi? Don't worry about Natasha. I met this Kapalski guy while I was in Moscow. I think Sarah is right. He impressed me. and I found myself trusting him. If he wants our help, he had nothing to gain from hurting her.

"Look, I'm absolutely exhausted. You'll have gathered that I disappeared because I was looking for Sarah. I'm sorry, but she's quite important. I had no time to start explaining things and I knew you'd try to stop me.

I told Jacob where I was going but not why. Nothing else seemed to matter. I'll tell you all about it but not now. Strangely enough, we seem to be making some progress, but a good friend paid the price and I'm finding that difficult to deal with. I'll see you tomorrow."

Jake and Griff were quiet on the way home. Back at Jake's, they opened a bottle of wine. "Make it a large one," said Griff. "I'll sleep on the sofa. Tell me what you're thinking."

"There's just one thing that bothers me," said Jake thoughtfully.

"Only one" replied Griff.

"So far. "She must have known that Hubert would be beside himself with worry. Hell, it's something they've both been worried about for years. Have you read some of her articles? She is no fan of the Russian Presidency. Why didn't she send a message, a text. Three words would have been enough."

"Maybe she didn't have her phone with her."

"Come on, Griff. On a trip like that?"

"She said she was just expecting to talk in the car."

"There are phones at the airport."

"He might have stopped her."

"Why? If he is on our side?"

"She would have insisted."

"Yeah! You have a point. No doubt Hubert is asking her exactly the same things as we speak. He's besotted with her. He will want to believe every word she says, but unless she comes up with something very convincing…"

Chapter 17

Hubert was sitting opposite his wife listening to a more detailed explanation from his wife. She explained that she had left in a hurry and gone without her mobile phone. There were queues by the kiosks at the airport. She had asked the stewardess on the plane to send a message. "Had it not arrived?"

He was silent, then looked at her coldly

"You've never lied to me before. Whatever is happening to us?" He handed her the mobile phone, which he had found half an hour before in her dressing gown pocket. The record showed numerous missed calls from him, and a number of calls from Russian numbers, which had been answered by her, the day before, the day he had found her, but earlier.

"You ignored my calls." His face was ashen, and she flung herself at his feet and hugged his legs.

"I'm sorry, Hubert. I'm so sorry. I can explain. Please give me a chance. You know I love you. You know that. Please trust me."

Hubert sighed. "Yes, I think you do but convince me Tell me everything."

"I will but I need you to answer some questions also."

"Okay — shoot."

"What do you know about the ISC?"

"You mean the Intelligence and Security Committee?"

"Yes, the Organisation that spies on spies. Have you been involved with it at all lately?"

"No. I've been far too busy — and why should I?"

"Have you been approached by any of the nine members lately, or quizzed in connection with — well, anything?"

"No for heaven's sake, where is this going? There is an Act called the Justice and Security Act. If any of us is suspected of any kind of malpractice, they investigate. Quite rightly. I have a horrible feeling that I will be investigated very soon, thanks to you and Ivan"

"Never mind that now. Who is Konstantin? What do you know about him?"

"Konstantin? Why? Not much. He's just a gofer. He just turned up. He had various passes which would be required for him to be in the building and he made himself available to me. He must have been thoroughly vetted. He seemed to be able access anything he wanted."

"Did you never bother to check?"

"No, of course not, I have my job, he has his. One must take a certain amount on trust. When I needed information or assistance, he was pretty adept at getting whatever information I needed. Please don't ask me what. He was quick and efficient and didn't ask questions."

There was a sudden musical sound from Sara's phone, and she turned away to read it.

She turned. "Come and sit down." He followed her into the living room and they both sat.

"Konstantin is a newly recruited investigator for the ISC, the Intelligence and Security Committee. He is a recent addition to the force. He is investigating you, Hubert. That's why he is always there."

Hubert stared at her. "What on earth do you think you are talking about? Where is all this rubbish coming from. You can't know anything about the ISC. Do you honestly think they would rely on any person without the most rigorous checks? Especially someone with a name like that and the status of a driver."

"Please listen to me, Hubert. He is also involved in the Russia Report Inquiry which, incidentally, reveals that Russian involvement in UK public life is more damaging than we ever envisaged. He seems to have been appointed by one of the nine members, but he is more than just a driver. He has connections in Moscow. He seems to be providing each side with whatever information he chooses. That's how Ivan knows about him, because he doesn't always get it right. His motives are a mystery." She paused. "I was waiting for that message. Ivan is now quite sure that Konstantin has two faces and yes, he has been reporting to the ISC Committee that you are unsound and possibly vulnerable because of me and my parentage, and at the same time he is trying to convince Moscow that you could be bought, for the very same reasons. Fortunately, neither side is biting."

"Of course they aren't. You were thoroughly vetted over here. They know your history. They had to. They accept that you are a genuine British citizen now, loyal and reliable, so whatever Konstantin has been feeding them will have been filed away and forgotten. As far as the other side is concerned, I'm sure Kapalski will have dealt with that. We need to tell Griff about this development."

"I agree but I don't want to become embroiled in any investigation. I thought I had left all that behind. I had no idea that Ivan had been quietly checking up on me ever since I left Russia, not because he intended to use the information, but because he cared about me."

Hubert was about to speak but she held up her hand

"Let me finish. Konstantin has been very carefully doctoring any information that comes out of Russia. He knows exactly what the ISC is looking for and feeds them false information. He is also feeding the Russians classified stuff from your department, carefully edited, of course, some of which is patently misleading or untrue. He's on two payrolls. Ivan has made a connection, but he won't divulge until he has concrete evidence, especially by phone. He thinks he knows who is pulling Konstantin's strings.

"My God, Sarah," Hubert said. "I need to go in. You must come too, I'm afraid. You'll be questioned. Just tell the absolute truth. They will want to know every detail and I won't be there to help you. Whatever you tell them will be in confidence. They will be very interested in Kapalski, and I'm warning you that it may not be pleasant."

"I don't see him as a traitor, Hubert. He doesn't like what is happening to his country and its' people. Please don't be too quick to judge. He will be able to justify his actions. I know he'll be able to do that, Hubert. He's a decent man. I just hope he leaves soon. If anyone of the President's close associates suspect him, they won't hesitate before reporting him. He's not popular with the Inner Circle. The whole world is aware of the way Russia deals with rebels and troublemakers. It's either poison or inexplicable disappearance. As far as Ivan is aware, he is not under suspicion yet. He' always plays his part well. I'm sorry I didn't call you from Russia. He begged me not to, in case you said the wrong things to the wrong people. He could never contact you directly, of course, and my poor mum dying was just a matter of coincidental timing. She would be horrified if she had known what was going on."

"Maybe not," said Hubert holding her close. "She wanted you to stay here, didn't she? Maybe she knew more about things than you thought. As for Ivan, I'll just have to contain my anger. He must have known from the start that I would have been frantic, although I confess that he did impress me when we met. Anyway, if everything you tell me is right, we need to get him over here and make sure that Konstantin's treachery is revealed. I need to divert him if I see him tomorrow. I mustn't let my feelings show in any way, although I might allow myself one punch when his cover is blown." He sighed and put his arms around her.

"I don't want to leave you here alone ever again. We're going to risk leaving together. I think we'll go to Jake's. He can get Griff over, then we can decide who to trust, which after what you have told me will not be easy."

The meeting at Jake's was tense. It was quite late now. Kate was fast asleep upstairs, and Griff had been about to leave when the call had come.

"Bloody hell, what now," he muttered. "I haven't seen my partner for days."

"It sounded pretty vital. There must have been a third-degree investigation after we left. Sarah is coming as well. Get some coffee brewing, we need to wake up."

Hubert's expression was grim as he walked through the door and Sarah looked defiant as she described again what had happened in the last forty-eight or so hours, and the information they had received from Ivan after Jake and Griff had left. Griff listened without interrupting until the name Konstantin came up. Then he sat bolt upright. Jake looked stunned and turned to Hubert, who held up his hand

"I can't come to terms with this yet, Jake. It didn't occur to me that he could be a plant. I led him to Joseph. He must have gone there to trace me. He was never involved in anything faintly sensitive. He was just a useful skivvy. Why was I so gullible, so stupid?"

"He was always there," said Jake "Seeing who you met or contacted — like Joseph. Now he's disappeared. Uncontactable. Where is he, I wonder?"

"In Moscow, I guess," said Griff "Putting in his carefully edited reports. Not that he needed to go there to do so, but if there's the remotest chance that he has somehow cottoned on to your cousin's leanings, we need to get him out fast."

"I need to get in touch with ISC," said Hubert, standing up. "I hope to God they are all clean. First of all, I need to find out who enlisted him and what checks were made — if any." He put his hand to his head. "Who can I trust? Who can they trust? Will they even listen to me if he has already sowed the seeds of doubt into their minds? This is a nightmare."

"Hubert," said Griff, "if MI6 had the vestige of doubt about you, I would have been the first to know. There was concern in certain quarters about your brief disappearance, but it was brushed aside with almost indecent haste. I'm just wondering if they are one step ahead of us. I have questions to ask them myself. Now go home. Get some sleep. Do nothing. I'll be in touch tomorrow."

He turned to Sara. "Have you a safe way of contacting Ivan?"

"I have now, yes."

"Ask him if his immediate departure is necessary. If he feels it safe to stay over there a little longer, well, he can be the best judge of that, but we need to be told when and how he's ready to leave Russia as soon as possible. I'm guessing he is not without friends there.""

"Yes, he has, of course, but not necessarily in high places."

"Well, it looks to me as if Ivan is a survivor. We'll just have to hope for the best. Don't contact him too often. I am going home. I need to sleep. Can we meet here tomorrow?

"Of course, but I'll have to explain all this to Kate."

"Do you need to just yet?" demanded Hubert. "It will all be passed straight on to Charlie Knowles.""

"Kate is totally trustworthy, Hubert," said Jake coldly. "If I ask Kate to keep quiet about something, she will. I can assure you."

"Yes, of course? I'm sorry, Jake, I'm worn out and worried. I know Kate is fine. Tell her whatever you like"

"I know, Hubert. I'm sorry I snapped. We're all knackered. Tomorrow! Let's say eleven. That will give Griff time to do some digging and then we can decide how to handle this. And thank you, Sarah. You've been brave and resourceful. There's no denying that Ivan would be an asset, but he may need just a little plastic surgery if he's going to survive the move. If it gets out that he's helping us here, we'll be knee deep in Novichok in no time at all."

Chapter 18

Kate came downstairs early next morning, and Jake followed with Ben

"So, what was all that about?" she asked as she came out of the kitchen with cups of tea

Jake explained as they drank and suggested that it might be better not to tell Charlie just yet.

"Absolutely," she agreed. "He has quite enough on his plate at the moment and it really doesn't concern him anyway. Hubert is back, so as far as he is concerned, that's one of our problems solved. He has problems of his own. He is quite excited about Ahmed, though, you know, the kid you met at the station when you were called in to account for your involvement in the Epstein killing."

"I wasn't exactly involved in the killing. Do you mind? Get your facts right."

"Yes, well you know what I mean. He texted me earlier to say he had received a message from Ahmed, who believes he saw someone on a motor scooter who may have been involved in the fake message about the Arab Prince's visit. Laver said Ahmed had noticed some mark on the helmet that the rider of the scooter who delivered the message to the Westminster Police was wearing. He'd had been showing the boy how we can track vehicles using the roadside video cameras. Ahmed says he had seen a scooter rider wearing the same helmet. He was positive about it. He himself was on a pushbike, but the traffic was slow, and he kept up. He saw it disappear into a place somewhere on the outskirts of Richmond — a private house, very large with extensive grounds.

"Charlie is picking him up so that he can show him where, then Charlie can go straight in and ask some questions."

"Sounds good but what if it's not the same bike? Suppose he's wrong about the mark."

"It's not just the mark. He wrote down the registration number. He couldn't remember what it was from the video shots, but we checked, it is. It's the same."

"Wow! That was a bit of luck, almost too good to be true. What was the kid doing there in the first place?"

"Well, it seems that Ahmed managed to get over here with quite lot of money stuffed into an old teddy bear. He used some of it to buy himself and Sharon's little rescued boy bicycles. He was on his own though when he saw the moped. He had been looking for the mosque. He seems to be determined to find the man who killed his mother, or at least any of the men who he saw on the trek across Europe. It will be nigh on impossible on his own, but Charlie is going to introduce him to his team of Muslim terrorist-trackers today so that should make his mission possible."

"He's not a Muslim himself, though? Is that right?"

"Quite right, but he lived as one, went to school in Iraq with Muslim friends and is quite happy to behave as they do. As far as he is concerned, it's no big deal. It's not religion that makes people bad, it's people.

"How very refreshing. We must have him over to meet our friends upstairs — both the rescued boys."

"Yes, but let's give them time. They have both suffered incredible trauma in the last few months. Griff is on the case and"…" She was interrupted by the buzzing of her mobile phone.

"Hold on, it's Charlie."

She listened for a few moments and from her expression, Jake could see that it was something significant. He sat down.

"He's not here," Kate was saying. "We saw him yesterday. I think he and Sarah have a meeting arranged with Hubert and the ISC."

She listened again and Jake saw her face pale

"Oh my God. Stay online, Charlie.' I'll get Jake to call him now." She turned to Jake

"Get Griff on the line now please, Jake. Tell him to drop anything else. This is vital."

Jake was already on his phone and was holding it to his ear. He looked at her enquiringly.

"What the hell do I say?"

"Just tell him to call Charlie. When you nod, I'll tell Charlie to expect an immediate call. If he argues — just say Novichok!"

Jake's expression was one of astonishment and horror. He did precisely as he was told and switched off his phone.

"He's on it. Didn't stop to ask questions. For God's sake, Kate! What's happened?

"They found a man slumped over a steering wheel in a large supermarket on the outskirts of London. He told me the name. I can't remember. It was reported to Charlie's unit, who asked why the hell they were bothering him with it. Told them to call an ambulance, get him to hospital — just in case he was still alive, and to take the car to the police pound which wasn't far away, I think. I'm not sure of the strategic details. Anyway — the guy was dead. They did a post-mortem and couldn't see any obvious cause until they took blood samples. Found it was some sort of poisoning, which could only have been absorbed by the skin. By then, they were really worried. This was a couple of days ago, give or take an hour or two. To cut a long story short, they examined the car and found it on the steering wheel."

"Oh my God! Are any of them affected?

"They always wear gloves. They're okay. Just shocked."

"Well, assuming the guy didn't choose such a horrible way to die, we can only assume that he didn't put it there himself."

"Quite. They are checking the cameras, of course, but it looks as if whoever drove there was savvy enough to avoid them."

"So, there must have been a passenger. The guy wouldn't have gone there alone and committed suicide in such an extremely unpleasant way. The passenger must have persuaded the driver to get out and disappear for a while, to go to the loo or something, while he anointed the steering wheel with poison."

"There was a spilt coffee cup on the floor at his feet. It's an all-night store. He could have been sent to get that, or fags or anything. There must be cameras covering the entrance. Obviously, they will be able to recognise him, they know what he looks like although his face is somewhat contorted, but the passenger must have left on foot, giving the cameras a wide berth."

"Unless this was pre-planned, and the passenger had an escape car there already."

"I don't think so. There would have been other less conspicuous places, but who goes round with Novichok in his pocket? Anyway, Charlie will deal with all that. We'll just have to wait and see what develops. The car must be taken away and minutely examined. The crew who did the initial investigation were, thankfully, all wearing gloves, of course, but they will nevertheless be under observation, and for now this matter is not under any circumstances to be made public."

"God no! There would be massive panic countrywide. Who is the guy? They must be able to check his identity from the number plate."

"Hell! Getting murdered by a Russian poison in a British supermarket car park! They'll have to close it down while the investigation is proceeding. I hope it wasn't Waitrose."

"I don't suppose we'll hear a word from Griff for a while. In the meantime, you had better go and help Charlie. I'm staying at home with Ben. If I hear anything from Griff, I'll let you know, but I guess he's going to be much too busy to deal with Hubert's problems. They will have paled into insignificance compared to this bombshell. Wear gloves."

"You too. As soon as I know anything I'll call you. With a bit of luck, we'll be able to identify the corpse quickly from the car registration or stuff in his wallet. We may even have details on record, but I'll make sure I'm not the one to take his prints." She smiled, hugged him, kissed Ben, and left.

Chapter 19

Griff had been at Vauxhall House long before Hubert was up and about. They had all agreed to wait until he called, and then either to join him there, or at Millbank, the MI5 building by Lambeth Bridge.

Hubert had agreed that Griff should share the bare bones of his visit to Moscow, with trusted colleagues and then let him know when and how he should disclose the staggering information from his in-law, a possible defector. He himself would almost certainly be interrogated by ISC at this stage and so would Sarah — but separately.

Griff's first enquiry earlier that morning had been about Konstantin. Precisely how had he become involved? Who checked him out? What was known about him? And how could it possibly be that a Russian agent could have been employed, not by them, but by an arch enemy of the State, to spy on one of their own high-ranking officers, and managed to get away with it? If the Press got wind of that, GCHQ would be severely and irretrievably damaged. Griff shuddered at the thought.

It was on record that Konstantin had made contact initially by providing information regarding a recent attack of one of their agents, who fortunately had survived a deliberate hit and run. He (Konstantin) had disclosed nothing that was not already known. He had been arrested as a suspect as a matter of course and then released for lack of evidence. Once released, he had asked if he could speak to someone of a higher rank. He inferred that he had information, which he had not divulged during interviews. He said he was from Belarus. His brother, a journalist, had been imprisoned in Russia for writing an article criticizing the regime's annexation of the Crimean Peninsula for self-serving purposes, whilst ignoring the poverty in regions far outside the centre of the country where thousands were struggling to survive the fierce and freezing winters with little or no support. This information had been impossible to confirm but was persuasive.

Once given the chance to talk, Konstantin was able provide other information about agents operating in the UK. Some of the information was well known, the rest was of interest and credible although so far not confirmed.

They took him on board with reservations. At first, he did small-scale investigations for MI6, checking on new, possible suspect's' arrivals into the country, where they went, and what they did. He was methodical, reliable and astute. He didn't stand out in a crowd. He seemed to see things without looking. After a while, they offered his services to ISC, but always sceptical, ISC tested him by suggesting that he checked out the one man they believed to be totally sound — Hubert. Hubert was not in the loop but in any case, had not noticed or reported anything suspicious. Konstantin's name was not on the register of checked and reliable drivers because he was being trained for a more important role, but Hubert was impressed with the reliability of the new recruit. He was always available at short notice and seemed to be discreet. He didn't ask stupid question, or any questions. He just did as he was told, but Konstantin had his own agenda.

He gave it time. He waited until he became invisible amongst those he served. He took instructions from a higher source, and then, independently, quietly employed a man called Louis, a thug, all fists and very little brain, but muscular, probably due to the ingestion of steroids. This man was to be Konstantin's own gofer/protector/driver and general run-around. Louis used his own vehicle. He had records for grievous bodily harm, armed robbery, and drug trafficking. He was loyal to whoever paid him enough. He was on permanent call twenty-four hours a day and was told never to discuss the source of his income with anyone at any time. The payments he received were more than generous and he was quite happy to concur. Konstantin took taxis to work and never revealed to Louis what his occupation was. Louis was given a mobile phone and was on call twenty-four hours a day. He dropped everything when he was called. He asked no questions.

When Hubert disappeared, Konstantin was frantic. He had seen him home safely the day before and had no idea where he could have gone. His credibility was at stake if this news got back to either of his own paymasters… He snatched his mobile and called Louis.

"Get over to the usual meeting place now. I need to pay someone a visit."

When they got to Jacob's, the house was in darkness.

"Try the back," ordered Konstantin. "There's a way round. There's a lane."

They parked. The gates were closed but with Louis' help, Konstantin was able to scale the wall. There was a light on the top floor and the back door was not locked.

"You stay right here in the yard," he instructed Louis. "I'll be as quick as I can. If I'm not back in ten, just open the door and check." He disappeared inside.

The sound of his back door closing brought Jacob downstairs immediately.

"What the hell are you doing in my house," he demanded of Konstantin.

"I'm sorry to disturb you. I did knock but there was no response. Er, Hubert sent me. He thinks he left something here."

"You're his driver, aren't you? Konstantin? I saw you from the window upstairs the other day."

"Yes, indeed I am, and sorry to trouble you but Hubert needs you to write down an address that he was instructed to visit when he got to, er… he thought he had it but must have left it accidentally. I'm sorry, but he said he would text you to let you know I was coming. Did you not get a message from him?"

There was a pause.

"When he got to where?" enquired Jacob. "And if it was a matter of an address, which incidentally he would never forget, he would have called or texted me — and I would have responded immediately. You have no idea, have you? And if Hubert had left anything here, I would have noticed. The last thing he would do in any case is send somebody else to collect it without informing me first and I have had neither text nor phone message. In any event, there are at least three other people he would have contacted first. So, what is it you want?"

Konstatin sighed. "Mr Epstein," he said quietly. "Hubert has disappeared. They have sent me to attempt to discover his whereabouts. And suggested that you may know. I'm truly sorry to disturb you."

"They? Who are they?"

"You know who he is and for whom he works Mr Epstein. Please don't waste time. This is urgent."

"Do you have any identification? Is there anyone I can phone to check your identity? What about Jake — Mr Scott? I'll call him now." He made for the stairs and Konstantin followed quickly. "Just a minute please Mr Epstein" Konstantin was halfway up the stairs in pursuit when he heard the door open. He looked down and saw Louis.

Already at the top of the stairs, Jacob looked down, and seeing another man enter his home without permission, immediately knew something was not quite right. This whole visit was suspicious. He remembered Jake's and Griff's disquiet about 'the driver' and darted into his bedroom, attempting to slam the door in their faces. It was too late. Konstantin was through. There was a struggle. Jacob was punching out, defending himself, and had his back to the door. Louis pushed through and Jacob felt an arm round his neck, then an agonising feeling in his throat. He fell.

Konstantin looked in horror at the body writhing on the floor. There was blood spurting from its neck. He couldn't speak. This was a nightmare. He looked at Louis, lost for words, Louis folded a blade, put it in his pocket and shrugged. "He went for you, boss. I had to do something. I didn't mean to kill him. It was his own fault, he struggled." Konstantin stared at him, lost for words while the horrifying significance sank in. He breathed heavily, sighed, and then said, "I told you to stay outside. Give me that knife. Get out now, you bloody useless idiot. Turn the car. Be ready to move. I'll be down shortly." Louis disappeared. Konstantin washed his hands in the bathroom and took a cloth. He wiped every surface he might have touched. He ran the blade under the tap and watched a small amount of pink-tinged water run down the plughole, hesitated, and dropped it into a waste bin. Not something to have in his possession if he was stopped. He must not be stopped.

There was a footprint in the blood on the wooden floor upstairs. He left it. It wasn't his and there was no time to clean it.

He looked briefly in the office for anything that might give a clue to Hubert's whereabouts. There was nothing —

he left. Outside he stood for a while thinking. Mission abandoned. He could hear the sound of the car engine idling in the lane. He took his wallet from his inside pocket and removed from it a small plastic sachet containing white powder, which he put into his coat pocket. He remembered his instructions. *Never use it unless it is a matter of life and death.* Well, his life, an idiot's death.

He closed his eyes, sighed and hoisted himself onto a dustbin, climbed over the wall and down the other side. Louis leaned over and opened the passenger door.

"Let's get out of here," said Konstantin. "I need a coffee. Drive to the all-night store near the museum, the one we passed on the way here. Get as close to the door as you can."

"Sure thing," replied Louis, relieved and rather surprised that the tone was not more acrimonious. He hadn't meant to kill that bloke; it was just a case of a sharp knife and struggling victim. If the guy had had the sense to keep still.... All he was doing was protecting his boss, for heaven's sake.

The supermarket's car park was almost empty. Louis did as he was instructed and parked at the side of the building, near the door and close to large disposal bins. Konstantin handed him a ten-pound note. "Large, black, no sugar."

Once Louis was out of the way, Konstantin put on his fine leather gloves and carefully took the sachet from his pocket. He sprinkled a very fine powder — barely discernible — onto the leather-covered steering wheel and then with gloved hands, took a cloth and once again he wiped everything he had touched. He then climbed out of the car, dropped the sachet and gloves into one of the bins, pulling some other rubbish over the top. When Louis came back, he was standing beside the car.

"Look, Louis. I need to walk home and calm down. Lots of thinking to do, and it isn't far. You get in the car and drink your coffee then just go on home. I'll call you in the morning." He saluted and walked away. It was almost midnight.

The police were called the following day at about ten in the morning when the bin men noticed a man slumped over the steering wheel of car parked in a discreet corner of the car park. They raised the alarm and then proceeded to empty the two large bins outside the store. The police and ambulance arrived within minutes of each other. Louis was rushed to hospital but pronounced dead on arrival.

Chapter 20

Kerim was all packed and ready to go when Grace arrived but looked a little apprehensive. She had explained briefly during a conversation they had on the phone that Ahmed was fine, that there were things he, Kerim, should know which Ahmed would prefer to tell him personally. She said that Kerim would understand when he knew the details. Kerim had looked unconvinced.

Ahmed had come to her the day before to ask for her help and advice. He had been gripping his teddy-bear round its middle at the time and asked for a pair of scissors

"I would like you to help me open a bank account if you please. You have been so kind. You bought new beds for us, and I know I probably eat more than you and Sharon put together, but there is no need for you to keep me. I have money."

He took the scissors and began, to Grace's surprise, to dismember the bear. She was even more surprised when she saw rolls of high denomination dollar bills pulled out.

"I have about five thousand dollars here. I will pay my way, but I want to buy a surprise for Kerim before he arrives."

"Wow, you're rich," she had exclaimed.

"There is a beautifully furnished house in Iraq which is rightly mine. But I suppose I will never inherit it or anything that might remind me of the parents I loved and the life I left behind," he said sadly, "but this will help for now"

"We'll have to get in touch with the Foreign Office about that, Ahmed. There are still laws. Iraq is not a failed state. You said you and your family had good friends there. We must try to get in touch. Anyway, yes. Come on. We have time to get to town before I go and sort out an account for you. They might even be able to issue a debit card straight away, although I doubt it. For the time being, they can change some dollars for you."

Grace had left Ahmed in the hands of a helpful bank clerk and set off for the Stables. It was a long drive and chances were that she would stay there overnight. She had suggested football boots as a gift for Kerim and written down the size.

She did stay overnight because the boys had organised a goodbye party for their budding little football genius and Spike and Pippa were keen for her to stay. They were eager to know how she was coping with Ahmed, and both devastated to learn what he had gone through.

"Oh God forgive me," said Spike, his head in his hands. "If only I had known. I was an absolute swine to him."

"No, you weren't, Spike." Pippa gave him a hug. "You were a little distant, that's all, and who could blame

180

you? He revealed none of this, and the story he gave was thoroughly unconvincing."

"He said you had restored his faith in humanity," interrupted Grace. "He saw what you did for these boys. I know he would like to visit. He is an amazing young man, really, and now that he has unloaded to a certain extent, his grief, he is finding himself again."

"Please tell him he is welcome any time, to stay for as long as he likes. Tell him I need him to come so that I can make up for being such an insensitive bastard."

"I will," laughed Grace. "Now can we have a drink? Scotch would be great, then bed. I want to get an early start."

They were on the road by seven o'clock, missing breakfast but supplied with sandwiches, biscuits, coffee, and water. Kerim enjoyed the ride. He had been in the country for about a week and Grace was astonished at the amount of English he had learned and the confidence he had acquired. They didn't speak about Ahmed though and Grace noticed that the closer they got to home (he had asked how far now at least three times), the quieter he had become

When they arrived, Grace tooted the horn and Sharon came out beaming.

"Now can I give him a hug?" she asked, smiling.

"Yes please," replied Kerim

As he approached, they heard the sound of a bell and Ahmed drew up on the pavement with a shiny brand-new expensive-looking bicycle."

"What do you think?" he said, grinning at Kerim

"Wow! It's amazing," Kerim replied, gazing at this brand-new machine. There were bikes in Idlib, but nothing to compare to this. "Can I have a ride?"

"Oh gosh, I'm really sorry! It's a bit too big for you," replied Ahmed, looking regretful. "Come on. I bought some football boots for you and a shirt and shorts — all Manchester United colours."

"Really?" beamed Kerim. "Fantastic. Thank you."

"We'll go in the back way," said Ahmed, pushing his new acquisition and winking at Sharon, who was suppressing a laugh."

"What's going on?" asked Grace as she heard shrieks coming from the back of the house. She ran through the front door and into the garden where she found Kerim standing by an identical, but smaller bike, just right for him. He was crying with joy and hugging Ahmed. This was something that even in his wildest dreams he could never have hoped to own.

"Is it really mine?" he was saying to a smiling Ahmed.

"Of course, little brother. When you can ride safely, we will explore this amazing country together."

Grace's fears melted away. She had two boys now, different but both very special. Her responsibilities were here. Maybe in time she would go back to Syria, but not yet. Not for a while. She had told Ahmed about Kerim's mother, and his eyes had clouded. "Don't tell him yet," he had said. "When the time comes, I will tell him. He knows some of what happened to me — no details but enough.

He knows I feel the same pain. We are brothers now and we can comfort each other."

Grace nodded. "Yes," she said, "that' sounds like the right thing to do."

That evening was one of the happiest she had had for a long time. Ian happened to be in the country and came to meet Ahmed and to say hello again to Kerim. He was amazed at the change.

"Things are not improving in that part of the world," he said sadly. "I'm taking hospital supplies to so many countries now. Yemen is a nightmare. I can hardly bear it, but what sort of guy would I be if I turned my back?

"I feel guilty coming home to a table laden with food and a comfortable bed. The aid we send over barely scratches the surface, but we do what we can to help while the powers that be there seem to be intent on decimating their own people. They're all the same race, the same religion, for heaven's sake. It's crazy."

"Calm down, darling. You do what you can. The news is full of the new virus that is sweeping across China. I hope to goodness it doesn't arrive here, but it might serve to make governments reassess their priorities."

"Yes. I heard about that. Anyway. This is not the time to contemplate worldwide problems. Let's concentrate our minds on one lovely evening together, with these two new responsibilities we have. Let's try to make everything right in our little world today and sort out the rest of the world tomorrow. What's for supper?"

*

The next morning Ahmed and Kerim wheeled their bicycles to the park. Ahmed was insistent. Rules of the road and bicycle control first. His first thought, however, was to sense the moment when it would be appropriate to speak to Kerim about his mother. He knew Grace was reluctant to do so before the boy had settled in, but he realised that she was just putting off the moment. He had asked himself several times whether he would have preferred to have been told after the event than to have witnessed an episode he would never forget. A sight that haunted his dreams might after night. He didn't cry any more. He thought he would probably never cry again. He was inured to pain and grief. He tried to tell himself that his parents were at peace now, but it was difficult. He knew they would want him to move on, but he couldn't. Not until he found and killed that man — that brutal man who had slaughtered his mother and his sibling.

"Ahmed! Ahmed. Are you okay?" Kerim's voice penetrated his thoughts. He looked down at that happy little face, hands clutching the handles of his new shiny beautiful bike.

He looks down and forced a smile. "Come on, let's sit down on that seat over there. It's lovely and sunny and warm. I'll test you on the highway code"

They propped the bikes against the back of the seat. Kerim turned and patted the handlebars lovingly.

"I wish my mum could see it. She was brave. She would have wanted to try it."

Ahmed smiled and ruffled Kerim's hair. He had noted Kerim's use of the past tense.

"Maybe she can see it, little brother. Maybe she is seeing us now, together, and she is happy knowing that you are not alone, and that I will look after you."

Kerim hesitated. "Do you think she is dead?"

"Do you?"

Kerim sighed. "Yes, I do think so and I am sad, and I know you have lost your parents too. Grace told me. She didn't say what happened and I don't want you to tell me, but I am happy that we met and that I have you as my friend, so we can look after each other and not feel alone."

"Agreed," said Ahmed jumping up. "Now get on that bike, ride ahead of me and then signal right. Keep your arm out straight and count to five. Don't wobble and try not to run anyone over."

As Kerim did so, a little dog ran over in front and barked at him. He manoeuvred round it, made the signal, stopped and turned round, grinning. How was that?"

"Not bad," replied Ahmed. "Not bad at all. Let's have an ice cream and then go home."

"I have no money."

"Well, being your big brother means that I have to give you pocket money every week. Let's say three pounds, but you'll have to work for it."

"What do I have to do?"

"Tidy the bedroom."

"It's a deal."

"And clean the bikes."

"Okay, that's fair."

"And wash up after dinner."

"Really?"

"No, just kidding. Let's go. I need to talk to Grace. She's been worried about you. We can tell her that you know about your mum, so she doesn't have to talk about it unless you want to, of course, and I think we should take her some flowers, don't you?"

"Good idea. We can buy them with my pocket money."

Dinner that night was relaxed and happy. Even Ahmed was able to set aside his past and was looking forward to seeing Chief Inspector Charlie Knowles the next day and taking him to the spot where he'd seen the messenger on a scooter with cats' whiskers on his helmet. He had told Grace about the conversation with Kerim, and although it was a huge relief, both knew that it didn't stop there. Once Kerim had digested this information, he was going to want to know more. Where was she now? When could he go to see her grave, hers and his father's? Were they together? He would want them to be together.

Muslims were never cremated, at least never deliberately. His mother had been arranging, as far as she could, the burial of her husband. She had been in contact with the White Helmet Organisation — volunteers from all parts of the world and local Syrians, whose activities consisted of the evacuation of civilians from danger areas and essential services — like burying the dead. Such was the horror of the situation in Syria then, that they spent most of their time digging graves in advance. Russia, Iran and President Bashar al Assad of Syria portrayed the White Helmets as terrorists and launched misinformation campaigns to discredit them. When the White Helmets had published genuine proof of a terrible attack on the people of Douba, when their own President encouraged the use of Sarin and Chlorine gas, Assad declared that it was fake news. People on the ground were not fooled. They saw the bodies and knew that the White Helmets saved lives, losing hundreds of their own members who were killed while performing what they saw as their duty. Grace knew some of these brave men and had wept for them. Kerim's mother had died in hospital. They would have buried her certainly in accordance with Muslim tradition.

For the time being, thanks to Ahmed and Spike and her mother, the little boy was not broken. He knew the facts and was able to accept that his much-loved parents were at peace. Whether or not Ahmed would ever feel the same was something that only time would tell, but she sensed that he needed closure and that only Griff could assist him with that.

Chapter 21

The body of Louis had not yet been identified. His clothes and shoes had been carefully bagged, checked for any signs of dangerous substances, and sent to the forensic science laboratory. Fingerprints had been taken with acute care and were presently sitting on Charlie Knowles desk beside a tough plastic bag containing pair of boots.

There were distinct traces of blood on the soles of the boots, which were patterned with ridges. Typical heavy boots size fourteen. Charlie was smiling grimly. Things were falling into place, but that 'place' threatened to be terrifying. There were traces of Novichok powder on the steering wheel of the car. That car, the assumed owner of which was currently stiffening in the morgue, had been the wearer of those boots and presumably unknowingly had grasped the steering wheel whilst it was parked outside the supermarket. It was certainly not suicide. He had not been alone. There was no sign of a struggle. He must have left the car for a while, and someone else had decided to ensure his swift demise without giving a second thought to the risk to anyone else.

Novichok was usually in liquid form, he had been told. This was powder form and would have been accessible only to a high-ranking Russian. It was unthinkable that it would be available to anyone in this country outside Porton Down and since the Salisbury incident, it was unlikely that any responsible foreign agent would be randomly using it here unless he was desperate. It was a high-risk operation. Had it been planned beforehand or was the culprit always carrying a rare and deadly poison around in his pocket just in case?

He called Laver.

"Look, this is urgent. I want a fingerprint comparison, if possible, without delay." He explained the situation. "The 'stiff' in the car was murdered. They are aware of the means and must of course be careful, but we need to identify him as soon as possible. It's too much to hope that he has a record, but he certainly moved in questionable circles, so here's hoping. I'll call the morgue."

Prints were available without delay and transmitted to Laver. He was back within minutes.

"I do love computers! Got a match, gov. His' name is Louis Maclaren. Just an ignorant thug who acts as a heavy for anyone who pays him. The car is registered to him, and I have his address."

"Good work! That is great. Look, I need to make a couple of calls. Meet me in the car park in about twenty minutes. Try to find out where he operated and where he's done time. Never mind, we'll talk on the way. Bring disposable gloves, will you please, several pairs, and that knife we found in the bin at the Jewish guy's place."

"Joseph Epstein. Was he Jewish?"

"Bound to be with a name and a conk like that. Not that that has anything to do with anything. Go on, bugger off. See you in half an hour. Bring a flask of coffee."

Griff, at the same time, from his office, was in touch with Heathrow and other UK airports that ran flights to any Russian airport, to ask for detailed passenger lists. Whoever had used that powder would not be hanging around, and as far as he was aware, no other country had reported any connection to it. Not yet, anyway.

"Yes?" he snapped as his mobile chirped.

"It's Knowles. I tried to get you on the landline, but you were obviously busy. I have information which should interest you and questions in relation to our joint investigation."

"Oh, hello, Charlie. I'm all ears."

"The victim of the poisoning has been identified. I'll text the details. I'm going to his address very shortly and I'll keep you in touch. What I wanted to ask you about were the footprints you mentioned at Epstein's. By the time we got to the scene, most of the evidence had been disturbed by you buggers. The area round the body was scuffed but I recall a footprint in the blood pool. I guess you would have taken dozens of pictures before anything was touched. The thing is, I have the dead guy's boots — and there are bloodstains on them. There are a number of small stones wedged in between the tread on the soles. It's a long shot but worth investigating. Especially as the hidden camera shots in his studio were unclear."

"Yes, definitely. I'll send them over. There are two or three shots of the footprints — nice and clear, and I did notice some small white patches in the blood stains. The hidden cameras were trained on the office where the lights were off. Pity he didn't have one covering the landing, which was well lit, but it looks like there's a link, Charlie — if those boot-prints match, there'll be no doubt about it.

"Talking of cameras. I might have made some progress myself. I've been checking airports. Those facial recognition devices are bloody clever. They reveal three trips to Moscow by a man with three different passports. Same face, three different names. One of those names was Konstantin The third one travelled late, the day before yesterday, just hours before the car was discovered. It's our man; I'd put money on it. The reservation was made just an hour or two before the plane was due to leave. He was lucky. It was only half full."

"Can you identify him? Can they send you prints — of the faces I mean?"

"Well, it's not like a camera. It registers a kind of mathematical formula that can be used to identify or check individuals'' identity in just a few seconds based on their facial features. The software will confirm that this is the same man. It's kind of a mixture of geometry and geography — spacing of the eyes, bridge of the nose, the contour of the lips, ears, chin, et cetera.

"They call it a face print. They will send the algorithm or code and hopefully we will be able to decipher it and come up with a face — or three versions of the same face and the name. Can't wait. In no time at all, you will be using it yourself, Charlie. Detecting faces in crowds. The machine will pick 'em out for you."

"Bloody hell! That sounds useful. No doubt you'll need a science degree to use them. I'm only just getting my head round computers."

"I know, Charlie. Don't worry. There'll be teams of kids fresh out of uni — and you always have Jake on call; he's the unparalleled expert, don't forget. By the way, we are hoping the Press doesn't get hold of this. There didn't seem to be much publicity attached to the Epstein business. My team are used to being discreet. How was it when your guys arrived?"

"Well, I think by the time we left, neighbours had all gone home to bed. Luckily it was late and dark. People die and nine times out of twenty there's nothing suspicious about it. The Press are unaware of anything interesting so far. God help us all if the Novichok business is made public. Anyway — must go. Send over the boot prints. If there's a match, we're going to have to have an immediate meeting to discuss, so keep your mobile handy."

Charlie opened the cupboard under his desk, gazed at the bottle of scotch, sighed and closed the door.

Later, he thought, grabbed his jacket and headed for the car park.

Louis's pad looked uninviting — decidedly grubby. Access was through a door in an alleyway through the middle of a street of small, two-up, two-down red brick houses built in the early twentieth century. The lavatories were in the back yard then, but most had been updated since.

"Gloves," said Laver, handing over a pair of police disposables — large. "What are we looking for?"

"I'll tell you when we find it. Right now, I haven't a clue. Anything that might reveal associates, income — I don't know, let's just get on with it."

It was more or less as expected, smelly, dusty and very untidy, but there were indications that Louis was being well paid — a very large, curved screen TV was on brackets on the wall at the end of the bed, a brand-new dishwasher, unpacked but uninstalled was in the middle of the living room. The sink was full of unwashed plates dishes and pans and the bin was overflowing with takeaway food packaging. In the bedroom, thrown onto the unmade bed, was an expensive leather jacket and in the corner a heap of unwashed clothes.

"Right! We need to go through every one of those smelly pockets. Don't stop to read stuff. Grab one of those bins bags and put everything in there. Keep your gloves on. I know he never came home from his last excursion, and he's ninety-nine percent unlikely to have any fatal substances here, but let's take no chances. I'll do the kitchen and do the same with the contents of the trash bins, then let's get out of here. We'd better take a used cup to match prints and a toothbrush or comb for DNA comparisons.".

He paused. "Actually, if you do see any white powder, just take a swab. It may be heroin or cocaine. Best to know what we're dealing with, and it might lead us to some of his unsavoury mates."

"What about this?" said Laver, pointing a handgun at the window. "It was in that dishwasher. It's okay — not loaded but there's ammo and a knuckle-duster."

"Put 'em in a separate bag and let's go. Are you prepared to work late? If so, we'll grab something to eat on the way back — on me. What I need sooner is a large scotch and you're driving so I'll make it a double. There's a place round the corner. Keep your ears open in there."

Back at the station, and in a calmer mood, Charlie found the photos Griff had sent on his desk. There was no doubt. There was a perfect match. Louis's boots had paddled in Epstein's blood. Sadly, he was no longer able to explain why, or to reveal the identity of his companion. Charles leaned back in his chair. The knife they had found in a waste bin at Epstein's offered no clues, apart from the fact that the forensic buffs had agreed that the type of blade could match the cut, but so could a number of others. In fact, probably any sharpened knife. It had been rinsed, but it looked like a superficial job. It would be minutely inspected later. Partial prints might still be on it from the natural oils in skin. Why stop to wash it, why not just take it away? Was a man like Louis likely even to think about it? He certainly hadn't been alone. Maybe the unknown companion had rinsed it and thrown it away. It could have been Epstein's. Who would think otherwise? Did he just run it under the tap? If so — yes, prints might still be there. Charlie grinned. There was always a moment when a piece of evidence presented itself, something that was bound to lead to something else, something that signalled success. He worried just now and again, when he went home full of glee to tell Jill, his partner, that he was hot on the trail and she had to remind him that somewhere, someone was probably grieving — that a precious life had been lost. He shrugged — *well, not in this case*, he thought. Louis had been a lump of human detritus and anyone grieving for him should think themselves lucky. There had been little in his home to indicate that he had any kind of partner.

He went to pick up the phone to let Laver know the examination of the knife handle was urgent when it began to ring. It was Griff.

"Are you sitting down, Charlie?"

"Yeah — do I need to be? Are you going to tell me the mysterious late passenger was Vladimir?"

"No chance. He doesn't travel with the hoi-polloi. Anyway, he's skiing this week. Keeping his image nice and shiny. Has Jake ever mentioned the name Konstantin to you?"

"Several times. The mysterious driver! Is it him?"

"No doubt about it. Konstantin was with your Louis guy at Epstein's late yesterday and one or both of them killed him.

"We are supposed to be introducing Hubert's wife to the Investigators this morning — she has a bit of explaining to do but that's going to have to wait a while. Can you get over to Jake's, Charlie? This is going to be a dual investigation and there are things you need to know.

I think Kate is at home today. Ben is a little off colour apparently."

"Yes, sure. I'll just get things moving here. Give me an hour and I'll be with you."

Chapter 22

They were all assembled around the dining table except Kate, who was upstairs with the baby and would be given a comprehensive synopsis later.

Griff summarised. "This has become a Case Grade One now and it is vital that we deal with it as quickly as possible. It will inevitably go public. We can take no risks. It is more than likely that any packaging of the stuff..."

"Call it sherbet," interrupted Jake.

"Yeah, okay. There is a possibility that the container of the, er, 'sherbet' and protective gloves and stuff may have been chucked into the skip at the side of the car park. Once used, he needed to rid himself of anything that might jump back and bite him with fatal consequences. The skip was very close to the spot where the dead bloke's car was parked. It was emptied early this morning. We've located the spot where the contents were deposited at the edge of the landfill site, and we've cordoned off an area around it. We have had to explain to the staff — and there are dozens of them, that there may be a murder weapon in it somewhere. We have stressed the fact that nothing should be disturbed by anyone save the team that are going to do the search. They, of course, will be wearing the kind of protective clothing that will invite all sorts of speculation and I felt I had to tell the manager precisely what it was just in case any of them were tempted to go raking around looking for something. He is sworn to secrecy. I've asked the police to post a twenty-four-hours-a-day watch there.

"Anyway, Charlie, you aware of most of this, but for the sake of fluidity and just in case anyone has something vital to add, I'm going to summarise.

"When this all kicked off, Kate had gone to Paris to with the baby to see her mother. At the same time, and probably deliberately, Hubert had arranged for Konstantin to pick up Jake from his MI5 office. He didn't warn Jake, but he had had a brief discussion with him a couple of days before and expressed his concern about security. He hadn't gone into any detail but had warned Jake that something was wrong somewhere and that Jake might have to play along and keep out of the office for a while. You know all that, yes?"

Charlie nodded. "Yes. I didn't take all that very seriously. It was out of my jurisdiction really and I had cases of my own to think about. It's different now we have a body."

"Of course. Well, from the beginning, Griff was aware of the situation and confident that his friend was not in any way under suspicion. He advised Jake to act as required. They were discussing the matter in Jake's office when Konstantin turned up. Neither of them recognised him but he was able to satisfy them that he had the authority to remove them from the building, and that he had been instructed so to do. He drove them to Joseph Epstein's place. Neither had been there before and Epstein was another complete stranger to them. We assume that Konstantin was just obeying orders and had no idea that it was a strategy devised by Hubert.

"At Epstein's, they found Hubert. He then went into more detail. He told Jake about the unusual message that he had found on Jake's office laptop which he had for the time being, confiscated He explained that while he trusted Jake implicitly, he wanted to appear to suspect that Jake needed to be investigated and must be suspended pending enquiries. He assured Jake that this was for show only but also disclosed that he, Hubert, was now certain there was a traitor in the system and that the mysterious message, must have been deliberately placed there as a warning. Why on Jake's? — because they knew enough about him. to know that he was trustworthy.

"I don't know what they expected him to do but I did realise that they hoped to contact him privately, away from his desk. I banked on his brief suspension giving them the chance to make contact — which they did, through Kate, when she visited Paris. That was just lucky.

"Well, it turned out that he was right. Jake and Griff met two young people over there who possessed and revealed evidence involving a Russian agent who was transmitting information from London to Moscow. They themselves felt no allegiance because although both were employed by the Russian State, they were clearly not happy with developments regarding their own part of the world, Crimea, which had been annexed not so long before. They could prove to be very useful allies especially the girl. This stuff is not really of any interest to you, Charlie, as far as your investigations are concerned.

"When Jake and Griff returned home, they found Hubert had disappeared. They went back to talk to Epstein, and it was clear that he had been concerned about Hubert's unusual rather secretive behaviour and stressed manner when he had dropped by the day before. He had revealed the fact that he had gone to Moscow and had left an envelope for Jake with contact details.

"They promptly made that contact. When Hubert responded he didn't explain what he was up to but assured them that he was on the level. He expressed concern that he had lost touch with Epstein which was worrying and asked them to check on him. They made a further visit and found Epstein had been murdered. Alarm bells rang. You know the rest. MI6 were there like a shot, and you followed. I have promised to update you on that one Charlie as things develop.

"Hubert did return and has explained to us that his wife Sarah had disappeared and that he was convinced that the Russians must have her because there was a history. Sorry, Charlie, this is stuff you didn't know. His wife was born in Russia but left years ago. She is fine. She was in Moscow. She had been to her mother's funeral. She is safe now, but she has disclosed the fact that her cousin Ivan is a high-ranking Russian Secret Service Officer who would like to come over to us. Hubert had absolutely no idea about this family relationship and is still in a state of shock. You may well meet both Hubert and Sarah later today unless they are both instantly deported after the interview, but I don't think that will happen.

"As far as Konstantin, your chief suspect is concerned, he was a plant. He has hightailed it back to Moscow. Hubert and Sarah are meeting the investigators sometime later today to discuss the possibility of her cousin coming over. He himself is not quite ready and has no idea who controls Konstantin but has been digging since Sarah mentioned his name. He has discovered a connection. It is a danger signal to him. Up to now he had been top dog. No one moved unless he knew about it. He pulled the strings. He wants to find out what is going on before he makes any move. So, you see, it is all very complicated and quite honestly, I am beginning to wish I'd done what my parents wanted me to do and trained to be a doctor."

Charlie was silent, staring at notes he had jotted on his pad.

"Why did Sarah not tell her husband where she was going and why?"

"Good question! She said that she'd been driven away by the cousin who turned up at the house when she was alone. He'd told her he just wanted a chat in the car. He had a passport in her Russian name and whisked her away to the airport. She trusted him. He had been her favourite relative. I believe her now that I've had a chance to quiz her. She had no idea that her mother had died until they were well on the way. She had cut all ties for personal reasons. No need to bother you with those. It seems that Cousin Ivan had been keeping tabs on her since the day she left."

"How did Konstantin and Louis meet up?"

"Well, that's something only Konstantin can tell us now. I just hope we get to ask him."

"So, the situation now?"

"Well, a lot of this doesn't concern you, Charlie, but as far as your murder investigation goes, the best witness you have is probably eating caviar in the Kremlin. If he ever comes back, the airports will advise us immediately. Whichever name he uses, his face will be recognised and he will be detained. I'm giving you all the extraneous details because I trust you and it's only fair that you have some of the background. It's complicated, but the use of Novichok and the death of Louis does involve investigation by you, so you need to have the big picture.

"Yes, thanks, I'm grateful. I will of course keep you informed one way or the other. When Novichok turned up, you were the obvious person to contact. Believe me, I wasted no time."

"I know," smiled Griff. "I swear your voice was trembling when you did. You have two contact numbers for me, yes?"

"Yes."

"Use the new one if it concerns this case, Charlie. I have things to do and people to see. Thanks for coming. See you soon with Ahmed, I think. Once I've delivered

Hubert and Sarah to the investigation team, I'll be able to concentrate on the terrorists again."

Charlie found Laver parked outside and they were back at the Yard within half an hour. There were no questions asked or information given.

Chapter 23

It was with a sense of relief that Griff parked in front of Grace's house and tooted the horn to announce his arrival as agreed. Ahmed lost no time and was out within a minute, smiling happily as he climbed into the passenger seat.

"Hi," he said to Griff. "How are you? I've been told not to ask you questions about what's going on, but that is going to be difficult because Grace didn't give me any clues as to what it might be, so! What is going on?"

Griff laughed. "She probably means to remind you that lots of my work is confidential, so probing is forbidden. Without giving away any secrets, I can tell you that I'm extremely glad to be out and about and not stuck behind a desk trying to be polite and reasonable to people who tend ask stupid questions."

"Like what's going on?"

"Like, 'Where precisely were you at three-fifty-five p.m. on January 17th, 1992?'"

"No! Surely not."

"No, just kidding. It feels like that sometimes. In fact, I have just been listening to some friends being quizzed about their precise movements over the last few days, and feeling very sorry for them. Every time they said they couldn't remember, they looked guilty."

"Do you think they are?"

"I know them well. I'm absolutely sure at least one of them isn't." He shrugged. "But I could be wrong. I may have been fooled by him for years. History is full of clever persuasive liars. Sometimes they do it for money and sometimes out of loyalty to another person or a country or from fear. Anyway! I want to give my brain a rest. Sometimes I feel I should be doing something else. Something that doesn't require me to doubt the integrity of my friends. What have you been up to? Tell me about this scooter rider you saw."

"Quite honestly, I know nothing about him. Not long ago, Sergeant Laver was showing me some films taken from street cameras. He was trying to track a scooter. He was quite right, it was ninety percent tedious and eye-watering work, but there was one shot of a guy on a motor scooter who had made a delivery to Scotland Yard, which turned out to be fake, or a trick of some sort. I don't know the details. Anyway, they had managed to follow his route from one camera to the next and one shot was quite close-up. I saw a strange mark on the back of the helmet. Like a dark grey scratch or something, and it looked rather like a cat's ears and some whiskers. Well, it stuck in my mind. A few days later I was in town on my own bike keeping close to the kerb when a motor bike overtook me. I wobbled because he was a bit too close. I stared at him from behind and then saw the same cat whisker mark on the helmet. As he raced away, I made a mental note on the numberplate, which I hadn't registered when I saw the film at the station, but apparently it was the same. I kept him in sight him for about three miles. There was a lot of traffic. He turned off into a side road. I was pedalling like mad. I managed to stay on the trail but was quite a long way back. The lane continued through a couple of streets of houses and then it was countryside. He was well ahead of me by then, but I saw him turn into the grounds of a very big house with a huge garden. I could see tents and caravans there. Then I went home and phoned Sergeant Laver."

"Well, you sure are in Charlie's good books. Best not call him Charlie, by the way. Not unless he invites you to, and that is highly unlikely. It's almost like being awarded an Oscar. Actually, I think you will make a very good copper. Is that what you want to do?"

"I have a mission first, Griff, you know that. Is it okay for me to call you Griff?"

"Sure, but as far as the 'mission' is concerned, bear in mind the fact that it is a dangerous one and that it could ruin the rest of your life. You need to accept that there are degrees of evil and that sometimes circumstance can have an enormous influence on how one behaves. Let's just suppose that you have that man in your sights. That you kill him and then find out that his children had been bombed after some random attack by an American pilot — who was 'just obeying orders.'"

"Yes, but it wasn't like that. He was laughing. He loved what he was doing. All the way across Europe from

Turkey, I saw desolate people. People who had lost parents, children, loved ones. They comforted each other. Shared whatever they could. But that man bullied, stole, and laughed all the way over. I will never forget his face in my garden. My mother bleeding — dying at his feet. There were three of them there. The other two looked shocked. There is no excuse for any of them, but I think the others felt shame. Their war was not with women and unborn babies. They weren't with him on the journey here. I may never see him, Griff, but I can never forget."

"Listen, Ahmed. I made a promise to you, and I intend to keep it. You saw something that will haunt you for the rest of your life. I can only begin to imagine what it was like for you. In your place I would feel the same determination to destroy him but..." He paused.

"If, when the time comes, if it comes, if it is not possible for you to do so without either of us getting into serious trouble, or without putting your life or freedom and my career at risk, I will break my promise. Do you accept that?"

Ahmed stared out of the window. "Yes of course. As time goes by, I have to admit that although the pain is still there, I don't want to die. People like you and Grace and Detective Inspector Knowles have made my life worth living again. My parents would be furious if I threw away the chance to achieve something worthwhile."

Griff grinned. "Okay, well let's just hope we find the bastard miles away from any witnesses and we can use him for target practice. You get the first shot."

They were still laughing when they parked near Scotland Yard and made their way to Charlie's office.

"I'm going to have to leave you here, Ahmed. I have things to do and people to see. Charlie will be down soon. I sent a message to tell him you are in reception. Have a good day and I'll expect a report later." He waved and left. Ahmed climbed the steps into the building and arrived at the door just as Charlie came out.

They shook hands. "It's really good to see you, Ahmed. I was going to send Laver, but I suddenly needed to get out of the office. It's a sunny day and I'm sick of hearing complaints from the Crown Prosecution Service. Lawyers can be such a pain in the neck. Now we're going in an unmarked car so as not to give advanced warning of our interest. So where are we heading? Richmond way?"

"There was a place called East Sheen. I saw it on signposts. If you can get me to the high street there I'll know exactly where to go next."

"Perfect. I know the way there only too well. I used to go there to watch the Boat Race — Oxford V Cambridge. I just need to stop for some petrol. It's the BMW over there. Can you drive?'

"Yes, but I don't have a licence. Dad had a Jeep. I loved it. We used to…" He stopped. "Well, that's all over now. I'll see about getting a driving test next week. For the time being, my bike is great. I don't think I could have followed that guy in a car like this without being noticed."

"Not so easy to manoeuvre in heavy traffic either. Yes, get your driving licence, but more importantly, first things first, what about exams? Are you applying to universities? What was the situation in Iraq? Do they have O-levels, A-levels, stuff like that.? You need to go to university. Have you researched entry requirements for foreign students? If not, do so as soon as we get back. I suggest a couple of A-levels, say in Law and English. That should do it. That will go you lots of options. Lawyer, detective, teacher…"

"Teacher? No thanks, but the other two are tempting. Yes, I did have the requisite entry requirements over there, but in any case, Mum was determined that I should come to a university over here, so they organised a British Tutor for me. I was about to apply for a place at Durham just before the troubles began."

"Durham is excellent but too far away". How about a Law Degree? If you really want to be a detective, that would be a great start. That and English perhaps. You would walk that one. To tell you the truth, you need to be deeply interested in Criminal Law to be any good as a detective. So many cases fail because we forget the rules. Disclosure, for example. Only last week we had to drop an ABH case."

"ABH?"

"Stands for Actual Bodily Harm. You see, the defendant has a right to examine any unused material, that is stuff that we know about the alleged offence but feel we need not use it because it's irrelevant or more than we need to get a conviction. All the evidence that we are going to rely on is handed over — or served, as we say, on the defendant's solicitor, and details of the unused material are also served. If we fail to do that, we can lose the case. In fact, over the years, we have lost quite a few that way."

"So, you really have to play fair to the bad guys. That must be really annoying for the victims."

"My feelings exactly. We had one a few weeks back. There was this old lady who lived on her own. She lived in a road of substantial houses. She had gone to bed at about eleven o'clock and was reading a book when she heard a noise downstairs. She had a phone by her bed and when she heard more noise, not loud, but enough to worry her, she dialled her neighbour's number, to ask if they would pop round and check. There was no answer so after a minute she hung up and decided to get up quietly and go and investigate the noise herself. The only 'weapon' she could find was a lavatory brush from the bathroom next door so clutching that in her right hand she tiptoed downstairs and saw a man holding some hideous ornament which had been on top of a side table. She rushed at him waving the weapon and he saw her coming and pushed her away. She fell and bumped her head and was concussed, only for a while, then she managed to call us. The burglar scarpered of course.

"Well, we found fingerprints in her house, which identified him, and we found the ornament at a local junk shop which had a camera over the door, which showed him going in the next day looking very shifty, and actually carrying it, so as far as the theft was concerned, we had him bang to rights as we say, but the thing is, the old lady never mentioned her phone call to the neighbours. In fact, it was the neighbours who told the police about it. They said that when they did pick up the phone, there was no one on the other end. They recognised the number of course and in case the old lady was ill or in any kind of trouble, they went to investigate. Once outside they saw a blue car parked outside her house. They assumed it was her son's car and that he was visiting, because he did have a blue car, so they went back inside. They weren't asked to make statements because it wasn't until much later that the police found out about it. The old lady hadn't mentioned it and had no recollection of making the call. The officer dealing with the case made a note of it in his pocketbook when the neighbours told him about it days later. He should have disclosed this to the defence lawyers, but he didn't. He knew we had evidence enough and he didn't think it was relevant. The guy was charged with ABH and burglary.

"When the defence checked his pocketbook, which they are entitled to do, they pointed out, quite properly, that the neighbours should have made full statements which should have been formally served as unused material. The owner of the blue car may have been the old lady's assailant. She was unreliable as a witness, as her recollection of the assault differed every time she described it. This was weeks later. The blue car owner was never identified, and the old lady's' memory was questionable. In the end, we dropped the ABH, and he got six months for burglary. He already had a record for similar offences."

"Couldn't he have claimed he was acting in self-defence anyway? She might have put his eye out with the pointy end of a lavatory brush?"

"Well spotted! When he was interviewed, he said he was threatened and just protecting himself by pushing her away. We gave him the toilet brush and asked him to demonstrate just how she was threatening him with it. He held the pointy bit in his hand and waved the brush end. We have that on film. He had to accept that she couldn't have done much damage with that. We got the old lady to demonstrate, too. She did the same although she had no idea why she was doing it. So, you see, the law is complicated. You need to anticipate problems, which is exactly what you did there.

"Anyway, if you decide that it will be one of your subjects, we will take you on as a sort of novice trainee and involve you in current cases without breaking any rules, of course, and you can study old cases where we made complete cockups and tell us where we went wrong — subject to any reasonable objections from the Gov. After a couple of months, you will have to decide whether you want to be on the side of law and order by joining the Police or, of course there's always the Crown Prosecution Service. The other option is to become a Defence lawyer."

"Or a well-prepared crook," replied Ahmed with a grin.

"Ha! Look, we're in Sheen."

"Yes, I recognise this road." Ahmed sat up. "Keep going for a couple of miles. I'll tell you when to slow down when we are closer to the left turn. Don't overtake anything. It isn't far.

"Hey!" He laughed suddenly. "Just look at that." He nodded towards a motor scooter a little way ahead, indicating a left turn. "I'm pretty sure that's the same guy."

The house looked enormous and the grounds extensive. Acres of manicured lawns, home to immaculate wooden chalets and caravans of all shapes and makes. At the back and the sides, thickets of bushes and young trees were nestling in natural beds of wildflowers. It was a successful marriage of nature and order.

"And not a gardener in sight," remarked Charlie. "Let's go in and say hello to the scooter boy if we can find him. Where's the front door? There'll be a butler, I expect. I'm going to park near the stables — they're all closed, so I guess there are no horses in residence. It looks like some top-class holiday camp. Come on, let's find out."

As they climbed out of the car, a youngish man approached, looking puzzled but not unfriendly. Knowles held out his hand

"Good morning. I am DCI Knowles from the MET, and this is a young friend of mine who has guided me here. We were for the last few yards following a young man on a motor scooter with whom we would like a chat if that's possible."

"I see." The man paused. "He's not in any trouble, I hope. I'm his — sort of guardian. May I sit in while you speak to him? Look let's go into the house and I'll find him and perhaps you would like a cup of coffee?"

They followed him towards the front door.

"This is an amazing place, quite beautiful. Is it a sort of up-market holiday site? All the vans are immaculate, not like the usual mix," observed Knowles.

"They are all mine, but I let them. You'll see. Come on in."

The entrance hall was wide with polished parquet floors and lines of hooks along the panelled walls, some bearing coats and jackets. The man ushered them into a large room at the back of the house with French windows overlooking formal well-tended gardens.

"I'm sorry! I haven't introduced myself. I'm William Evans — sadly not the wonderful jazz pianist Bill Evans to whom my father listened avidly whenever he had time, and I prefer 'William' anyway — or 'Will' if you're in a hurry. Now what is all this about?"

"Well first, could you get the lad here so that I don't have to go over it twice?"

"Okay. What's his name?"

"I don't know. All I can give you is the reg number of his bike"

"Well, that might do."

"Ahmed. Can you remind me?"

"FT21 CWU," said Ahmed and held out his hand with a piece of paper. "The rider was wearing a white helmet."

"Ah. That would be Jason." He went to a table in the corner and spoke into some sort of gadget "Hello. Will here. Could Jason present himself in my living room in ten minutes please. That's Jason B. Nothing to worry about."

He made another call requesting coffee and biscuits and then sat down. "I'd better give you some idea of what goes on here, hadn't I?"

Knowles raised his eyebrows. "Goes on? Yes, please, I'm all ears. I hope I shouldn't be suggesting that you have a solicitor with you."

"Well stop me if you think I'm on dangerous ground, but I think not. I am lucky enough to own this house and all the land around it. After I left university, both my parents died within ten years. They were both magistrates and came home with all sorts of sad stories about kids who weren't rich and privileged. I had promised them both to do something worthwhile with my life and so I help young people who have had — well, let's say a difficult start. They get to live here on condition that they find a way to survive without harming other people, and from the outset, they have to accept and abide by the rules, the first being to keep the property immaculate. Then together we investigate their skills. They get training, board and lodging free while they are here, but they must contribute in some significant way to the upkeep of this place - gardening, cooking cleaning, whatever it takes to keep it looking as you see it today.

"My standards are high. I don't run a school. Those with an obvious talent get apprenticeships or even go to university if they are clever enough, or they may just cook or work in the garden clean the house — whatever. Believe me, it's worth it for all of us. They love this place and look after it well. They are of course free to leave whenever they want to. Jason is one of our 'collectors'. He'll tell you all about it. I trust him implicitly.

"I would be grateful though if you could give me some idea of what this is about. As I said, he works for me — maybe he was just obeying orders."

He smiled.

Knowles looked thoughtful. "Okay. Let's get to the point. Did you, at any time, instruct Jason to deliver a letter to Scotland Yard?"

There was a gentle knock on the door and a young man came in with a trolley with coffee and cakes. Evans thanked him and waited until he had left then sent out another message to delay Jason until further notice, but he was not to leave the premises until notified.

He then returned to the sofa and sat down.

"It's a complicated business but I'll come clean. Firstly, I want to apologize if this has caused a problem."

"Mr Evans," said Charlie. "An apology may not be enough. I am a senior police officer with more work on my hands than a dozen officers could deal with. I am snowed under. I should be doing countless other things, so don't waste time. Just explain as briefly as you can, and then I can either arrest you or get back to my desk. I will be very interested to hear however about your connection with a non-existent Saudi Prince and an armed escort."

Evans put his head in his hands. "Oh dear! I really didn't mean it to work out like this." He leaned back in his chair.

"I told you Jason is one of our collectors. We have arrangements with local supermarkets and hotels to collect all the food and other items which would normally be thrown away and use it ourselves. You know, out-of-date food products — those past the sell-by date but perfectly safe to eat. We rarely have to buy food, we have a wonderful range of meat, fruit and vegetables and nothing is wasted. Three of the guys collect, and yes, they do other errands on the way or further afield. One of our collections is from an hotel in Richmond. The owner is a friend of mine."

"Yes, all very commendable. I applaud your motives, but what does that have to do with the message, which had our gun squad lining up to deal with armed Arab maniacs.

"Evans picked up the internal phone again. "Jason, no need to worry. Just carry on and I'll explain later." He turned again to Knowles.

"All the kid did was deliver an envelope as instructed. He had absolutely no idea what the message was about. He was slightly uncomfortable about donning the uniform of a well-known delivery service but excited about delivering to Scotland Yard. I told him it was information that might be useful to you.

"Look, please hear me out and speak to him later if you think you need to.

He settled into his chair. The owner of the Richmond Hotel is Sebastian Lovell. He is fifty-four or five, I can't remember. We don't do birthdays.

"When he was in his twenties, he travelled a lot. His parents weren't short of money. He married a French girl, and they had a daughter, a lovely girl, Suzi. She did a degree in languages, met a bloke from God knows where, an Arab country, Oman, I think, very civilised and off they went together. Her parents got postcards and the regular phone call for some months, and then suddenly — nothing. No contact at all. They were frantic. The wife had a nervous breakdown. Sebastian hired a detective to try to find the daughter. He tracked her from the last contact point which was Bahrein but then nothing... until a few weeks ago." He stopped and looked at Ahmed and then at Knowles. "It may be best if this young man goes and has a look round at the estate now."

"Don't worry, I can vouch for him. Believe me. You have nothing to fear."

"Well, if you're sure." He went on "Sebastian had a visit from a group of Syrians just a few days ago — at least that is where they claimed to come from. They weren't scruffy, two of them spoke English. They just turned up and asked for rooms. There were three vacant and they took them. Two shared and the other two had one each. They ate a lot but didn't drink alcohol. The day they intended to leave, the leader Rahman, went into the office where Sebastian was preparing the bill. When he handed it over, this Rahman looked at him, tore it in half and dropped the pieces on the floor. When Sebastian stood up, the guy said, 'Please sit down and listen to me.' Sebastian sensed that something significant was coming and did as he was told. Rahman said they had his daughter, that she was safe, and it was possible that her parents might see her again, but only if they arranged something for him.

"At that point in time Sebastian would have done anything to be able to tell his wife that their daughter Suzi was alive and well, so he listened. What he was required to do was to arrange a gathering, put on some sort of performance in the hotel gardens — a concert, anything that would attract a crowd. Seb was stunned. He pointed out that the grounds there weren't spacious enough for a very large crowd but was told that area was big enough for a hundred or so. The closer people were to each other the better. At this stage, Sebastian was beginning to realise what they intended. He told them some stuff about not being able to do what they wanted because he needed a licence if it was a public event and that his place would never get one because of the size. He was playing for time. Then he thought of me. He said he knew someone with much more space. The perfect venue. The guy said he would be back in a couple of weeks and that if Sebastian cared about his daughter, he must comply. He was told that he would be watched constantly.

"Sebastian begged me to help. I said I would but knew I must do something. Their intentions were transparent. I thought if I could just get the police involved without risking a riot, it would be a start. He was furious when your inspector arrived on the scene. I tried to explain, and we talked about the worst things that could happen. I pointed out that there were no guarantees that his daughter would be freed. She may already be dead. We didn't know what to do next and the last thing I want is a massacre in my grounds here, and of course he feels the same. I am relieved that you are here. There must be some way we can stop this and with luck, secure the safety of Suzi too."

"Well, there's not a lot that I can do" said Knowles, "but I know a man who can. I'll get in touch with him. He won't hesitate to help, and we'll keep a low profile. We need to get Sebastian here, and I'll arrange for a chap called Griffiths to be here too. Let's not waste time. Don't worry. He won't hesitate. We must liaise and it must be soon — like tomorrow. Here is my card. Keep in touch."

Ahmed had been sitting on a chair by the coffee table, listening intently. He got up and followed Charlie out of the room. They both shook hands with Evans and headed for the car.

"Please let me help with this, Mr Knowles," he said quietly.

"Call me Charlie," said Charlie quietly. "And yes, I will let you help as long as you do as you are told. Come on, get in the car, I need to get in touch with Griff without delay. We haven't much time."'

Chapter 25

Griff had invited Hubert and Sarah into his office. "You'll be glad to hear," he said, "that it is I who will be vetting your story myself. I do most of the interviews when someone gives cause for concern but in your case, it is a mere formality. They know about Konstantin now — insist that they had their suspicions all the time, and probably did. His access to any information was limited, and you knew you had to be careful, Hubert. Tell me honestly, did you have any doubts about him at all?"

"No," replied Hubert, "I had too much to think about to worry about him. He was a good driver, always turned up on time and never asked me questions. If he was a spy, and managed to unearth anything useful at all, he was brilliant, but he got very little from me. I'm still reeling from the fact that he killed my friend. It was I who directed him to that address after he'd picked up Jake. I'll never forgive myself for that."

"Well, you weren't to know, and it may have been his associate, some thug called Louis, who killed him. I can't imagine why, though. Anyway, Hubert, there's something I need you to tell me. Would you mind waiting in the outer office, Sarah? I'll get someone to bring you a coffee and we won't be long. I promise." He came back and sat down at his desk.

"When you sent that text to Jake about the girl you met in the park in Moscow, you said something about the sun coming out which sounded totally out of place and surplus to requirements, but significant. What was that about?"

"Ah! Yes. It's been at the back of my mind ever since. I'm. hugely relieved that it is you conducting this research, Griff, because what she told me is that she suspects that it is a member of the ISC who has interests on the other side. If only I had known about Ivan's inclinations, I may have found a way of talking to him about it. But all I could think about was Sarah."

"What on earth could have made her come to that conclusion. Did she give you a name?"

"No, but in one of the reports that she dealt with, the source had said something about managing to get close to the prime target as arranged. She suspected that the target was Hubert but giving him Konstantin as a driver could only have been arranged at a higher level — or by you, Griff, I suppose. What do you know about them? Who do they answer to? They're civilians, aren't they? Quite honestly, I wouldn't know them if I bumped into one of them."

"You should know all this, Hubert. They oversee policies, expenditure, admin, but most importantly they oversee us: MI5 and MI6 operations. They can interview anyone they want to. The PM nominates them, and

Parliament appoints them, so they are answerable to Parliament. There are nine of them. They have access to heaven knows what classified material. I suppose they have a panoramic view of all the minute and specific details we amass and quite honestly, they should be able to point us or me in the right direction if they feel uneasy about anyone. If there is a traitor in their camp, the others would surely become aware. There is a limit to what they can access, of course. It just wouldn't do would it to have a bunch of inflated egos playing at being James Bond. They do deal with minor matters very efficiently, of course, but something like this, for example, is resolved at a much higher grade. They point the finger and we do the rest. They do the unwrapping, and we examine the contents. Quite honestly, they are just dressing. Don't quote me!"

"Do you know any of them?"

"Yes, I've had cause to provide information a couple of times. I would definitely vouch for the guys I met. If you're curious, their faces are plastered all over Wikipedia, which as far as I'm concerned makes them dangerously vulnerable. Some of them will be familiar."

"Well, how are we going to handle this, Griff?"

"Not sure but first, I will have to submit a report about you and Sarah, and I shall make no mention of your meeting in the park this stage." He put his head in his hands. "I think it's time to give serious consideration to getting Natasha and her partner out of there. I know they are keen to escape. Look, let's get Sarah in here. She can do things we can't." He turned quickly and stared keenly at the man he had known and trusted for years. "Can we trust her, Hubert?"

Sarah entered clasping a cup of coffee and sat down beside her husband. He took her hand.

"Sarah, when did you last contact your cousin?" Griff asked. "If he is planning to defect, we are thinking that he might be wise to move out sooner rather than later. Has he given any indication that it could be soon?"

"I tried to contact him this morning to update. There was no response, but that often happens if he's with someone. He keeps the phone we use in his jacket pocket. His usual one is in his desk if he's at work. He would prefer not to reveal the fact that he has two. In any case, we usually make contact at night, but I was worried that I hadn't heard from him for a couple of days. I've had no emails either. Shall I try again?"

"Yes, please do — er, just suppose he wanted to leave without flying? I mean, could he take a train to Rostov and cross the Black Sea to Turkey, or head for the Baltic States?" As far as you know, is he more or less free to travel? Is he kept under observation at all?"

"As far as I know, he goes where he likes. Is there any indication that things have changed?"

"Maybe! There have been developments. In short. He needs to make a move now or stay where he is and keep looking over his shoulder for the rest of his life. Is there any sort of signal you can send?"

"Like what? Hell! I don't know. The picture of an 'alarm' clock maybe. Or a print of ''The Scream.''" She stood up and paced around the office. "If he's in danger, I'd rather not contact him at all. It might make things worse.

""Seriously. If and when you next get in touch, just tell him briefly what has happened here. Mention the disappearance of Konstantin and the manner of the death of his associate. Ask if he has heard anything regarding a suspicious death without mentioning the N word. Tell him that if we can help, we will. There's an address near Heathrow which is safe. I can meet him at the airport and take him through the private route. Just let us know. We can arrange safe passage as soon as his feet touch British soil. Wait until he is likely to be home this evening and try again. He would only answer if it was safe to do so. Is he married?"

"Divorced — no children."

"Good, leave the rest to me. Hubert, take a couple of days off as sick leave. I'll update you. Off you both go. Interview satisfactorily concluded. I'll file my report."

They were just about to leave when a message flashed up on Griff's computer screen. It seemed that Griff had a visitor who was anxious to see him without delay. The camera in reception showed a smart dark-haired man at the desk. He looked up and smiled at the camera. Sarah gasped and grabbed Griff's arm.

"It's Ivan," she gasped. "He's here."

Hubert turned and stared at the screen. "She's right. Good Lord! Cool as a cucumber. Shall we go down?"

'Yes, but listen carefully. We will go to the lobby. You two will leave immediately without looking left or right. Just straight ahead. Go home. I'll call you later. You don't know him. Is that clear?"

"Yes, but will I see him later?" demanded Sarah, unused to being addressed as if she were a wayward schoolgirl.

"Possibly! I'll be in touch. Now go."

They went.

Chapter 26

Griff strolled over to the desk where Ivan was chatting to a receptionist. He turned as Griff approached.

"Ah. Mr Richard Griffiths, I believe." He held out his hand.

Richard took it and the shake was firm but brief.

"Forgive me," said Griff. "Have we met before?"

"Not in person," replied Ivan. He smiled. "But I've seen your photograph so many times. Is there somewhere we could have a chat? I'm in a bit of a quandary right now and I think you could help me."

Griff smiled back. "Well, I'll try. Come with me."

They went to the top floor. Rooms there were not equipped with discreet cameras and microphones although Griff's minute device hidden in his shirt collar would pick up and transmit their conversation to a receiver in his office. Only he had the code to recover it.

"Well!" said Griff as they sat in the comfortable leather chairs. "I never imagined that I would be sitting here with the head of Russian Intelligence at any time in my life. Am I dreaming?"

"Yes! It's a nightmare. May I smoke?"

"Sure. And then tell me why you are here, blatantly recognisable, undisguised, and apparently relaxed, in the offices of MI6. If I hadn't known that you'd be checked for firearms and deadly substances on the way in, I might be shaking in my shoes."

"Well, I have always conducted myself in the manner of someone who has nothing to hide. It's the best possible disguise. Looking furtive is fatal. Brazen it out, that's my strategy. Normally at home, no one would dare to suspect me of any kind of misdemeanour anyway — and over here? — Well, you might know who I am, but very few people outside this building would have a clue. I'm simply here on business. Just suppose my presence here was noted and reported back home. Well, so what? I have come to discuss business with you. To tell you a few feasible lies. I do what I like."

Griff laughed. "Good for you. But I'm sure you noticed a couple, both of whom you have met before, albeit separately, leaving just before I approached; and I suspect that you know perfectly well that one of them would have already paved the way for a discussion between us. Am I right?"

"Spot on." He sighed and leaned back in his chair and closed his eyes. "Quite honestly, Mr Griffiths, I am absolutely fed up with the state of the world." He sat up. "Remember Mikhail Gorbachev — remember Perestroika? We were allies. The world seemed so much safer. Your Queen paid us a visit, for heaven's sake, in '94. It all made sense; and then came Vladimir in 2000. Safety, civilisation, confidence in one's future? All have diminished every day, ever since.

"I looked after myself, of course. I can't deny it. I tried to keep things on an even keel, said the right things, supported the right people, lied through my teeth to my superiors, appeared to be ruthless, just to keep some sort of control, and yes, to protect myself, but it's hopeless now. Everyone is suspect. If they don't toe the line, they die or rot in prison. I can't change things. I've tried so I'm getting out." He looked at Griff and raised an eyebrow. "So, I need your help, and I can certainly help you."

"I would so love to believe you," Griff said, "but if you've fooled the President for all these years, with breath-taking success. You could be sitting there feeding me top-quality bullshit. What do you expect?"

"If you weren't suspicious, you'd deserve to be fired, of course I know that." He stared out of the window at the river. "Why don't you ask me about Konstantin?'

"Why don't you tell me about him?"

"He's dead. When I found out about the death of Hubert's friend and how he died, I knew I had to deal with Konstantin. Suddenly this figure skulking in the background became a significant hazard. I became aware of him from contacts I have here. I have agents who have agents, but all are registered, in my files, and I make sure that no one has access to those. None of my people had anything but whispers. There was a tenuous link to Moscow but nothing concrete. This was a shock. I guessed he would have to leave the UK pretty quickly after the recent Novichok incident, which came as a huge and horrible surprise, and guessed the safest place for him was home. Cameras at the airport proved me right and I was able to have him tracked. We had a chat which was enlightening, and he was perfectly well when I left him, but not for long, I suspect. He seems to have had a nasty accident. I can assure you he is no more. What had bothered me... When I say bothered, I mean terrified, was — who pulled his strings? Who gave him the poison? I had to find out. That stuff is not for sale at the corner shop. You have to jump through hoops and scale mountains to get it. Anyway, Konstantin was helpful. I now know who was behind it all."

"I'm listening."

"You may have heard the name Hector Polanski."

"It sounds familiar, but I don't know much about him. I've never met him as far as I know, it's just one of those names that bandied around. If he's a pop artist, I wouldn't be interested anyway, so why are you? Wait a minute, isn't he some sort of oil magnate? What's this all about?"

"Oil, drugs, people, currency, you name it. If there's money to be made, he's into it. He owns massive estates near the Black Sea and in Ukraine and heaven knows where else. He skis with the President — when he's there. But recently he isn't.

"Isn't what?"

"Isn't there. He disappears. He has a double identity. It's taken me some months to discover where he does go and to identify his alter ego. He is a very clever man and I

230

predict that you will be reluctant to believe me, but I swear it is the truth. To start with, google his name and tell me how many photos there are of him."

"Erm — none, and very little information either. Are you going to divulge?"

"Are you going to help me?"

Griff sighed. "I've already had discussions with Hubert and your cousin. I've taken advice and sought the approval of the management, with the caveat that if we find any holes in your information, we might just send you home, wrapped and labelled, with the address of the Kremlin on your brow — so yes. We are prepared to do anything to keep you safely here. So, who is this Magnate?"

"Open your computer and find the faces of the nine members of your Intelligence and Security Committee." Griff stared at him.

"Sorry?"

"Trust me, just do it. One of them is completely bald. In Russia he wears a very expensive wig. His contact lenses give him brown eyes and he is much thinner. I think he wears padded vests in public over here."

Griff moved to the computer and found the page and stared at the nine faces. Ivan pointed at one. A man who had been introduced to him some time ago as Harding or Hardy, he couldn't quite remember.

"You may not know that he has estates over here too, and a private jet which can take him anywhere in double-quick time. There are hundreds of private airfields, as you know. Since he was appointed, Mr Polanski hasn't been seen in Moscow much, but nobody wonders why, or would dare to ask anyway." He paused. "Konstantin was employed by him, Polanski, or Hardy if you like. He persuaded the other members of the committee to take him on, after all the usual checks were made. He sold him on the basis that he could be useful in making sure that everything in the organisation was financially above board. He suggested that as a trial project, Konstantin could check out Hubert. It seemed a harmless enough plan."

"Good God! Wait a minute, are you telling me that this man is... You can't be right. His name is Harding, Hardy? I was introduced. I shook his hand. He didn't say much."

"Exactly. He keeps a low profile. I don't think he got very far in his quest for information, but I don't know exactly what was intended. What puzzled me was that killing someone would not have been sanctioned under any circumstances. Polanski must have been horrified when he found out, but that was one puzzle that Konstantin cleared up for me before we parted. It seems that he had a hired helper, some crook who chauffeured him around. I don't know the name, but the Jewish man's death was due to an over-enthusiastic attempt by this crook to protect his employer. After that, Konstantin saw no alternative. He had the means. The man had to go. No great loss to the human race, I think, but if Vladimir knew that one of our agents carried some of the death-powder around with him and used it, he would not be pleased. He knows there are lines he must not cross. He loves taunting the Americans and delights in hacking into their computer systems, but he values his reputation too much to take a step too far. He almost got away with it once in Salisbury, until the culprits were identified, and although they deny it, Vladimir knows that what you Brits broadcast through the BBC is usually accepted as valid.

"Anyway, when Sarah's mother died, I saw the opportunity to make contact with my slender links over here. I had already decided that it was decision time. When Hubert came hunting for her, and I confess that I hoped that he would, which is why I begged her not to contact him, he did what I would have done in the same circumstances; he came straight to the top. Perfect! Doors opened for me. It wasn't the time or place to confide in him then and there. I had already primed Sarah, so here I am!"

"How soon is your absence going to be noticed? Who do you report to?"

"Only the President." He's not stupid. I have actually kept him out of lots of trouble over the years, persuaded him not to make rash decisions. He knows I am here. I told him about the killing of Hubert's friend and that Konstantin had been drawing attention to himself. He agreed that I needed to get over here make sure that it wouldn't all result in the exposure of Hector, our ISC friend — let's refer to him as Toby to be on the safe side. That would be a complete disaster."

Griff was stunned. "You mean your President has personally installed one of his cronies into our Intelligence Services? Good God!"

"Precisely, but don't rush in and expose it. Use it."

"Use it? That's going to take some planning. Look, there are people I need to talk to. Where are you going to stay? With Hubert? No! I'll organise a discreet hotel and have you delivered there. Pay Hubert and Sarah a visit if you like, that will appear normal, but I'm going to lend you a driver for your stay, one who knows what he's doing and what to look out for. I'll be in touch as soon as I can. Take this phone for calls between us only. In the meantime…". He paused.

"Welcome to the United Kingdom. I hope I don't have to kill you."

"We are as one with that. Lead the way."

Chapter 27

It didn't make the headlines the next day. The tabloids didn't mention it at all, but somewhere inside some of the broadsheets was the mention of a light aircraft having crash-landed in a remote part of the Lake District. The wreckage had been removed for investigation by accident inspectors and the pilot, who had suffered fatal injuries, had not yet been identified, and of course would not be named until relatives had been traced and notified.

Days later, when the press were informed that the pilot had been a member of the Intelligence and Security Committee, there was much more of a fuss, but there was an absolute assurance with the information provided by the government spokesperson that it had been a genuine accident. There was no evidence of interference by terrorists or anyone else. So far, his identity had not been divulged, but of course members of the Fourth Estate were digging furiously. It was only a matter of time.

"Oh God! What have you done?" said Ivan, leaning back in his chair in Griff's office. "I'll have to go back.I was supposed to meet him today. The President is going to be so suspicious. This is exactly what he would have done.

He's very good at phony accidents — not personally, of course. I'll have to go back. I still have relatives…"

"Stop," said Griff. "You must see that we simply could not let this situation continue for another day. A Russian plant in our own Secret Service. We'd be a laughingstock for centuries. Calm down and I'll share a secret with you. If what I'm going to tell you becomes public knowledge, you might just have a nasty accident yourself!"

"I'm listening."

"He who shall be nameless, or Toby if you like, is, as we speak, tucking into a good breakfast somewhere in this building."

"So, he's not dead?"

"Not the last time I looked. Actually, he's thrown his breakfast at the wall and is refusing to speak, but that's okay. Thanks to you we know all about him and he can't do any more harm."

"So, what are you going to do with him?"

"I don't know, it's not my problem. What we must think about now is what's going to happen to you."

"If I'm going to be any use to you until my cover is completely blown, I need to speak to Vladimir. I must go back — well, I'd rather not, but I will. By way, I think you should get the girl and her pilot friend out of Russia as soon as possible. She's not a top priority at the moment but things could change. It might be a good idea if they visited her mother very soon and you can take it from there."

"Yes. I'm on it."

Jake had been in touch with Natasha's mother the previous day and the couple were on the way to Sebastopol. Natasha had a few days' leave due and her immediate controller had been quite happy to let her go.

"Mr Griffiths."

"Yes."

"Who knows, besides yourself, what is going on? Can you trust them?'

"About the accident with the plane which never happened? You, me and my superior. No one else needs know.

"Or about the Russian plant? Well, the other members of the committee will have to be told eventually but not yet.

"Or about your decision to join us? Well, you, me, Hubert and Sarah, of course, and two or three others know. I hope to keep it that way for the time being. Safer for you, and I don't have to reveal my sources. That is a given."

"And what's going to happen to, er, Toby?"

"I have no idea, but I guess he'll get used to toast and marmalade eventually. He has committed serious offences here, but I suppose it depends on how cooperative he is. We don't randomly kill people, you know. This is a civilised country still, although quite a few of us forget that sometimes. What I don't understand is why he's doing it! Is it for the love of Russia?"

"Might be. His mother was Russian. What has he been involved in officially?"

"That would not be revealed to me without good reason."

"Are you searching his place?"

"As we speak."

"I expect the boss will be calling me today. What am I going to say about it?"

"You mean your President? Absolutely nothing. You know nothing. Say you hope to speak to him later. One good thing about semi-recluse characters is that nobody ever knows where they are. Nobody but us on this occasion. Remember. The plane crash didn't actually happen. It was just a device to explain his disappearance here. You never know, we might turn him and send him back to Russia to work for us. If you feel that you must go back one more time, to sort stuff out, you'll have to bluff it. Say you just haven't been able make contact with "'Toby'" in the usual way. Come on now. You don't need me to tell you how to wriggle out of tight spots. In fact, the more I think about it, the more I'm wondering whether I should put you in handcuffs and send you down to join him for lunch."

"Okay! I'll go back tomorrow. Lead me to a phone and I'll book a flight before I go and say goodbye to Sarah."

"Yes, I will, but before we go, what can you tell me about her father?"

Ah! My beloved uncle Vadim. I still miss him you know. I was in my late teens when he disappeared in apparently suspicious circumstances. The relatives were upset, well, more than that, they were terrified, all expecting to be taken in for interrogation, but strangely, there were no repercussions at all. Not even a friendly chat. They didn't talk about it much. I tried to find out from my parents what it was all about, but their lips were sealed. After a while, he was more or less forgotten. The Russians don't like to admit that they are perplexed. They prefer to keep silent and look as if they are keeping secrets."

"But you remember him."

"I'll tell you what I know now. He was a closet Anglophile. He was mad about Shakespeare. His English was very good. He was good at most subjects at school and had a mind of his own. Against the advice of his parents, he came over here to the UK and got a job working for a theatre company. They were putting on a performance of Romeo and Juliet. He loved Shakespeare.

"He came back after a couple of years. By that time his English was so good he could have been English. He did translations for the Russian government. Nothing that would have been any use to you, I guess. His problem was that he just couldn't resist a beautiful woman. His wife, Sara's mother, was stunning, but she was, forgive me, quite boring. Vadim would disappear for weeks, ostensibly for 'special government work'. In truth he had another home in Crimea. Another woman and a daughter. He disappeared from them for weeks too, hopping from one family to another, lying through his teeth about where he was and what he was doing.

"Then the female American agent turned up — a reporter she said. He just couldn't resist her, and I think she was equally attracted to him. When her cover was blown, they were genuinely in love. She got him out of the country fast and he was consequently labelled traitor. It hit the headlines in the States, of course, and gave him a status he didn't really merit. I'm sure he made the most of it."

"Does Sarah know all this?'

"Well, not from me. I think she's better off not knowing, and I would think twice before you introduce her to the young lady on her way from Sebastopol, if I were you."

Griff stared at him for a moment. "You mean…"

"I mean that Sarah has a half-sister that she didn't know existed and it would be a bit of a shock for Natasha, too."

Chapter 28

When Charlie called, Griff was on his way to River House. It took him less than three minutes to find a turning spot and head for the given address in Richmond, 'The Manor House', with the appropriate postal code. Charlie was already on his way and had alerted Evans to make sure that his friend, the manager of the Richmond Hotel, was also heading towards the same place. The information provided by Evans was a recipe for carnage, but at least they had a chance to prevent it. *Not only that, but prevent the perpetrators from planning more*, thought Griff, *but it has to be handled with care.* They could stop it here and now, quietly arrest the hotel manager for being involved in criminal activity and be ready to round up the terrorists when they came back — if they came back, but if they didn't come back, there were no details of credit or debit cards. They hadn't paid. There was nothing at all which might help to identify them, apart possibly from fingerprints, but they could not be isolated from heaven knew how many other prints. They had indicated that Seb would be under constant watch but by whom and from where? Was it right to run terrifying risks in order to catch a bunch of murderous…? He braked sharply and parked in a garage forecourt and picked up his phone.

"Change of plan, Charlie. We need to meet somewhere else. Even in plainclothes, there's something about you that screams policeman, and it's just possible that someone questionable has already been planted at Evan's Manor House. Let's meet at Jake's.

"They might be keeping an eye on the hotel owner. If he goes to the Manor, that's only to be expected, but if we turn up, it's going to be obvious that we are aware that something is going on, especially as you've already been there once and identified yourself. Give Evans Jake's address now. I'll have someone check that they are not being followed from there. If they are, then my guy will follow the tail back to his source. I'll need an hour to fix that, so please tell them not to leave till eleven-ish."

"Yes, got it," Charlie replied. "That had occurred to me too. Give me a second, and I'll come back to you."

All was arranged and the two pulled up at Jake's within ten minutes of each other, Charlie first. He waited for Griff, and they went in together. Both Kate and Jake were at home, and they all had about an hour before Evans and the hotel owner were due. Fresh coffee was on the table. Little Ben had already gone upstairs.

Kate and Jake were briefed.

"It's imperative that a police presence is imperceptible. I can see that," said Jake "But just suppose, when these guys are informed of the proposed venue, as they are bound to be, they're going to snoop around and make plans. They're bound to draw attention to themselves."

"Not as easy as you think," said Griff soberly. "Evans will be on the alert. There are cameras covering all areas. Strangers are carefully vetted. He's going to be very concerned about the safety of his people. He might even refuse to be involved."

"Well, you'll soon find out. I think they've just arrived," said Kate from the window. "I'll let them in."

When they had settled into comfortable chairs and been given coffee, Evans and the hotel manager were given the run-down. Evans had prepared his friend, but with no detail. He himself made it quite clear that he was prepared to help as much as possible but only on condition that none of his tenants would be at risk.

"Hopefully by the time this thing takes place, you will be confident that no member of the public will be injured in any way?" Evans enquired without any degree of confidence.

"Believe me, I don't want anyone's death on my conscience. It would be the end of my career for a start." Griff turned to Kate. 'We may need our friend upstairs to pose as a gardener in a day or two. Do you think he would mind getting involved?"

"Like a shot," said Kate, "or is that expression a bit too close to reality?"

"Well, we hope not to end up with a carnage party. The other side tend to use bombs and knives. The bombs do by far the most damage in a crowd, as you know, so finding and disarming them is a priority. They will be much more likely to carry knives than guns. Anyway, we'll discuss tactics later. All we need to know today, Mr Evans, is how the concert would be arranged. Where the stage would be, how visitors would be checked in, et cetera, plus anything the manager might have to help identify the terrorists. Like when they call, how they call and anything that might be useful. Do you have anything in mind yet?"

"I have a rough plan in mind, yes. The stage would be set up at the front of, but a good distance away from the house. I thought of roped sections in front of the stage to stop a surge forward. I will have strong lights at each corner and pointing at the stage, of course. They will be controlled from the house.

"I've brought photos of the layout with me. You see there are clumps of trees and bushes at the sides, but the area where the stage will be facing is all lawn. In front of that is a gravelled area where visitors can park.

"The residents use a field down the lane which we rent from the farmer. I'm thinking that any attack would probably take place when crowds are leaving? I would imagine that it is then when they are most at risk, so I'm trying to work out a plan that would require them to leave in small groups. So far, I haven't managed to do that unless people pay for specific places. Each row would have a different colour ticket, and they would be allowed to leave row by row."

"Hey! That sounds like a plan, Mr Evans, but I need to plan a strategy. I'll be in touch again very soon. The bushes and trees at the east side could be useful. Could you fix a very bright light that shines on the area at the side of the house which is out of sight? That particular switch to be controlled by one of my team."

"Anything you say, of course, and please call me Will."

"I will, Will." He grinned "Thanks. Kate, will it be okay if we all meet here in future? In about three days? If anyone is keeping an eye on the manager, it might look suspicious if he pays too many visits to River House and I think my face may be known to the wrong people."

"Do you wear a vest? I mean a bulletproof one?" asked Jake. "Quite honestly, I spend so much time with you, I think I ought to have one myself.'

"Don't worry," laughed Griff. If the need arises, you shall have the latest model, but if Kate lets you anywhere near the place on the night, you'll be stationed in the house with some others who will be responsible for recording the entire proceedings, including the music probably. There's a hell of lot to plan and we don't have enough to go on by any means yet." He turned to the hotel owner

"Mr Lovell, or may I call you Sebastian?"

"Seb will be fine," Lovell replied

"Thank you, I'm sorry to have to ask you this, but do you think your daughter is still alive?"

"I'm not confident of that, to tell you the truth. He did show me a picture of her with her partner, they looked happy. They were in a restaurant, so I assume it was before she, or they were captured. To my shame I didn't ask about him and he wasn't mentioned."

"Is it remotely possible that he could be involved in this?"

"You mean on the wrong side? No! I'd stake my life on it.'

"Good. I accept that you believe that, and I tend to agree with you. What I need to know is whether she is still alive. I'm truly sorry, but I can't risk lives unnecessarily. When this Arab comes back, you must tell him that you suspect that his plans are to do harm to people, and that you are not prepared to risk other lives if your daughter is dead.

"He may already wonder whether or not you have reported this. We must make sure that all appears to be going to his plan. He will realise that the only chance of succeeding with it is to have you under his control. He can't do that unless you know you have something to lose. You must stand firm on that. He has not given you any contact details, but he will be back, unexpectedly. Hopefully you have a spare room at the hotel.? I'm going to have someone stay there. She can act as your receptionist. I guess these people will be unlikely to book in. They'll just pop by to check on you unexpectedly."

"Now Will, I'm going to give you further details of the measures we're taking here. Have you any vacancies at the moment?"

"No, we're nearly always fully inhabited. There's a waiting list."

"Would it be possible for you to get a couple more static vans? Or maybe get a couple of residents to stay elsewhere for a few days. My expense, of course? There's a young man I know who would be very useful to us and he speaks and understands Arabic…

"You've met him already, Mr Evans," interrupted Knowles. "He was with me when I visited you."

"Ah yes. Well, I can certainly make one van available immediately, but why two?"

"I may be wrong, but I suspect that once they know the venue, they will want to have someone there to monitor the arrangements we are making. I think the best way to do that would be for them to have a resident there, so we need to be able to allow that to happen. Suppose residences here are snapped up pretty quickly, yes?"

"Too right. Word gets around but I vet everybody. How am I going to know who to accept and who to turn away?"

"I've been thinking about that. If the van for Ahmed is available now, he must move in today, without delay. He must look as if he's been there for a while. The new available van must be next-door to his. Ahmed will be allocated some job in the house. When the applicants arrive, we will have had time to do brief checks, but if you keep them waiting in the entrance hall for a while until you are ready to interview them, Ahmed, who by the way will be called Mike at that stage, can stop to chat, ask if the guy would like a tea or a coffee. His English is perfect. Trust me, Mike will be able to tell. He's had the right kind of — well, you don't really want to know, but I for one would trust his judgment." He paused "Then of course if they are on friendly terms, Mike will have an excuse to pop round to his to neighbour to say hello, although I suspect the door will close in his face.

"Both vans will have discreet systems to reveal to us everything that is said and done. Mike will be our ears and some other sophisticated device will be sending pictures to his van and to another receiver in the house. Your new cook will need that room indoors, please. Oh, and if the guy has visitors, would your installed cameras be pointed in the right direction to catch them? Check every day, and if a visitor carries anything into the target van, see if he carries it out, but don't worry too much, all comings and goings will be recorded and monitored 24/7. It's just the sooner we get info, the better."

"No problem. I'm feeling better already. The sooner your people move in, the safer I will feel."

"We must do everything conceivable to make this safe and do absolutely nothing that may arouse suspicion. I'm going to install someone in the hotel today, Seb. It's the Richmond Park, isn't it?"

"Yes, that's right."

"Well, for us, for message purposes, it's the, er...the Resteasy Inn. Is there another one with that name in the vicinity?"

"Not that I know of."

"Okay. Well, if there is it will put them off the scent. Can you call your manager and make sure that a room remains available? She will be your secretary and receptionist. You'd better give the current one a week's holiday in case any of these people remember her. I need to know how and when they make contact, so let her answer the phone, then when you take the call, she will be able to let me know if it is significant. Now I must go. In the car I have some pay-as-you-go phones. I'll get them, Kate, and you can distribute

Charlie walked out with him.

"I need to get back, Griff. I have other matters to see to. I need to get back to the office in the car I have."

"Yes, of course, so have I. I'm dealing with two nightmare situations right now. Even they are getting confused."

"Anything I can do?"

"Well, as far as this pending nightmare is concerned, I have the seeds of an idea in my mind which is quite exciting. That team of young plainclothes detectives you have been nurturing... how many can you round up? I'll need a couple of hundred."

"Tell me more."

"Can't yet but I'll call you later, I promise. What we all must do is keep it under wraps. Can you reel Ahmed in, so that we can give him his orders? Tell him he has been renamed Mike. Let him know precisely what we want from him. I suspect that he's going to love this." He leaned onto his car and pulled out a bag which he handed to Kate who had joined them. Knowles left with a wave of his hand.

"I hope you don't feel left out, Kate," Griff said, "but this could get nasty, and I dare not put you at risk. To start with, Jake wouldn't have it, but more importantly we need a message hub, and you are brilliant at that. Just sit at home, cuddle Ben and make sure everyone is in the picture as things develop." He gave her a hug.

"Actually, Griff, I'm fine with that, and thanks." She waved him away and hoped that one day in the not-too-distant future they would all be raising a glass to celebrate a successful mission with no casualties. Just a few arrests.

Chapter 29

The meeting about the ISC interloper, which took place at the M16 Headquarters had been gruelling. Opinions were conflicting and after two hours there was no consensus. That was hardly surprising.

"The Prime Minister had to be informed, surely?"

Or not, argued Griff. "He would explode with rage, insist on taking over, and do heavens knows what. He appoints these people without any knowledge of them at all. He's probably been talked into to it by some crony with an agenda of his own and who has a lot to gain. I'm not saying the PM is corrupt, I'm quite sure he is not, but he is impulsive. This is something that must be kept under wraps until a fully considered and feasible course of action is clear."

"But Griff, how do we explain the sudden and complete disappearance of a member of the committee? We are the very people who would be expected to know where he is, and yes, we do know, but broadcasting the fact that we have him locked up downstairs in a cell, without the remotest idea of what we're going to do with him would cause a bit of a stir."

"We have the rumoured air crash. If we circulate the fact that there is a degree of evidence which might connect him to it, that could solve all problems. Our investigations will produce no further evidence at this stage. The public will come up with all sorts of theories and it will gradually become one of those historical mysteries that is never solved."

"But what do we actually do with him? He's a nasty bastard. If we let him go, he'll have the time of his life. Can't we stuff him in a helicopter and push him out as we fly over the lake district — Windemere would be a good spot. We could weigh him down."

"Yeah, great idea. Seriously though, maybe we just need to come clean. He fooled us all. The facts are these — Hector Polanski known to us as George Harding lives in England and presents as 'a very private person. Until his name was put forward as a member of the committee, we hardly knew he existed. No other member is admitting to being his nominee, but it must be on record. The PM appointed him but that was just a formality. He naturally expected the man to have a clean sheet. We assumed that he had — and it's not our business to interfere in that procedure. The fact that he and Vladimir are cronies is the kind of shock that would shake the whole of Westminster to its foundations and unless security in this country has fallen apart, we must find out who proposed him and whether there was any follow-up. Time for the fox to chase the dogs. I've asked to meet three members of the committee in a couple of hours. I'm quite looking forward to it."

"You better have a defibrillator ready."

"Is he talking at all?"

"Not really, except to tell us to fuck off. He must know we can't keep him locked up for ever."

"Well, I suggest we give him back to Vladimir. Not openly. But if we fly him to Estonia, say. Near the border he can hitch a lift back to Moscow. Then we will then broadcast the fact that we had become suspicious of his activities and acted without delay on the basis that he may pose a threat. Unfortunately, we can claim, he disappeared without a trace before we could interview him. That is a polished-up version of the truth.

"And when the time comes, when we know he's safely back home, we can the disclose the news that this Russian agent, who realised he was under suspicion, had provided us a list of names and sources in this country which would be of interest to us. We were suspicious of at least three names on that list and were delighted to have our suspicions confirmed. Three men had since been arrested." All rubbish, of course, but it wouldn't do him any good. And when we do disclose the fact that one of the President of Russia's close friends was a member of ISC, because it is bound to come out sometime, at least we can claim to have known it all along and used it to our own advantage. Vladimir might even believe that."

"Do we actually have three Russian agents in our sights?"

"More than three, what matters though is whether or not Hector P. has any idea that Kapalski might be a turncoat. If he gets to Moscow and sows the seeds of doubt in his President's mind, heaven knows what the outcome could be. We must keep him here until Ivan has been home and returned. Once he is safe, we could leak some story about our nasty Russian intruder giving us lots of very useful information about his President in a desperate attempt to gain his own release. Then we can consider arranging his escape. Vladimir may just polish him off himself before he starts making trouble. But it is vital that we do not reveal Ivan's presence here now, or later if he actually gets back unscathed. Vladimir is not going to accept the sudden disappearance of one of his top agents, and if he discovers that Ivan is a defector, he is going to look so stupid that there'll be a huge price on to pay."

"We've created new identities before now with great success."

"True, I'm working on it."

"What are we going to do with Polanski's property here?"

"Seize it, and his plane. We've arrested his pilot. He's being very helpful but had no knowledge of what was going on. He's just a pilot. Although he was told he'd lose his job if he told anyone anything."

"Well, I'm going to have to go," said Griff. "I need to see Ivan. He might have some good ideas as to what information Polanski might disclose under pressure. He's determined to make one final trip back to Moscow so, for heaven's sake, keep Polanski incommunicado till he's safely back."

"Are you sure we can trust him?"

"Ivan? Ninety-nine percent yes."

"Why does he need to go back?"

"He has relatives there. They could suffer. He wants to get them out. Not necessarily to the United Kingdom, but he has other options. Ukraine would be best. They have no idea what he plans to do, of course, and some of them will hate him for it, but I admire his sense of responsibility."

"Well, keep him monitored. Just remember some of the nice guys we've trusted before!"

*

Ivan had been placed in a safe house in the New Forest. It was well equipped, stocked with food and he wasn't alone. His appointed driver was staying there too, just to keep an eye on things! For the time being, Griff had retained Ivan's mobile phone. No point in taking chances. When he arrived, Ivan was pacing up and looked pleased to see him.

"Thank God you're here. I'm going out of my mind. Does Sarah know where I am?"

"Not yet, why?"

"Keep it that way, please, for now."

"Are you saying you don't trust her?

"Of course not, but I'm troubled by these Russian lessons she's giving weekly. You see, one of the ways I kept track of her was through one of her students."

"What!"

"Yes, I know, stupid, but it worked. I don't think he is dangerous. He is one of mine, but he believes that I am a Russian stalwart, staunch, loyal, faithful to the Russian cause. He speaks Russian fluently, of course, but disguises the fact very well. Sarah loves him because he seems to learn so very quickly. He sends me monthly bulletins. They often have coffee together and chat. It will probably be fine, but maybe you could have a word with her"

"Yes of course — don't worry. We're going to see them now. I suspect that you will have to meet our Prime Minister at some stage, but if you insist on making that final trip to Russia, this will have to wait until you get back."

"Okay. It will be nice to get out of this place for a while and have some decent food. The driver seems to exist on sausage beans and chips."

"Okay, well in that case we'll leave him here to pursue his culinary delights and stop at The Pig where, I promise you, the menu is varied and the food delicious."

"Great! I could murder a plate of Kamchatka crab."

"You may have to make do with stroganoff."

"Hmmmm! That'll do, but first a vodka with some caviar."

"Are you absolutely sure you want to live here?"

"I'll tell you after lunch."

*

"Lunch was good, Mr Griffiths," said Ivan, wiping his mouth with a napkin. "But quite honestly, if they had served up a plate of battered lizards with turtle-dung sauce and chips, I would have begged you to accept me, although I may have left the chips. I'm seriously worried about where my country is going and the lack of any genuine opposition. Ukraine is always on the menu, and for what? We take everything we want from them anyway. There's no hunger for war in Kiev. Where would it end?"

"Well, if there's no provocation, surely he wouldn't take action."

"He took Crimea with supreme ease! Anyway, with your permission and assistance, I'm heading back first thing tomorrow. I'll see the President, give him my report which I will compose on the way, sort out my relatives who are of no interest whatsoever to the Kremlin, and then head back on the pretext of investigating the disappearance of Polanski, so please keep him under wraps."

"Don't worry. Bon Voyage. Keep in touch through Sarah, if necessary, but preferably directly with me, and if you can, please let me know when to expect you. I can't really deal with our unwanted guest until you let me know how then land lies."

Chapter 30

It was quite late that night when Griff called Sebastian on the designated phone. "I have a plan," he said, "but it's complicated. Do you have any means of contacting these people or do you just have to wait until they contact you?"

"The latter, unfortunately, it's very frustrating."

"I sympathise. Could you meet me at Jakes's or somewhere closer if you prefer? I'll have you followed just in case."

"I'll go to Jake's. That's fine, but I'm busy all morning. Would two p.m. be okay?"

"Perfect, I have calls to make first. See you later."

The calls took up most of the morning. By lunch time Griff was feeling encouraged. The technicians were more than happy to oblige and were anxious to get started. The most difficult part of the plan was proving to be more of a challenge. He needed a celebrity. Someone who would be expected to draw a crowd. He knew two or three who would have been only too happy to help but they were tied up with various engagements here or out of the country. He had ruled out a concert. It would involve taking too many people into his confidence. The terrorists would not be interested in how he attracted the crowds, as long as there were crowds. He needed a name, a personality who was well known, just in case they did some checking. If he couldn't find one in person, perhaps one who would be quite happy to permit his name to be used in such a good cause.

First of all, Sebastian needed to sell this to the enemy. If they wanted to succeed with their vile plot, they needed lots of adults, all in a group. Whatever it was that attracted the audience to the Manor gardens would be of no interest to the terrorists at all, as long as they were there, lots of them all huddled together.

A message appeared on his laptop screen. A technician needed access to the hotel attic and couldn't find the manager. Griff arranged it and then went out to his car. He was going to be slightly late. Later in the day he would address the volunteers who, according to Charlie, would be only too delighted to take part.

Jake and Kate were both at home, chatting to Sebastian when he arrived. Will had been invited to join them and was on the way.

"First of all," said Griff when they were all settled, "what do we want to achieve? We want to avoid any fatalities, even those who have forced us into this nightmare. It is not going to be a concert. There will be no singers or musicians. There may be piped music just to set the scene. These guys do not give a damn about music, all they want is a close collection of victims, the more the better.

"I have decided that the type of person who would draw the crowds will be a comedian. One who is well known and very successful. Sadly, the ones I personally know who would be willing, even eager to do it, are all otherwise engaged. I'm pretty sure that the conspirators are unlikely to have watched that sort of stuff on TV. Our humour is beyond their comprehension. I have, however, asked a well-known funny man if he minds us using his name. If this all goes to plan, his ratings will go through the roof. There'll be canned laughter. The guy who will be playing his part is busy with his feet on his desk at the yard, learning his jokes. Any questions so far?"

"I like it," said Will. "If it works out, it will be so much easier to set up the stage and so on. What about tickets?"

"Ah," replied Griff. "There will be no sale of tickets, and there will be no publicity, but there will be a crowd. Trust me. Over the next few hours, Charlie Knowles and I are meeting groups of young police officers, male and female. Each one will be sworn to secrecy, and believe me, they are as keen as we are to make this work. The sale of tickets would have been by phone anyway and we can sort that out as we go. All our selected guests need to do at the gate is flash their warrant cards. As far as your near neighbours are concerned, Will, nothing is happening although they will see people arriving on the night, and assume it's a private party

"If the Terrorists turn up at the hotel for an update, Seb, one of my boys has arranged an ad for it on your TV.

I have a friendly film director to supervise. He needs a date and time for the event so we must arrange that. It's very convincing, this short advert, but it will only be on your TV, Seb. No other. I didn't know they could do that, but it's a special TV that plays discs. There's a slot at the back. The ad is all on a disc. It lasts about three minutes. Assuming they won't want to sit and watch the news, it will be fine. You look at the clock, switch it on, it will show the end of some soap opera and then there will be local adverts, including the one for the show. There'll be a phone number for tickets. I've prepared tickets for you to give them. Switch off immediately after the advert finishes.

"Don't ask me how it works. I have no idea. Just in case he wants to see it again, say the programme is live and you can't wind back. Hopefully you won't need it but it's there, just in case he wants some kind of evidence that plans are being made. I'm trying to cover all eventualities. The girl I have staying in the hotel will inform me of all arrivals and departures. If any of them turn up, they'll be followed when they leave."

He turned to Seb. "Have you made any progress, Seb?"

"News about my daughter, you mean. No, but I have told them that unless I have proof that she is alive, there will be no concert and that I will go to the police with everything I have — which isn't much, I'm afraid... but if she is still alive, that would be her death warrant, wouldn't it?"

Chapter 31

The call came at six the next morning. Griff was sound asleep, and it took a minute or two to gather his wits. It was Sebastian and he sounded frantic.

"They've sent me a film of her. To my phone. She looks so distraught, Griff. They've wired her to a bomb! What..."

"Seb! Calm down. First, forward the film to me, straight away, then come here. I'll send the address."

The video was as described, a once beautiful young woman, the anguish obvious from her face and demeanour, trying not to look at the camera, as if to do so would be to acknowledge the desperate situation she was in. He studied it for five minutes and then called Seb.

"Listen, there are two things here which are quite encouraging, Seb. First of all, she is alive, and second, she is in England."

"How can you tell that? It might have been taken weeks ago."

"I don't think so. Did you not notice the newspaper? It had yesterday's date on it somewhere. I recognise the headlines. Are you coming over? We can talk about it then. Come on, don't waste time, it's not far but try to stay calm and drive carefully." He contacted his technicians and forwarded the video to them.

"We need all the information you can get from this — location and time and anything else I may have missed. Lives depend on it. The location of the sender should be easy enough, but where was the film itself made? Definitely in the UK, I'd say. But we need a precise address. The room is typical post-war style and size. I imagine it's a terraced house in the suburbs somewhere. Judging by the time on the clock and the sky you can see through the gap in the curtains, you should get something. Contact me when you have more."

Seb arrived, dishevelled and bleary eyed. He listened to Griff's deductions from the piece of film and collapsed into a chair. "They told me that if everything did not go as planned — as they've planned, they will send me another video of her…" He paused. "Her destruction. I was sick. I just threw up, so forgive me if I must look and smell revolting. I should have showered and changed but…You think she may be here? In England?"

"I think she is quite close, Seb. It is amazing what you can tell from something like this. I'm waiting for further information, but we should be able to pinpoint at least the area." He glanced at the message he had received only moments ago. It read:

'*Hi Boss. Sorry mate, the video has been stripped of metadata at source. There is nothing but pixels. These guys are computer savvy, I'm afraid. However, not that savvy.*

You were right. The sunlight shining through the window confirms the time visible on the wall clock and we have a date too. The furniture in the same frame is mass-produced generic stuff but that works for us. We have exact specs on the height of the furniture. We can work out the direction of the window, and from that and the shadows cast, the declination of the sun, do some sums and voila! Voila what? You may ask. Well, we can calculate the line of longitude. From that and the age of the construction, west-facing room etc we can extrapolate a number of possible sites. Four in fact. I'll text you what I have asap.

Cheers
Scallywags.

Griff's response read:

'I don't want the bloody recipe, just send me the pie. Might need your help in physical form soon. Thanks Simon.

PS. Get an aerial view.

Griff turned the screen of his phone towards Sebastian.

"It's all here from my experts and they're still working on it. You can read it if you like, but it's just a mass of cyber babble, like a foreign language to me, but I believe the area is within travelling distance. Maybe an hour's drive."

"Really? Oh my goodness." He buried his head in his hands and then looked up. "I can't tell you what a relief...

Well, I'm sure you can imagine. Thank goodness for them. I'll repay them somehow."

"You don't have to think about it, Seb. They love what they do, and if they happen to save a life in the course of their work, it's a huge bonus."

"Indeed! Just one other thing that bothers me, Griff, is, when the man called, I was about to tell him where the concert would be and to talk about the likely date and so on, but he interrupted and said they knew where it would be. How could they know? Is somebody leaking information? I have never given them any idea of where Will Evans lives, oh, and another thing. He is going to call tomorrow and wants the date."

"Hm. Interesting. Your car is outside, yes? Let's go and have a look."

The tracker was easy to see. Griff removed it and they went inside. Griff made some coffee.

"When was the last time you went to see Will? Have you been at any time since we planned this new venue? They wanted a closer look, I expect."

"Just two or three days ago but Will was out. I stayed there for about five minutes just looking round."

"Will has one car, one van and a number of scooters, yes?"

"Yes."

"And he will have details of each one — I guess he's pretty methodical. Tell me, does that lane lead to anywhere else or does it tail off when you get to the Manor?"

"There's a farm, that's all. It's not a through road. Will bought the field behind the house. His residents and visitors park there."

"Okay. You were followed, but not closely enough for you to notice. We need to get webcam pics of the main road close to the entrance to that lane. I'll arrange that, but we need Will to identify any vehicle that was not too far behind yours, which is not his or connected with the Manor. I'll arrange the viewing and you get Will there. When he sees your car, he must note the registration of whatever follows you in, and later emerges shortly after you do.

"I've removed the tracker device but if they check, they'll know you've been in this area, which is a pain in the neck, but I'll sort that later. If we can identify the vehicle that followed you to the Manor, we can trace its owner or user and perhaps they will lead us to your daughter, but..."

"But what?'

"Well, Seb. Firstly, the bomb vest you saw on that video was a fake. Just to terrify you, which it did. They wouldn't attach her to a live one in case she accidentally or on purpose blew up the lot of them, but once we know where she is, which we probably will, within a couple of hours, you will expect us to rush in and rescue her. Yes?"

"Of course."

"And as soon as we do, they will know they've been rumbled, and scarper, unless we are lucky enough to find them all assembled there, which is very unlikely."

"What do you expect me to do then, Griff? Do you want me to leave her? How could I?"

If we extract her now, the whole plan fails. No gathering at the Manor. No hope of capturing fervent Islamists who are happy to blow themselves apart together with numerous people surrounding them. No hope of capturing the bastards who control them who will do it all over again. I know you think it's easy for me to talk, she isn't my daughter, but it's not easy, Seb. My first instinct was to go out this morning, suitably armed, to find her and rescue her. I have to look at the big picture. These people are not only slaughtering our citizens, but they are creating massive racial prejudice. They are a tiny poisonous minority who achieve nothing but misery."

He paused and put his head in his hands. "It's a matter of timing. Once the party is up and running and we have identified the likely suicide victims, and their controller, then, we can go for it. Take them by surprise, get them disabled before they can do any harm, then we can target whoever has been left to guard your daughter. They will be waiting for news. News will be transmitted to them, that explosions have taken place and officers will be poised somewhere very close to where she is, waiting for a signal from us. Then, they will go in. It is highly unlikely that she will be bomb-rigged, but whatever we do, we'll make sure she is safe, and I promise to keep you in the loop. Now go talk to Will and tell him what we're arranging to do today. He might need to make a list of names and registration numbers to work from and he can just tick the one we're interested in. We only have a day or two left. Does the man usually call at a specified time or just any time?

"He knows I have a business to run. Not that he gives a damn about that. It's usually just after lunch is cleared. I more or less set aside time for that."

"Well okay. It's nearly two. Why not stay here and scribble notes? When he calls the hotel tomorrow, you will be there, and you will give him a date. If he doesn't like it, be firm. It's Saturday and you can't change it. Your newly appointed receptionist can keep us in the loop, I'm sure. Time is running out. We have three days to complete preparations. Try to find out whether he is going to be there. I expect he will keep well away, but somebody will be reporting to him throughout. You can bank on that."

*

Plans were in place as far as it was possible. Ahmed, or Mike as he was now called, was installed in a van in the front row about a hundred yards away from the house. There was an empty one next door. A stage had been set up, as well as lighting, some of which was well concealed for the time being. Two of Griff's staff were in the house and the van, making sure that everything was wired and unobtrusive. Mike was impressed. "I'll be able to hear him pee," he said. "It is so sensitive. I just wish one of them would turn up. What if they don't, Griff? What if they've rumbled us, and are planning something else? What if they are just playing us?"

"It's not the way they work. It's this or nothing for the time being and Seb's secretary has just called to say the Arab guy has been. He has the date. She saw him give Seb a nasty look and said something like 'I hope for your daughter's sake that nothing goes wrong.' If they had any suspicions, he would be off like a shot. Probably would kill Seb on the way out.

"We have twenty-four hours to get this right. They know where and when the event will take place. They need to know the layout. They will get someone installed here. No doubt about it."

It seemed that Griff was right. Will took a phone call the same morning from someone who was very interested in renting a chalet or van. Will, detecting a slight accent, tried to sound unenthusiastic. "I am sorry," he said. "I have just promised our last empty van to a young lady. There may be something next week." There had been a long pause and then another voice. "Please forgive me for interrupting; my friend is in a terrible state. His wife has just died, and he has been ejected from their rented house. He has nowhere to go."

"Oh dear," said Will. "My sympathies. Could he stay with you?"

"Yes, of course, but I am in Scotland."

"Well," said Will. "In that case, send him along at about two o'clock this afternoon and I'll see what I can do. No promises."

At a quarter to two, everything looked calm. Griff was chatting to Mike who was desperately trying not to respond to the name Ahmed when Griff threw it in as a test.

"That's enough please, Griff. I was 'Mike' at home, so I prefer it. I was only Ahmed at school."

At two pm, Will was outside talking to one of the technicians, pointing at the guttering while they quietly discussed the security plans. The usual occupants of the vans and chalets had been sent to town on the pretext that there was a suspected gas leak. They were suspicious but had been booked into a smart hotel, all expenses paid, and were happy to enjoy a little bit of luxury at the expense of their landlord. All the vans were locked and residents unable to travel had been temporarily housed indoors with access to the private garden at the back. The stroppy ones who just wouldn't comply were to be addressed by Griff at a later stage and threatened with expulsion if necessary. Since they all liked and respected Will, they concurred with little more than a raised eyebrow. They knew something was up.

At two o'clock, the scene was set. Will was talking to a technician in overalls outside the front door on the gravel drive. A temporary stage had been set up on the lawn and a large number of folding chairs were leaning against the front wall.

A few minutes after two o'clock, a shabby Ford Escort drew up by the gate and parked. Will strode towards the gate and motioned the driver to drive on into the field just behind the house. The lane was too narrow for any overtaking.

He waited until the cat was parked and then greeted the driver, expressing his sympathies. There was a puzzled expression on the driver's face, just for a moment, and then he took a handkerchief from his pocket and held it to his eyes. Griff was chatting to Mike in front of his new lodgings. Mike was responding and taking no notice of what was happening behind him.

As Will and the applicant approached, the man beside him gazed at the rows of vans and chalets.

"Nobody there?"

"All at work," Will replied.

Mike was about to turn his head when Griff stiffened, gripped his shoulder and said, "Look straight ahead. Do not turn." It was the tone of his voice that caught Mike's attention and he continued to stare at straight ahead, at Griff.

"What the—? What's the problems for heaven's…?" His voice trailed off. By now Will and the visitor had gone into the house.

Griff gave a sigh and looked down. His face was pale. He looked up and stared at Mike, and suddenly Mike knew.

"It was him, wasn't it?" He felt sick.

Griff nodded. "I think so, yes. Come on, let's talk in the van. First I need to let Will know that we have the right man, then I need to get you out of here."

In the van, Mike leaned back and closed his eyes. He was trembling. Griff was talking about getting him out to his car and leaving without delay, but Mike wasn't really listening.

"Could you just be quiet for a moment, please, Griff? I'm thinking."

"There's no time to think, Mike. You travelled across Europe with that guy. He'll recognize you. Everything will fall apart. I can't risk your life. I'll get someone else in here. Come on."

Mike sat up. "He won't recognize me. I was a scruffy long -haired kid. I've changed. I'm older, cleaner, slightly fatter. He won't recognise me."

"Well, You recognised him."

Mike stared at him. Griff sighed and hung his head. "I'm sorry. I'm so sorry. Look, tell me what you want to do."

"I'm not sure, but I'm staying here. I'm just going to act like the others here. I have a job to do, here in this van. I'm going to do it just as we planned. I'll cope, I promise and at least I know that his days are numbered."

"If I agree, it must be handled according to plan. No impulsive acts. Remember, if you kill this man out of the context of our legal arrangements, you will end up being charged with murder, and if it was deliberate and not accidental or in self-defence or in defence of another, then you have no defence."

"I know, I know; Charlie has given me books to read. Look, Griff, I'm okay. I just wasn't ready for that. Let's have a cup of tea and plan our next move. How long have they been in the house?"

"I have no idea but assuming nothing has gone wrong, he'll bring, whatever his name is out to look in the van next door. I haven't seen or heard anything outside yet." He stood up and peered through the curtains. "Eyup! They're coming out now. Come on then, let me put you to the test. Let's say hello!"

He opened the door and went down the step onto the lawn outside. Mike followed and strode ahead. "Hi, Mr Evans, is this the new resident?"

He was standing in full view, but about two yards away from the Arab who looked straight at him. There was no flicker of recognition.

"Yes Mike," Will replied, "but we're in a bit of a hurry." He turned to the man, "This is Mike, your neighbour." And then to Mike he said, "I'm not sure I can get my tongue round the name, but yes, this gentleman will be moving in and staying for a short while, maybe just a couple of weeks, but I'm sure you will help him to find his way around if necessary" He ushered the man past and they walked towards the empty van.

Griff breathed out slowly. Mike was half smiling, and kicked at a stone

"See! It was easy. It was almost like coming to the end of an exciting film. Minutes before the end, you suddenly know it's all going to work out, and the end is going to be perfect."

Griff sighed. "I need a coffee and then I have to go. Things to do, people to see. I'll be back later. Get in touch with the team here as soon as I've gone. Tell them what's happened and arrange when and how to keep in touch. After he's gone, they need to make final checks."

Upstairs, they sat with coffees and watched the front from behind a muslin curtain. After about five minutes, Will and the man emerged from the van, Will walked to the house and the man walked off towards the gate.

"Will came into the room looking anxious. "It seemed to go smoothly, don't you think? He's gone to get his luggage."

"Couldn't have been better," said Griff, still looking through the window. "Here he comes with a big wheely case. That's a hell of a luggage for two weeks. What is his name?"

"Abdullah, but call him Abdul. He said all his possessions are in there. He wants to go back to Syria."

"I bet he has a couple of waistcoats in there, but I have no information to suggest he's a bomb maker. Did he say anything about expecting visitors?"

"Yes, as a matter of fact he did. Some relative or friend is bringing his passport, possibly tomorrow."

Griff smiled slowly. "Did you tell him about the show tomorrow evening?"

"Yes, but it was as if it was no surprise. He just nodded and said he'd probably stay in his van. It wasn't his kind of thing!"

"Right, well, both of you. Keep me informed of anything that might support our suspicions but don't interfere. We have discreet cameras all over the place. He will be putting in a report to his masters by phone, I suspect. Watch him carefully. See if he investigates the shrubbery at the sides, and all possible exits." He sighed and put his head in his hands.

"Look, why don't you go back home now, Mike? Come back in the morning. Kerim will be missing you. The indoor crew will be able to monitor anything going on in the van. If he makes any calls, they will be recorded. We won't hear the responses, but we'll get the gist of what's going on from what he says.

"We've checked his transport. There's a tracker on there now and if it is registered, we'll have an address. I really think you need a bit of time to come to terms with things. This new development is totally unexpected. You need to consider just how far you want to go. I need someone calm and composed in that van next door, Mike. There's still time to put in another Arab speaker, people's lives depend on us, Mike."

"Yes! I know, and yes, it shocked me to the core to see that face. I still want to kill him, but I know how important it is that we make no mistakes. I promise that I will call you when I've had time to think and digest. Maybe it will be enough to know he's been captured, or killed by someone else, but I want to be part of it, Griff. Please let me help. Please let me be there. He's seen me now. Someone else in there would look suspicious."

Griff was quiet for a moment and then pulled Mike towards him and gave him a hug. "Come on. I'm going to drop you off. I'll give you money for a taxi back tomorrow. We need a code word for him. How about Pigface?"

"Ha! He'd recognise himself straight away. How about Osama?'

They settled on Brian.

Chapter 32

It had been decided earlier that day that a meeting in the New Scotland Yard building was not appropriate. Fortunately, the manager of the old building, now a very expensive hotel, had offered the conference room there. It was perfect. Two plainclothes officers kept strict control of the corridor outside. The manager had very kindly laid on a buffet supper and the atmosphere was tense with supressed excitement as some two hundred young plainclothes police officers, male and female, listened to Griff's outline of the proposed strategy.

"Well, you've been told the basics. What I want from you lot," he said, "is a very good impression of a bunch of people, mostly strangers to each other, apart from the couples of course, dressed in whatever you like, looking forward to an amazing evening with a celebrity comic whose' name you'd better learn off by heart." He held up a photo. "This is what he looks like. Cheer and whistle as soon as you see him. He knows exactly what is going on and I hope he will not at any time be in a danger zone. He kind of hopes so, too" There was a subdued murmur and one or two brief laughs.

"To begin with, this is a private affair. No members of the public will attend. We believe there will be three suicide bombers. Three sad blokes who intend to blow themselves apart and take as many of you as possible. The man who hopes this will happen will be operationally absent, I suspect, but we know where he is now, and we'll be watching and waiting until it's time to pounce, but we can't pounce until this event is under control, that is, until we have disabled four people, the three already mentioned and one more who is already there, in place

"I'm going to be quite honest with you. This is how it is at the moment. I've told you where it will be, you have maps, photos and an aerial shot of where things are, including the car park. There is a guy in one of those vans in the front row at the end of a column. It's marked with a small x. As you can see, there are lots of vans and chalets, all fixed, with gaps between. They are in front of the Manor House but set quite a long way back. We are ninety-nine percent sure that this guy is the vest maker, although he might just be the dresser. He took in a large case yesterday which we think contained the kits. Obviously, none of the three chosen victims would expect to get past the gate if they were already wearing the bulky vests, so they will have to go into his van to be 'dressed'. I don't think they'll arrive together but if they did, would we be home and dry? Couldn't we just lock 'em all in the van and arrest them as they came out? Sadly, that is not an option, because the occupant would be straight on his phone to the organiser before we had time to stop him, and a young lady would probably die. She is being held hostage. A promise has been made that she will be released as soon this plan to slaughter a number of our citizens has succeeded.

"So — back to the plan. It's almost certain that they'll be dressed individually. They'll go into the dresser's van, one at a time and as they come out and move away, they will take up positions in the crowd. Once they have positioned themselves, one by one, we take action. If all goes to plan, they will be quietly shot with an anaesthetic gun, which will bring them down immediately and before they can do any harm. Experts will be standing by to safely dismantle. More on that in a minute.

"If they do come out singly, they will move in different directions. Their plan is for each to take down a bunch of victims of their own. Left, right and middle, I guess. The guys with the tranquilliser guns will stealthily follow until the opportune moment comes. The anaesthetic to be used will act immediately, so if a bloke suddenly falls to the floor near you, just stand back and let the experts in. but keep up the laughter and chat. Your job is to be a crowd of happy young people there for a night out and you need to keep it up.

"As soon as each is down, we have people who will discreetly take them to the side of the house where there are trees and shrubs. Way out of sight of the dresser. The lights there will be full on, and the explosive expert will disable. It doesn't take long if you know what you're doing. When they come round, they'll be in handcuffs and either in a police van or a cell. Any questions so far?"

"What about the guy in the van, the dresser? He'll be out watching them surely?"

"As soon as the three are out, and assuming he will have no idea what has, or will happen to the three, he will almost certainly stay in the van to phone in a report to the organiser. His van is bugged so we'll know.

"Once he has made his call to say that the three are loaded and in place, he will no doubt come out to watch and a burly plainclothes copper will be waiting outside with handcuffs. Assuming that the three have been disarmed and loaded into the van, he will be arrested and taken to the Yard. But timing is crucial. Just keep your eyes skinned. You'll have your usual equipment with you, so you'll be able to report back to your team leaders if you see anything sinister going on. Any questions so far?"

"What if the other two panic when the first one goes down?"

They won't know It's important to keep them separated. When the first goes down, several of you will surround that particular part of the garden, talking and laughing. Remember, the three will be tailed as soon as they come out of the van. Hopefully there'll be enough of a crowd around him and of course, you will make a point of blocking the view. Who's in charge?

"Hi, I'm Ben. We've already decided to split into three rough groups, with a leader. They'll be groups numbers One, Two and Three, in order of action. Now that we know the situation, we'll discuss positioning later."

"Exactly. Pick a couple from each group who could be standing chatting and facing the van and fairly close. Then they move in the same direction as victim one does, the rest follow, laughing and chatting until the gunners do the business.

"Okay, any more questions?"

"Yes, hi, I'm James. The three are going to go in one at a time obviously, what if the dresser comes out with the last?

"If he does, it will be brief. I'm pretty sure of that. He must make that call as soon they are mingling with the crowd. Obviously, they plan to press the buttons at the same time. One by one wouldn't work for obvious reasons. Mike in the van next door who has been listening in as they briefly discussed their plans, heard the dresser say, 'Yes, of course, I will let you know when they are dressed and ready.' And then later he heard, 'When I give them the signal, I will call you. My lights will go off and on and I will step outside and film it.'

"So, guys, watch the lights. By then, we must all know that the three are no danger to us. I just want to see his face when there is no bang. That's when I'll get him. The organiser who is safely about ten miles away thinking everything is going to plan will then be seized by a unit poised to act, and the hostage will be freed, while the bastard here is panicking because there is no bang and nothing to film. No pictures of a bloodbath — pray to God."

"Could Mike inside the next van give us a signal when the dresser makes the call? He could open his curtains perhaps."

"Good idea. Then we'll all know, and we can watch his arrest. The case he brought in yesterday may have contained a weapon. I'm ready for that but be aware and be careful. If I get the message I'm longing to hear, that the hostage is released, there'll be a party at headquarters tomorrow and all the drinks are on me, but before we go, I want to introduce you to a young lady called Poppy. She is going to give a brief educational talk about the anaesthetic gun she uses. She looks like a teenager, but trust me, she is a fully qualified veterinary surgeon and will give a demonstration if anyone would like to volunteer. It'll be biceps or buttocks. No? Cowards! See you all tomorrow."

Mike was quiet on the way home. Kerim was waiting at the gate.

"Where have you been? You didn't tell me you were going to be away so long, and Grace wouldn't tell me anything. I was worried."

"I'm sorry," replied Mike. "Look, grab your bike, let's go for a ride in the park. I'll buy you an ice cream." He waved as Griff drove away and went indoors to say hello to Grace.

"I need to tell Kerim something, something that will help him understand what's going on an. I think he's old enough now and I trust him. He's had to grow up fast. I think he's old enough to take all this on board and realise just how important this is. Apart from anything else, I hate lying to him."

"Well, I have no idea what is going on Ahmed but—"

"No!" he interrupted. "Not Ahmed, any more, Grace, I'm Mike now. That's something else Kerim will have to get used to. Trust me. We'll be fine. I have to do something tomorrow which will mean I'll be out again, all day and possibly for a night, I'm not sure. Griff will be looking after me."

Grace sighed. "Yes okay, but when it's all over, I want a full report, right?"

"Absolutely! I'll enjoy it. I'm off to the park now. We'll be back in about an hour."

"What time will Griff pick you up tomorrow?"

"He won't. I'll be going on my bike." It's not far." And off he went.

"Little Kerim," began Mike when they were seated on a bench with the bikes parked behind them'

"I'm not little," said Kerim. "Please don't say that."

"But I've always wanted a little brother."

"Well, little brothers grow up. Get used to it."

"Okay. It's just as well, really, because I have to tell you things that little brothers might find difficult to listen to."

Kerim turned to look at him and waited "Go on then. I'm ready"

"Well, to begin with, my name is Mike, and that's what you must call me now. When I was in Iraq, it was easier and safer for me to be like the other boys at school. I spoke Arabic. anyway, but at home I was Mike. My parents. I suppose. Would be classed as Christians: we weren't religious, but they were good people. I think that's all God wants from us, is to be good, kind people. All this hymn-singing, and praying is very impressive, but it means nothing. What matters is how people behave, what they do. I'm sure Assad says his prayers at the mosque every morning before he sends out his pilots to bomb schools and slaughter children." He paused. "I think Grace told you that my parents were killed?"

"Yes. We both lost our parents."

"So did so many children, Kerim, and all in the name of religion, but I don't think Grace told you what happened to my mother. I think both of our fathers died in the same way. In falling buildings."

"My mother, too," said Kerim sadly."

"I know," said Mike and pulled Kerim towards him. 'But it was different for mine."

He quietly gave Kerim brief details of what he had seen from the upstairs window of his home. "I saw his face, Kerim. I saw it. I will never forget it." He paused. "And I saw it again when I was travelling across France with the refugees." He took a deep breath. "And yesterday I saw it again. I saw him, Kerim, and I'll see him again tomorrow."

Kerim stared at him, his face pale with shock and fear.

"What are you going to do? Have you told the police? Does Griff know?"

"Yes, Griff knows. He already has pictures of him because this man has already done bad things in this country. Griff and his colleagues want to catch him and some other bad men together tomorrow. I am going to help."

"Can I come?"

"No. I'm sorry, but you can help me celebrate when I come home. I shall want chips, chocolate and champagne. You and I will share a bottle."

"And get drunk and play loud music, yes?"

"Almost certainly yes. And when you grow up, Kerim, we will go back to our countries and put flowers on the graves of our parents. You and me together. Come on. Let's go home."

Chapter 33

At six o'clock the next evening, in the grounds of the Manor, the visitors began to arrive, mostly groups of two or three. They wandered around the front lawn where an impromptu stage had been set up. Some of the chairs were lined up in front but Griff had decided that this audience would need to stand in groups or sit on the ground. Chairs would just get in the way, and no one was likely to complain.

The tech crew were in the house on the first floor. Cameras were in place and functioning. Eyes were drawn to the caravan at the front of a column, ready to look away should anyone arrive. By ten to seven, they were beginning to think that nobody would but suddenly they heard a noise at the gate.

"But I lose my ticket," a man was shouting.

"Okay, Okay," said Will at the gate. "Do you have any money? This is for charity."

"No money," was the reply.

"We have his ticket," shouted a voice behind them and two men, clearly of Middle-Eastern origin, handed in the three tickets which had been designed and printed by Griff's partner at their home in Stoke Newington. Will breathed a sigh of relief and ushered them through. The current occupant emerged from the caravan and walked towards them. Will walked away. There was a heated conversation, then two of the men wandered off and paused together a few feet away from it. The other went into the van together with its tenant.

"It's going to take a while," muttered Griff to Mike. "About fifteen minutes if he's adept. Let's wait and see, but remember, you must be in your van when the third man is dealt with. I need to know when he makes that call."

The audience were doing exactly what they should be doing, laughing and chatting. One group were positioning themselves to the left of the lawn fairly close to the van, with the central group, ready to take their place, when the first group moved away. Suddenly the door opened, and a man emerged slowly, clutching the front of his jacket as if he had belly ache. He wandered forward and sat on one of the chairs to the left of the front of the stage.

"I hope he doesn't bloody stay seated," muttered Griff.

"The second one has gone in," replied Mike. "Group One is mingling round that chair. Poppy is there. Quite useful those baggy trousers with the deep pockets. That gun has quite a long barrel. She's very pretty but she looks so young."

"I told you. She's a fully qualified veterinary surgeon. I just hope she's up for this. These buggers are far more dangerous than a lion with toothache. Ah! Number two is out heading for the centre and thank goodness; number one is up now heading left."

"Three has just gone in. Come on, Poppy, do it." He and Mike wandered to the left. "Yes!"

The first Arab was down. No one appeared to have noticed Poppy was reloading and heading their way. There was a flurry of activity at the side of the house and Griff saw two men with a stretcher disappearing down the drive.

"One down, two to go," muttered Poppy as she and her assistant wandered past them towards the centre ground. Suddenly Griff saw the last man emerging from the van. Number three. The man sauntered to the right-hand side of the garden, his eyes searching for his comrades. *Too soon*, thought Griff and went towards him. Mike already had gone to his van to catch that phone call

Out of the corner of his eyes Griff saw men with the stretcher making their way quickly to a spot in front of the stage. "Two down," he muttered. "They'll be out of sight in a couple of minutes. I just need to delay number three somehow till two is round the corner."

Mike approached and gave a furtive nod. The first phone call had been made. The organiser now believed that three suicide bombers were togged up and in place. *Just a little premature*, Griff thought, but moments later the third was down and in no time at all, he was out of sight and the process of disabling his deadly waistcoat was underway.

The dresser was out of the van, at the top of his steps, mobile phone in hand. Trying to decide where the best position would be to take a good picture. So far, he hadn't moved back to send the signal. The light switch was just inside the door. It wouldn't do at all to have a sequence of explosions. People would have time to take cover He was looking over the heads of the crowd, trying to spot his clients.

Griff hurried over and Mike followed. They wanted him on the lawn, away from his door. A muscular male whom Mike had seen at the police station was standing close by with his hands behind his back.

"Er, hi," said Griff. "I think one of your friends was looking for you." He pointed toward the stage and the man nodded and stood on his tiptoes, looking in the direction that Griff had indicated. He looked puzzled, came down the steps, then turned. "I turn off my lights please, just a minute."

They were a few feet away from each other and Mike was close by. Griff stepped forward "You don't have to worry about that," said Griff smiling. "Actually, none of your friends are looking for you. They are all taking a nap — in a police vehicle. Your first name is Rasheed, I think, but what is your full name please?" There was no response. Well Rasheed, I am arresting you on suspicion of attempted murder and conspiracy to…"

He got no further. There was a commotion at the gate and a boy came hurtling towards them. "Ahmed, Mike!" the boy called and rushed towards Mike. It was Kerim. The man put out his arms and grabbed him, holding him like a shield in front of him and pulled a stubby sharp knife from inside his jacket. He held it close to Kerim's throat. Griff and Mike were frozen with shock.

"I'm leaving now with this boy. If you want him to live, you'll let me go."

"Please," said Mike. "Please let him go. He is a child." He continued in Arabic. "But you don't care about children, do you? I saw you kill my mother and her unborn child. I was watching. You were in my garden and I watched you from an upstairs window. You don't remember me, do you? I crossed France with you. I wanted to kill you then, but I'm not like you. I'm not a killer. What would be the point in hurting this boy? It would be just another crime. They'll arrest you anyway. Let him go. Whatever happens you are going nowhere, except to prison"

Suddenly the man dropped the knife and slumped to the ground. Kerim flung himself at Mike and Poppy stepped around with a satisfied smile on her face.

"Got him right in the middle of his left buttock. It'll be quite painful when he does come round but I guess that will be the least of his worries."

"I saw you coming," said Mike. "It gave me the courage to say all the things I've wanted to say. I'm glad you took the shot when you did. I was running out of words."

"Yeah!" said Griff. "My heart was pounding. I have never been so relieved in my entire life as I was when I saw you sneaking up. Let's get this bastard in the van. We can tell our famous showman he can go home, he having not told a single joke. He will be delighted. I think he was getting cold feet."

"Where will the van be going with its four passengers?" Poppy asked. "Please tell me they'll get a health check. I don't want manslaughter on my curriculum vitae.

"Sure, they'll go first to a clinic to make sure we haven't killed them, and then on to nice cold cells. I think it's pork on the menu tonight — perfect."

"They're Arabs," said Kerim, happy to be safe with his brother. It had all happened too fast for him to be too shocked. "They don't eat pork."

"I know," grinned Griff. "Now, young man. Explain yourself. I turned on my phone to send a very important message to someone and I can see three text messages from Grace. She is frantic. She doesn't know where you are. I'm going to call her now, and tell her you are safe, you can use Mike's phone to explain to her where you are and why. This could have had a very different ending young man and it would have been your fault."

Kerim hung his head

"It's my fault," interrupted Mike. "I told him things. He knew I was going to see this person this evening. He was afraid for me. I should have waited until it was all over, but I had decided to tell him anyway. I just chose then wrong time."

"Well, it was a mistake, but credit to Kerim. He's a brave boy, and to tell you the truth, I probably would have done the same thing myself if my partner was in danger. All's well that ends well, Kerim, but I wouldn't want to be in your shoes when you get back. Let Mike explain, eh? I just need a few words with the crowd and then I'll take you home." He strode over and jumped on to the stage.

"Can I have your attention please, boys and girls? It's over. No mistakes. You were absolutely spot on all the way."

His phone rang and he held up his hand motioning for silence. It was a short call.

"And I am very happy to tell you that the hostage is safe, and on the way to be reunited with her father"

There was a huge cheer. Griff held up his hand. "Thanks to you all. Take the day off tomorrow but could all of you who witnessed or were involved in any significant part of this incident, please send in statements as soon as possible. We'll all meet on Monday. Same time same place. There is tea and coffee indoors if you need refreshment before you go."

He went indoors to thank the teams there who had been invisible but vitally important and who had their own bundles of evidence which would at some stage be produced in Court. Will, who was tired but hugely relieved and happy with the outcome, promised to lock up the two bikes and to attend the Monday meeting.

He had been in front of the Manor waiting by the front door while Griff addressed the plainclothes officers who had accomplished, without a noticeable hiccup, an exercise which would, without specific details, almost certainly hit the headlines the next day. The temptation to tell someone about it would be just too much to resist.

News like that spread fast. Griff knew that and so did Will. He just hoped that the venue would not be revealed. Two weeks ago, life had been so calm and uneventful. That was how he liked it. He strolled over to Griff who was giving some last-minute instruction to a small group. "I'll call Charlie Knowles as soon as I can, but if you three wouldn't mind going back to the station now to give brief details, I'd be grateful. He said he'd leave at ten if there was no news and rely on D.I. Meredith for updates. I'll call her in a minute myself.

Hi Will. How about a celebratory drink?"

Will laughed. "It's waiting for you. I did have a dusty bottle of the fizzy stuff ready, but I guess you'd prefer a stress-relieving scotch."

"I'll sample both and see which is best, but scotch first. Any more news from Seb?"

"She is unharmed and relieved to be home, but it's going to take a long time to recover, I think. They killed her boyfriend — in front of her."

"God! What bloody savages they are. Well, that will make a whole life sentence inevitable for at least two of them. As for the three with the vests, I'm pretty sure they would have been unwilling victims. We'll wait to see what they say."

"Of course. By the way, our guest entertainer is slightly tipsy and still drinking. He's not fit to drive so, assuming Mike will not need the van tonight, I've said he can stay there. Is that okay with you?

"Of course. I'm taking them home very soon — sober as a judge, of course. I have work to do when I get back. There's a man called Ivan who should be getting in touch with me soon and I am honour-bound not to miss his call. His life may depend on it."

Chapter 34

Ivan was in Kamchatka, a peninsula to the far east of Russia surrounded by volcanos and blessed with wildlife. Brown bears roamed unrestricted; the scenery was staggeringly beautiful, but it was very cold.

The remnants of Ivan's family loved it. They would be safe there and there was work, although Ivan had arranged to transfer enough roubles to keep them going for as long as they needed support. As a World Heritage site, there were visits by tourists with some decent hotels which were seasonal but provided work for carpenters and cooks the year round.

They had flown from Moscow to a nearby airport, finished the journey by train, and rented a well-equipped cottage there. Ivan was satisfied that they would be safe and happy. He left them and flew back to Moscow, satisfied that they were in a good place. He took lots of pictures to show Sarah, hoping that he would make it back to England before too many questions were asked about where he'd been and what he had been doing.

He had sensed a change in Vladimir's attitude when they had met three days before. The President was distracted, pacing up and down, ignoring questions, not listening to suggestions. Ivan was no longer his golden boy. Something or somebody else was gnawing at his brain. Returning to Moscow, Ivan found out what it was, and taking advantage of the President's distraction, took the first flight available, leaving a message at the Kremlin to suggest that he was on the trail of Polanski.

*

His safe house was in darkness. Inside, he locked the front door and leaned back against it with a sigh of relief. He was exhausted. He'd eaten well on the Aeroflot, pampered by the stewardess when he'd shown her his card, the one issued by the President to his favoured friends and staff and which commanded first-class attention for the bearer. All he needed now was a hot bath, a stiff drink and a long sleep. He sent a text to Griff.

Hi

Urgent info. available. Please contact me tomorrow — not tonight, I need to sleep and it's not that urgent! I'm at the safe house and the car is in the garage. Don't worry. Don't tell Sarah yet, but family all safe.

Goodnight.

Griff read the message and gave a long sigh of relief. There was something very likeable about Ivan and to know he had returned safely to UK was the best ending there could possibly be to this traumatic day. He put the car into gear and drove home to Stoke and to his very best friend. There were still calls to make. Charlie Knowles would have been given the good news about the night before by now, but they needed get together discuss strategy. Preparing the case properly would be vital. It was unlikely 'The Organiser' would be satisfied with a duty solicitor, and he had the means to afford one of the best. Was he going to rely on entrapment? Certainly, the whole show had been arranged to appear to be the perfect venue for murder, and although he hadn't been there himself, the recorded instructions said it all. He had been pointing a gun at Seb's daughter when the police had lobbed a banger into the room, and as soon as she was up to it, she would make a written statement describing how he had murdered her friend. He had no possible defence. His instructions and intentions were all recorded. Hopefully one or all the prospective bombers would be delighted to give evidence. They must be interviewed first. It was quite possible that other hostages were involved. Home at last. He parked the car, went into their superbly furnished home and fell onto a chaise-longue, holding out his hand to take the glass from his lover.'

"Look, take your shoes off if you're going to crash there. I sold it this afternoon for a very high price."

"God, why did I have to hitch my wagon to an antique dealer? Are we going to keep any of this stuff?"

*

Three weeks later, Ivan, still suffering slightly after his nose job, looked in a mirror and smiled.

"It's great. I love it and I can breathe more easily now. Not so sure about the hair colour. Did I have to be prematurely grey?"

"Well, it was that or ginger," Sarah said. "You chose. It's amazing, though, what a change it's made. You are no longer the cousin I knew and loved, but very attractive, really. Griff is outside. He piloted me. He said you can visit us at home very soon now that you've changed your identity, but only by appointment. Hubert is looking forward to seeing you. Griff said you have lots to discuss, so I'm going."

Sarah gave him a hug "It really was lovely to see you, Ivan. *Da svidaniya. Harosheva dnya.*"

"Sorry!" He grinned. "Could you speak in English please?"

Griff waved as she drove away and turned to Ivan. "You've had breakfast, yes?'

"Well, if you can call a slice of dry bread with green mould around the edges and some of your vile English tea breakfast, I suppose I have, why?"

"I'm taking you to meet a policeman, I need to speak to him about an incident last night, but I want him to see you anyway. You'll find out why, and if you're very good, I'll buy you lunch."

On the way, Griff gave him a resumé of the night before and Ivan rubbed his hands together with delight. "I love it," he said, "but you were lucky."

"Luck had nothing to do with it. It was just meticulously planned."

"Apart from the young boy turning up and nearly being stabbed to death."

"That just shows how good I am at dealing with the unexpected; and actually, if that hadn't happened, the bad guy might not have ended up with a painful shot in his arse. That was the best bit. Anyway, we've arrived and there's a space. Out you get and follow me. Charlie is expecting us. Address him as Chief Inspector."

"Charlie came forward with a smile. "I'm delighted to meet you but I'm not sure what I can do to help."

"Nor I, Chief Inspector," shrugged Ivan

"Please call me, Charlie — so come on, Griff, spill!"

"I just need you to know what's going on, Charlie. I know you are incredibly busy, but we need a favour. This man is taking huge risks and I don't have the reserves to fork out for a trained guardian/driver. We've been very careful to keep him safe while we modified his looks just a little, but he has work to do. He will have to be out and about and may need instant support. I just want to keep you in the loop. He does look different, but the chances are that agents embedded here will be instructed to search for him. To begin with, what I want you to do is listen to him. What he has to say is frightening, and we need as much detail as possible so that we are all prepared for the worst. Our next stop will be with the P.M. Carry on, Ivan."

Ivan shrugged "Okay! I have known the President for twenty years, from being a young translator and record keeper, to a close and trusted agent. I did not always see eye to eye, but I was always very careful. I always said the right thing. I buried my doubts and disapproval — often looked the other way. I saw my friends kicked out or imprisoned for not toeing the line. After a while I had no friends.

"As the years went by, he grew more and more authoritarian. His inner circle grew richer day by day. He was buying their support and that was fine by him. He was in total control and the prisons were full of those who challenged his views in any way.

"He became obsessed with the thought of re-establishing the Soviet Union. He hates all the NATO countries. He despises Europe. Democracy is the dirtiest word to him. I made my decision when I realised that Ukraine was to be his first target. If that succeeded what would be next? The Baltic Countries? Poland? He took Crimea so easily. He has a huge arsenal; he has chemical and the most sophisticated nuclear weapons. He relishes the thought of taking on the American President. Trust me. It's going to happen in a matter of months."

Griff and Charlie were silent.

"No," said Charlie. "He couldn't. there'd be world-wide opposition."

"He ignores opposition. In his own twisted mind, it is a signal for him to act. He longs to take on the President of the United States. He believes he is invincible. That is his weak point. There are Russians who will undermine him.

They are quietly planning his demise. They need a little time. Trust me."

"So the end of the world may not be nigh," said Griff. "I hope you are right, Ivan. I really hope you're right, but thanks to you we can start preparing and planning; then only time will tell."

EPILOGUE

Clissold, the new British ambassador in Moscow, leaned back in his very comfortable chair and rang the bell for his assistant. A man with prematurely grey hair came in, closed the door behind himself and sat down on a leather sofa.

"You didn't bow," remarked the ambassador.

"It's bad for my back,'" was the retort. "Any developments back home?"

"They've released him. He's on his way. Your fingerprints on his car were a brilliant idea. Enough with all the other stuff to hold him for days, but of course nowhere near conclusive. The papers are full of the news that the government has been unable to prove that Hector Polanski was involved in the disappearance, and possible murder of Ivan Kaplinski, so they were obliged to let him go. The press unwittingly has done a great job. Vladimir will be baying for Polanski's blood. Without going into details of course, it seems clear that Hector has provided MI6 with enough information to make the President of the USSR look even more unstable than he already is. Even his supporters will treat him like a pariah, and so they should. He is either insane or evil. As for Hector Polanski, he deserves everything he's going to get. A man who doles out Novichok for any reason whatsoever should be made to take a bit of his own medicine. He's being tracked anyway. When do you think will be the right time to contact your trusted friends?"

"I'm giving it some thought. They think I'm dead, of course, and since I don't look much like the man they knew, it might be difficult. But there are certain things that only the four of us know. I have a plan. I may need to pop down to Kyiv. I really would like to meet the President there, and he could help me. Can you arrange it? It would be unfair to meet my old friends here in Moscow, or in Russia at all, so somewhere in Ukraine would be safer, I think. Give him the facts about me — that I am very much alive. Tell him he has genuine friends in Russia. They are horrified. He already knows that. One of them is a doctor. We'll discuss plans safely there, and with luck, proceed to a satisfactory conclusion."

Within a year of that day, Russian troops who had helped to destroy the cities in Ukraine were helping to rebuild them. The people in Russia were watching filmed records of the devastation their army had caused in horror, and mourning the deaths of their own sons. Millions of pounds confiscated from oligarchs were being used to help the restructure of a devastated state. Ukrainians were going home.

The President was in a private ward in hospital, under constant guard, no visitors allowed. He didn't speak. He just looked confused. There was no treatment. There is no cure for failure.